Ulrike Dietmann

Jamaica

– ONE LOVE –
HOW I FOUND IT

spiritbooks

© 2020 Ulrike Dietmann, www.ulrikedietmann.de
Publisher: spiritbooks · www.spiritbooks.de · 70771 Lein-felden-Echterdingen
Editorial office: Gabi Schmid · www.buechermacherei.de
Typesetting/Layout: Gabi Schmid · www.buechermacherei.de
Cover design: OOOGRAFIK · www.ooografik.de
Illustrations/Pictures: #66008149, #66918353, #66917702, #66918348, #73408255, #2698066 | AdobeStock

Print and distribution: tredition GmbH,
Halenreie 40-44, 22359 Hamburg · www.tredition.de

978-3-946435-82-2 (Paperback)

Inhaltsverzeichnis

Shine for me, Jamaica,

Smile for me, oh glorious one, gentle one, pure one.

You are the land of the wellsprings that never cease to flow.

They came, stole her gold, killed her children.

They came ashore, they abused her, she kept shining.

She wanted to escape, but she was an island in the ocean.

Others came, abused her, she kept shining.

She could not escape.

They came, they used her, she kept shining.

She gave them her heart, her soul, her body.

Keep shining, my beautiful, my pure, my chaste one.

You are the land of the wellsprings that never cease to flow.

Just like the rain that never stops falling, like the sun that rises every day.

They come, they defile your wellsprings, the rain cleanses them.

They kill, they steal, your sun rises again.

Shine for me, Jamaica.

Smile for me, oh glorious one, gentle one, pure one.

They come, but you remain free,

the island in the endless sea.

Translated from German into English by

Angelika Taubmann

Ocho Rios, Jamaica, 7th January 2018

We all are wounded, deeply hurt. Is that true? Do we even have a soul that is born with a wound? Some say so. My answer to this question is my story.

My name is Viola. I'm one of these women who do everything as it is expected to be. I care for others, clean my teeth twice a day and whenever I get approached by someone, I smile.

Everything was fine until ... well, until my wound became visible. I personally believe that this happens to everyone. Sooner or later. At that very moment we become the real versions of ourselves.

If your wound hasn't become visible yet, it's possible you're living in a cocoon. Just like I did, in the old days. Sometimes I wish I could return there. But, that's not the way it is.

I'm Viola. I'm sitting in front of my notebook. My energetic system is trying to cope with a time lag of six hours, starting at CET (Central European Time) and arriving at EST (Eastern Standard Time).

I'm in Ocho Rios, Jamaica, and everything is smelling moist. Odors have no chance of hiding here. The humidity reveals them. Even the wood smells like freshly ploughed earth. There's nothing hidden. And that's a good thing, it gives me a feeling of security.

I moved into this cottage by the sea, where insects make music during the night, yesterday evening. I'd discovered it online.

Sometimes life just tells you: Now! Yeah! And then – you just do it.

Now I'm here in the home of an artist. She isn't among the living anymore – corporeal, that is. Her daughter is maintaining the house. But, the spirit of Annabelle is still there and utterly vivid so. The veils between the worlds are thin. Every single item in this house breathes beauty, even the umbrella stand. There are flowers on the table next to me that smell like the colour purple.

Have you ever felt the proximity of another entity who, although invisible, deeply affected you? This is what my story is about. How to discover an invisible world beyond the visible one.

Yes, I'm searching for love. Show me one person who isn't. For a love that is ruled by the invisible. To meet the invisible is very frightening, but it also brings forth miracles. I know the fragrance of miracles. Here, in Jamaica, you can smell it. It's humid and saturated with sun.

Annabelle, the former owner of the cottage, used to run an art gallery just a few steps from here. Harmony Hall, the pictures on display selected with love, pictures painted by Jamaican artists. The cottage walls are covered with them as well. One is a miniature of an everyday scene and there are horses in it, too. That makes me laugh a lot because they are the very beings who brought the invisible into my life: horses.

I'm an artist myself, a person living in dreams and there is no place on earth that could make me feel more at home than Annabelle's house. Far away from my life in Europe where the odors aren't as naked as here.

I'm searching for a place I can call home. Have been searching for several years, in fact. Since I lost my home, my family, my children, my horse. This is my story. A journey fueled by a yearning and the one question: Is it possible to find love again once you have been bereaved of it? Or will fear dominate?

I've lost my home, the feeling of being safe, I've lost everything I knew and was familiar with. Since then, fear has been my constant companion.

I don't bemoan fear. Although it is an overpowering feeling and has been controlling the course my story, it keeps bearing miracles. It made me come to Jamaica, to Annabelle's cottage in Ocho Rios.

Fear is the gate to truth. Every single one of us will stand in front of this gate, sooner or later. In front of the gate to truth, and this moment in time will be the one to reveal our deepest secret.

The wound I carry is loneliness. I'm like a horse that has been separated from its herd, searching in blind panic for my fellows. For some horses it's not a big problem to be on their own, but others are doomed. I'm of the latter, I almost died from it.

Will I find love, the one love? "One Love – One Heart," goes the saying of the Jamaicans, "One Love – One Heart," the song of Bob Marley.

There is only one kind of love. One Love. And I want to find it.

Chapter 1 – Who Are You when Everything Ends?

"Why did Hemingway commit suicide anyway? I mean, his writing is immortal, he could've been proud of himself."

"Please stop asking questions like these, it's depressing."

"No, it's good, it's helping me to put an end to everything. Just imagine – you're in good company ... Hemingway, good God."

"How did he do it?"

"Shot himself. With a shotgun he called 'my sleek, brown lover'."

"How on earth do you know things like that?"

"Ideas. Just looking for ideas."

These are the dialogues we had that night. It was friggin' cold, it was raining, the water was running down our faces. But we were there, nevertheless.

Frankfurt, on the rooftop of a skyscraper. A miracle had caused that situation. Yes, a miracle. That was three years ago. A miracle coming in the form of Michi. He was the janitor of this high-rise housing banks and insurances and he had the keys to open the steel door. There is no other way to reach those rooftops. And! The next miracle: Michi was as determined as were we. Otherwise it would never have worked.

I just thought: Never before in my whole life has fate played into my hands in such a way.

Everything had come to an end. Unfortunately, I cannot tell you the actual detail of what happened. I just cannot go there. I just cannot write it down, even if three years have passed in the meantime. It's too ... I just cannot do it. Maybe later. Just one thing: They were gone. The father and his two children. My children, my husband. Dead. An accident. I could only think of one thing: I want to go there where you already are, my family. But it wasn't that easy. I didn't have the strength. I didn't have enough strength to walk across the rainbow bridge. I didn't have the strength to live, much less to die. That was three years ago. I could only pray that a divine power might help me.

And then ... you know how it is. Suddenly it's there. And you know: Now! Yes! A miracle! This Facebook-group named "Wenn alles zu Ende geht" – "When everything ends" popping up on my monitor just like that. I've no idea which hobbies or cookies or apps led to their finding me; no idea in what state of mind I was when I clicked "join".

And this is how it worked: Michi was the moderator. Wanted to check who I was, for a start. Via Facebook chat. "Hey, Viola, we are on our way to paradise. How about you?"

Me: "Yeah, sure – me too."

Michi: "We are convinced about the fact that it's to be found beyond the commonly known reality."

Me (thinking): That's a cult? They're using drugs? Some sort of sex-obsessed people ...? I honestly tell Michi that I'm way to wiped out to consider things like this. But then I learn that "Who are you when everything ends?" is about a group of people who are tired of living. Just like me. Thus, I'm approved to join the group.

And then ... the second miracle. They already have a specific plan. Michi, the group's moderator, is in possession of the key to reach a rooftop of a high-rise in the City of Frankfurt where there is a certain spot from which one can jump down and land on a fenced speck of lawn. This way, you won't crash onto anybody's head. That's just brilliant, isn't it!?

I'm sorry for having to paint pictures like this, but I need you to understand where I'm coming from, what roads I've travelled so far. I just can't help writing everything down, for I believe it's the only way to get closure.

And now I'm sitting here in beautiful Jamaica. And so many of you already read the text I wrote yesterday and left genuine comments and kind sentences in Facebook and on my blog site and maybe, just maybe I will be able to deal with life after all. Even if it's somehow ...

Well, I learned in Michi's Facebook group that it's not too easy to cross that boundary to the other reality, that is, to walk across the rainbow bridge like Hemingway did, arm in arm with his sleek, brown lover.

Who are you when everything ends? That was the welcome-question of the Facebook group. "I'm Viola, I'm an artist and this journey to paradise is right up my alley. I'm fed up with everything here and you have planned a classy goodbye. Count me in!"

It was friggin' cold, it was raining, there were five of us. The Facebook group named "When everything ends" had a total of 59 members. But now, here on the rooftop, there were only five of us. Michi, Alex, Hannah, Severin and me.

My heart leapt into my throat. How many of us would arrive together on the other side? You need to know that my greatest fear of all is to be alone and thereof to die alone. And would I be all alone on the other side? Or would I see them again? Oliver and the children?

No, I wouldn't die alone. That was the third miracle: I would not die alone – that was just too unlikely. There were five of us. I wouldn't be alone when I finally climbed up Jacob's ladder.

Every single time I think of that night, my internal systems crash. I'm not sure if I can put you through this. But that's also an excuse because, to be honest, I'm not sure if I have it in me to write it down.

In Jamaica, dusk arrives at half past five p.m. and doesn't stay long. When the first insect starts to sing, you know the time has come. Just this minute, I've heard it. The darkness frightens me. Not the dark of Jamaica, I can deal with that one. But the darkness of my memories. I was here in JA (brief for Jamaica – everyone here uses it) for the first time two years ago. That was shortly after I had set forth on my journey to paradise, back then on top of the high-rise. And now I've started to write about it. But first, I need to make myself some tea and catch my thoughts. The tea is called Detox. It smells like recently harvested grass. I bought it at Progressive Foods, the supermarket in downtown Ocho Rios, yesterday.

The scent of Progressive Foods, the supermarket, is very subdued because of its aircon. It mainly accentuates the scent of the cleansers. Nevertheless, Progressive is paradise on earth for someone like me. Why?

Because nobody, or almost nobody, has the same skin color than me. That's incredibly soothing. I'm not afraid of the people here. Their skin color is different from those people who surrounded me when my heart was crushed. The Detox tea tastes good, it comes from paradise.

Yesterday, after I had written the first chapter of the book, I hit on the idea to create a blog and thus enable the readers to read along. Wow! There are so many comments in Facebook and the blog. I'm crying inwardly because I'm not alone. And suddenly I remember that I dreamed of a certain person the night before I went to the airport to go to Jamaica. A person who wrote a text in Facebook. The dream was about a theatre play with horses. So, I'm telling myself that this story is some kind of theatre play with horses as well. I'm a writer and usually I write about horses. This time, however, I'm writing about myself.

So, what happened that night in Frankfurt on top of the high-rise? Five people on their way across the rainbow bridge.

Severin – lawyer, soon to be divorced, three children, affluent family and a broken heart. With the wind blowing in such a fierce way, he is bending his knees and clinging to the waist-high balustrade.

"If we aren't careful, the wind will blow us away before we can do it ourselves." That's just his humor. Who are you when everything ends?

"All I ever wanted on this earth," Severin had written in FB, "was to find my one. I've found this woman and we have three children, but now she's gone. And I will never know why."

There were no comments on that post. Well, what's there to write? That's not to say that nobody was affected by it. There were just no comments.

Hannah – ran her career into the ground and really hates her job (as it would take about ten minutes to explain said job, I won't bother with it). Burnout, five years filled with talk therapy, daily meditations, two craniosacral treatments per week ... futile efforts, every single one. Who am I when everything ends?

"I know that there is something better waiting for me someplace," Hannah had posted, "I'm just not sure anymore if that place is here on this earth. In fact, I'm quite certain it's *not*.

"Quite certain is not enough," was the comment of someone who is not with us on this rooftop today. Hannah, on the other hand, is. She doesn't make promises easily.

"I don't fit into a world in which people keep promising things they actually don't intend to keep," she once wrote to me privately. "I've lost my job because for me it was always about the sake of the matter. For the others it was about power."

Hannah weighed at least 150 kilos. She couldn't be easily swept away by the storm. She had jet-black hair and snow-white skin. In a fairy tale and weighing 100 kilos less, she would have been the perfect Snow White. A princess. It's very sad that the people in this world have so few dreams. In a world with more room for dreams she surely would have found her prince.

And then there's me – a writer with her fear of loneliness. I cannot write anymore since my family is gone, since they died, were killed in that accident. Strictly speaking, since the wonderful picture of our family was painted over with this giant, shit-colored paintbrush. From that day on, the world hasn't been a fairy tale anymore, no longer a dream. And without a dream it's ugly, evil and cruel. And only now, that I've woken from that dream of life, I realize how many people are constantly forced to live in this cold, ugly and cruel world, unable to slip into a dream, contrary to me as an author. As I used to do when I still could dream. As I used to do when I still could write. After the accident had occurred, I couldn't write nor dream anymore. No idea where those dreams had gone.

The wind hurt, forced the cold into my pores and tears to my eyes. I felt like I'd been gutted. I wouldn't be able to take that very long, that fucking icy cold on top of that bloody high-rise. I would just go, one or another way. But certainly not back into that cold, ugly and cruel life.

And then there was Alex – in her mid-twenties, beautiful like a Madonna straight from the Renaissance period.

She was hopelessly in love with a married woman twenty years her senior. Who am I when everything ends? Her lover had informed Alex that divorce was not an option.

No shared future. A life so cruel and ugly. Who am I when everything ends?

"It's a miracle that I've met a person I can love this much," Alex posted. "That's more than I've ever expected from life. I know for certain that such a thing will never happen again. The rest of my life would just be an ongoing disappointment."

No comments.

It's not that the members of the Facebook group wouldn't have fancied writing. There were lots of posts about last recipes, last performances of church choirs and last visits to the movies. But when truth had its say, when it was about the question: Who are you when everything ends? – then everybody just knew that every single word would be futile.

Maybe that's the difference between a person still hesitating and a determined one. The determined one can sum up the truth in one single sentence and that truth will silence everything. A person still talking and telling stories will live on. The world of a person still talking and posting recipes isn't ugly, cold and cruel.

Even in that ghastly and friggin' cold storm Alex was stunning. She was glowing from within. She clung to Hannah's 150 kilos – a sight I will never forget. It looked like Hannah had brought her personal angel, suddenly corporeal in the storm.

And then Michi – in his early sixties, bald head, moustache, eyes like the leader of a pack of wolves. Michi is such an incredibly good person, it just makes you doubt

mankind for being responsible for his wanting to leave. It's always a bad sign if the best one's want to go. I hadn't really realized that before the night I met him in person. You only had to look into his eyes to look right into his soul which was too pure, too fragile to cope with this ugly and cruel world. Had I still been able to dream, I would have made him a character in a novel. Maybe I would've succeeded in bringing him back into the dream that can be found on this world. But there would have been a legacy. Michi defied the storm. He was a rock. A rock with a broken soul. Who are you when everything ends?

"All I ever wanted was to be of service to the people. But servants just get trampled on, exploited and laughed at. Nowadays everyone is a Lord, there are no servants anymore. This is my last duty."

That's what Michi posted. No comments.

Who are you when everything ends? I'm asking you. Yeah, you. What's your truth when there's nothing left to comment on? And how do you make your stand against the storm on the rooftop of the high-rise? What is it that crushes your soul? Maybe you don't have an answer to that right here and now, but someday you will have one. That will be a good moment because you will know that everything is ending. And then, something new will begin – whatever this may be.

To this day, I don't know what happened to Severin, Hannah, Alex and Michi. Because at that evening I left the cold, ugly and cruel world. A miracle, which I would never have expected, happened. A miracle beyond my wildest dreams. I'll tell you more about it in the following chapter. But first I need another detox tea.

Just one more thing: I have a feeling that I will see them again, my comrades who abided the storm with me: Michi, Alex, Severin and Hannah. When the time is right.

Chapter 2 – There Are Angels in My Life Now

I feel confused and amazed. I just had a look into the blog and found some really touching comments there and lots of comments in Facebook.

Marietta Tango writes: "I don't know what happened to Viola so that she lost everything she loved. But I had to suffer the same experience. All this grief. To this day, I feel it. Over and over I feel its throwback."

Or Nirupa: "And as every wound hardens our hearts, it now exposes itself, layer by layer, to be seen and to be felt ... Life says: Come home, come home at last ..."

I'm astonished at the extent of how the readers of the novel perceive and sense the topic already after the first pages. I've been writing my whole life, lots of books, and the writing has always been a very lonely experience. Me and the story with the potential reader far away. And suddenly ... It's a peculiar feeling. I'm not alone with my story anymore. I invited the readers and they came. Thank you, my dear readers. I don't know what to say. I'm filled with wonder.

I'm just coming back from a stroll through the area of Te Moana. Me and my small notebook that always accompanies me in case I'm hit by a lightning stroke of inspiration. And what did I do? I sketched the shape of the leaves. Perhaps you have a gum tree at home? You need to picture it like this: There are gum trees in inconceivable variety here. There are no apple trees, cherry trees, fir trees or elders. There are leaves as big as a towel, creased like a pleated skirt. And scrubs sprouting a myriad of those green pleated skirts.

Next to those there is a palm tree with a trunk thin like a match and tall like the neck of a giraffe. On the very top of it there's a bunch of fans exploding into all directions like fireworks on New Year's Eve. Down on the ground grows a palm tree with a red and brown trunk and leaves so giant-sized you could go boating on them.

Nirupa writes "Come home, come home at last." Yes, I've felt this sensation of "coming home" when I strolled through the gardens of Te Moana, right after I had sketched all those beautiful shapes. Eventually, it was a leave not bigger than a thumb. Just a small, elongated leave, lying on the ground next to various other ones the trees had shed. It's attracting my attention because of its neon green color. This color, the radiance of this color, affects me in a peculiar way. As if someone spilled a paint pot inside of me. It touches something. This is me.

I remember having the same sensation about the wallpaper in my nursery: Never ending copies of Mary Poppins covering the complete wall. The color back then was pink. Her umbrella was pink. Whenever I see these colors, a door will open for me.

It's as if I stepped out of the skin of one world and into the one of another. And then I feel like I'm home. Home is a hidden realm underneath the surface, and you can cross its shore by means of a neon green leave in the gardens of

Te Moana. There is no pain there and I also don't have to die to reach this place.

All my life I've been searching for this gate. As soon as I'll find it, everything will be alright.

There are many gates in Jamaica, an abundance of beauty. The wounded version of myself, living in an ugly world, doesn't exist here. The beauty of this Garden of Eden in its unimaginable generosity embraces me. And it comforts me.

Three years ago, that night on top of the high-rise in Frankfurt, I went through such a gate. I had planned to be dead but I am not. I will step through that gate again, this time with words. The words will protect me. I went through this gate and discovered an unknown and new world. A world that had me confused and enchanted at the same time.

People say that once the pain becomes too excruciating, something unexpected will happen to help you survive.

Three years back: I'm standing at the very edge of the rooftop. I'm ready. The storm is so fierce up here that I'm sure the next strong gust will carry me away with it. I put my life into the hands of the wind. Now, at this very moment. It's no longer in my own hands. That moment – I can feel it again, it's very close. The cold, the water running down my face. I've got a runny nose, I need a tissue. Can anyone hand me a tissue? I can't see the others any longer. Where are they? Michi, Severin, Hannah and Alex – where are they? I can't worry about them right now.

Any moment can be the one for me to leave this world. Now I know how it feels. I've let go. It's freedom. It's the same sensation as ... the phone call.

The doctor, speaking English with a strong accent. I could feel that he was very busy and very tired and that he had to tell me something he would've preferred to avoid telling me. It takes a lot of strength to be the bearer of news like this. I could feel it in the way how tired his voice sounded. I could feel that he was all alone with no one in his life to comfort him after he had to deliver such terrible news. News that drive the people concerned into loneliness, a loneliness they cannot survive. I cannot exactly remember the words he said, but I knew immediately that there was no hope left. That it was the end. They would never come back to this world, Oliver and my children.

And now on the rooftop, in the hands of the storm, in the fuckin' cold, it was just the same: There was nothing I could do. The wind had taken over. I was standing there, my knees pressed against the balustrade, my upper body like a blade of grass in the wind. I felt this freedom. I was one with the wind. The wind had taken command over me. I relented more and more, waiting for the moment when I'd lose my footing and just fall. Down ...

And then the storm ceased. Why? Why now? Damn! I had been ready to go. Why didn't it sweep me away? Why did I have to take care about everything myself, again? Why couldn't I even manage such a simple task like a jump over a balustrade on top of a freaking high-rise?

"We can help you," I heard someone speak behind me.

Michi? Severin? It was a male voice. "But you have to give your consent first," the voice continued.

"I'm okay with whatever it is," I replied, pissed off. "I'm sick and tired of this shit here! I just want to leave!" I think it was a first for me to talk to anybody in such a pissed way.

"How I hate this," the voice said. "It takes years to clean up this whole mess. The hole that's ripped by this action. Gosh, why did they have to send me again?"

I was confused. Who was talking to me like that? "No, I'm not willing to play these mind games. I want to go!"

The wind, that bloody traitor, just backtracked. I could even see a piece of cloudless sky, straight above me. And I swear: I saw someone there. A being of some kind with blurred lines and it ...

It was speaking and I heard it say: "For cryin' out loud, just make her sign the contract. You're a complete failure."

"I'm done," I say. "Until I'm dead, I'll certainly not sign any contract whatsoever."

I feel that the guy who talked to me is still standing behind me, but I won't turn around.

"How I hate this," he says again, and I have a feeling he's going to tap on my shoulder any moment. "Please sign," he says. But he really sounds like a loser. It's his voice. Nobody would sign a contract because of him.

And then, something very strange happens. I can totally understand if you think you've lost me when you read the following.

The rooftop, the high-rise, the cold, the storm and the

dark are suddenly gone. I'm somewhere else ... but where exactly am I? It's bright and warm and completely silent. There is noise, of course, but the noise is also silent. It feels like a place somewhere between heaven and earth.

I sign a contract, knowing its contents without having to read it. This is how it works here: you just know, you just do. The contract says that I'm surrendering my life into the hands of the angels. I look around. They are so beautiful – angels. Bright white they are made of light and they have wings. They don't have a clearly defined shape, no body like we human beings. Although I can perceive them as distinctly outlined shapes, I know that's just my personal perspective. They are made of light. I sign the contract.

I'm so very happy to be here. I'm not alone anymore. I even have the feeling that I will never again be alone, now that I've met them. This moment is so wonderful, and I want to stay forever. I'm so curious.

I recognize the angel who was with me on the rooftop, his sad face, even if I've never seen it. But it's fitting the voice. It was him who handed me the contract.

"Who's responsible for her?" I hear someone asking. A remarkable crowd has rallied around me, appearing like a congregation of medical specialists who've come to find out what my problem might be.

"She's from an old line," says one of them. "She really is totally exhausted."

I feel like I'm scanned by them, the angels around me, that is. And I think I hear a sigh from the one from the roof, despite everything happening in complete silence. As if he is thinking: Okay ... difficult case.

"Condemned," some of them exclaim, turning away from me as if they saw something sorely horrible.

"She is completely infested."

"To the last pore."

"That's a rare thing."

"He's ensnared her."

"I'm afraid so!"

"Awful!"

It goes on and on like that. You need to know that angels don't talk like we do, that is, with a human voice and human words. That's just the way I'm perceiving it. But they do mean it like that. It's kind of translated inside my head. Be that as it may, they see something inside of me they find very shocking, as if they discovered malign cancer. But it has a somehow calming effect on me because I trust them. And maybe they can find the solution. I'm just happy to be here. It's no longer cold and my pain has just vanished.

"What happened?" I hear them say.

"Look at her. He's ensnared her."

I don't know, what they're talking about. Who is *he*? And how has he ensnared me?"

Suddenly there is a great commotion. They seem to sense something that I'm not able to see. But I have a feeling that it's got something to do with me.

I hear them shouting "Oh my God!" although they wouldn't express it like this, of course. Or would they?

After all, they work for Him. That's what I'd always thought, at least.

"She is like a feast for him. To get one like her."

Hm, I don't know. A feast? Me? And for whom?

"She's utterly infested. That's out of our depth."

It's getting more and more mysterious by the second. The angel from the roof seems to be relieved. He's not the only one with a problem here. But why am I such a problem? Even for the angels?

Now a file is passed around. Energetical, you know. Energetical pass-the-file. They put a seal on it which indicates something like *highest level of difficulty*. Even if I cannot really read it, I just know it, like I know everything here somehow. Now it's official and they're all shaking their heads.

I see the file ending up on the desk of archangel Michael. How I would know it's him? You just know it when you see him. I recognize him at once although I hadn't ever seen him before and was only vaguely aware of his mere existence.

He scans the file. Archangel Michael! I stand in awe of him. He is incredibly beautiful. His light is beautiful, radiating, as if you selected the most beautiful colors in the world – purple, turquoise, magenta and the green of the leave I found this morning – and used only their very essence, their light. The result would be archangel Michael. The most impressive about him are his wings. They are like the wings of a million of swans illuminated by the light of the morning sun.

The other angels surround him and look at him in awe, just like I do.

"This case will be a useful lesson for all of you," he tells them. "She is precious to us. She needs special care. Do you understand?"

They nod.

These two sentences are taking hold onto me. "She is precious to us. She needs special care."

The next thing I hear is a grisly noise coming from the deep. The light draws back, and the angels suddenly look like they're feeling cold. And then I see *him*. At first, it's just like a cluster of dark energy but then, for only a fraction of a moment, I see a hideous face. I cannot really give a detailed description of this situation because right at that moment I didn't feel anything at all. All I can say is that He is ugly and that there is absolutely nothing amiable about him. I hear *him* laugh.

I wake up the next morning and I'm at home, lying in my bed. In the very flat I used to live in together with my family and that is empty now. Only the furniture, the clothes, the notebooks – in other words, the things that belonged to their lives – are still there.

I don't remember how I got home last night, back from the rooftop. If somebody took me, human being or angel. My wet clothes are lying on the floor.

Something is different. I'm different. I'm not alone anymore. I have angels in my life now. Archangel Michael, who is now taking care of me. To whom I'm precious. And I've signed a contract saying that I must follow their instructions from now on. That's the deal. They protect me and I follow their instructions.

I wonder if anyone else can understand any of this. Can you, dear reader? Do you have angels in your life? Did they offer you a contract, too? Did you sign it?

Have you ever been to a place knowing what's going on although you shouldn't be able to know? If yes, then maybe you can understand my words.

Or maybe you cannot. How could you if you haven't had this experience, yet? It's not important, anyway.

Out of all of this, there's only one important thing: I'm not alone anymore. I have angels in my life now.

ONE LOVE - ONE HEART

Chapter 3 – How I Came to Jamaica

The soul knows its predestined way, just like water. And we follow. Even if the conscious mind has no clue.

I signed a contract with angels but strictly speaking I probably just followed the call of my soul. It's not easy to feel your soul, to sense what it wants. Sometimes we even need no less than a high-rise and the intention to die. The soul doesn't concur with the mind – the mind wants something else. That's the difficulty. Had it been up to my mind, I would be dead by now. But I'm alive. I'm alive because of the epiphany I was granted. Because of the angels that marked me a difficult case and promised to take care of me.

Today I received an email from a friend who read my blog, the story about the angels. She wrote she couldn't agree with that. It wasn't me who was a difficult case, but the experience I'd had to suffer was difficult. Maybe our lives on this world are difficult in general. I think from the angel's point of view that may be the case. After all, they don't have a corporeal form and don't need to deal with the loneliness down here. I'd do everything conceivable to feel it, to hear the voice of my soul. Because without it I'd wither and die. The soul is the nourishment we cannot survive without.

I've found it in Jamaica – the soul. Why? Why here? I don't know. Yesterday a friend sent me an email: "I've learned to feel my dreams instead of interpreting them."

I went swimming. The ocean is only 20 meters away from my little house. There is a cliff of volcanic rock and some steps winding down a pass to a deck. From there I can slide into the water. Some places are shallow enough for me to stand on rocks or sand and others deep enough to swim.

The water is warm, and no matter how long I stay in it I never get cold. There are no other people there, sometimes a boat passes in the distance, a slim boat with an engine and swarthy men navigating it. Most of the time it's two of them, one sitting and the other one standing, sometimes both sitting, sometimes standing. Anyway, this picture always touches me. And if the boat is blue, I'm happy.

While I was in the water, I pondered his sentence: "I've learned to feel my dreams instead of interpreting them."

He's right, this friend of mine. When I try to interpret what happened to me, my mind recoils just like the water is repelled by the cliff.

So, what did happen to me? My husband, Oliver, and my two children, Saskia and Leo, lost their life in a car accident in Morocco while touring the country in a rental car. Nobody knows how it happened. The car veered off the road and crashed down a hillside in the Atlas Mountains. Presumably they were instantly dead. That's really all I can say. And I don't want to remember. I don't want to feel these emotions anymore.

I prefer being here in Jamaica where everything is so beautiful, where I started to write down my story and hit on the idea to invite the readers to join me.

I'm not alone – because of the readers of my blog where I post my texts. People I know personally, friends and people I don't know at all. Thousands of kilometers are separating us, but they're sending their answers on my blog site, nonetheless. They feel that their presence is crucial for me.

I'm torn. To write means to face the truth. Speech is merciless, I'm aware of this fact. There is nothing that cuts more deeply than the spoken word. To speak means to unveil a truth that was unknown until that very moment, and that's what I'm afraid of. But I'm also aware that I must face this fright because otherwise this feeling can and will never change. I'm frightened, so much so that I cannot stop thinking about a way to escape this situation. It's just ... I've made it public now. How insane must I be to expose myself in such a way. People are likely to hurt me again. They will destroy my protective shield and once this happens there won't be a place left in the world I can escape to.

Up to this point, however, they've only been full of sympathy and honesty, they've made me feel alive and they just see me. They make me feel loved and cherished. That's my medicine and I'm grateful beyond words.

I can see now why archangel Michael said: "She needs special care."

I've been living with this loneliness and this anguish for the last three years, afraid that any given moment could be the one to bring another phone call like the one from Morocco back then. Healing a broken heart cannot succeed without a sheer abundance of care and sympathy. And I wonder: Isn't every single one of us in need of sympathy and love and care to no end? Isn't every single one of us living with a broken heart? It doesn't matter how our stories go. My answer is: yes.

I believe that people feel that way and that's the reason they're sending their answers. It's also the reason why I keep on writing.

If you separate a horse from its herd, it will inevitably become depressed and ill and finally it will be too weak to gather the strength to break through the fence and find a new herd. The same applies for us humans. And I believe many of us have lost their herds, spending their lives desperately trying to find them again.

Thank you, Corinna, for reminding me of this with your comment. A comment in a blog or in Facebook, an email arriving at the very right moment – those are the things that change our lives. Seemingly insignificant things we do with great impact, with love.

So, what happened after I had signed the contract with the angels? What was next? That's what several readers have wondered.

The answer is: Jamaica happened. The way of the soul. Looking back, I can see clearly that I didn't come here just by happenstance. Even if my mind cannot proceed it, I know that it was the only possible way to survive. I'll tell you the story. Maybe you won't be able to understand it, but you will be able to feel it.

After that night on top of the high-rise I became a different person – something indefinable had happened to me and my everyday life kept showing me that fact.

Suddenly, my work as a personal coach, that I pursued besides my writing career, became very successful. The angels made sure of this. For some years past I've held workshops showing other people how to find a true connection to horses by connecting with themselves through personal development. It's a satisfying and beautiful work as it touches the soul. After that night, when I met the angels, I had a deeper understanding of things. I want to tell you three short stories about what the angels have brought into my life.

The first one is Manuela's story.

She approached me in search of a coach. Let me shortly explain here what's my concept of being a coach: A coach is someone who enables other people to achieve something they couldn't achieve on their own. Manuela was married to a guy who had cheated on her openly for years and who exploited her naiveté so much that she would probably have lost her parent's home, in which she lived, as well as the custody for their two teenage children when getting divorced. I'm not going into details here, just let me mention that such situations occur even in a state of law like Germany. Further on, Manuela owned three Arabian horses, thoroughbreds, which she loved very much. In this regard she was just like me and so we formed a bond of some kind.

When we started the coaching sessions, Manuela told me she wouldn't be able to pay me unless a miracle happened, and she was awarded the house in court. If that happened, however, she would pay me double to thank me for being able to help her. I agreed. The following night I had a dream in which an Arabian thoroughbred cantered along a busy road without showing any fear at all. And there was a very special detail as well: Manuela was sitting on his bare back, guiding him without bridle, without saddle. The horse trusted her completely.

Three months later the house was returned to Manuela during the court hearing. Four months later she was given the sole custody for the children and half a year later she got divorced and could finally start a new life. I talked to Manuela very often on the phone during that time and I became aware of the fact that she was allowed indeed to learn things that wouldn't have been possible without all the pressure, the pain, the fear and the humiliation. The success, however, was there because I'd had the absolute certainty that everything would fall into place. People think the angels help by waving a magic wand and thus conjuring happy endings. But that's certainly not the case.

The angels bestow you with the gift of faith. Nothing more and nothing less.

During every single conversation I had with Manuela – when she was crying, cursing her fate and wishing her husband to hell – I always had the unswerving certainty: She will ride through the city on the back of her horse and everything will come out all right.

The second story: Sabrina was fed up with her job. For years she had been dreaming of starting her own business and had made a solid business-plan; the one thing missing was the starter cash of 50,000 Euros. And no matter how many haircuts she did in her job as a hairdresser, she just couldn't save up this amount. But then, a repeat customer of the shop made her an offer. He would grant her a loan in the amount of the sum needed for an indefinite amount of time, the one condition being a profit participation of five % after five years.

Her business concept was brilliant as well. She would offer online advice of how to find the perfect hair style. The customers would send a picture and some details concerning their hair and she would provide exact instructions for the customers hairdresser. This way people all over Germany could use her service.

The problem was just, now that the money was within her grasp, she got cold feet. She had to decide within one week if she'd accept the offer, otherwise her investor would withdraw it. I learned about her story because Sabrina had a horse sharing at the same place my horse was stabled, and she asked me for advice.

I told her: "You know, normally I get paid for such advice. And if you want this advice to have any value, we should arrange an appointment.

I think she thought me a money-grubber and unfriendly person – after all, we both love horses and if you deal with horses, it's not appropriate to nit-pick.

But I also think she understood that free advice is nothing more than an insult to your own judgement. So, I stated date and time, and she called. She described the risks of her plans in all detail. Deep inside, she was dead certain that she would end up heavily indebted on the streets if she gave notice. When she finally, after about half an hour, had to pause to breathe, I seized the moment to ask her if she could see a squirrel outside her window.

She replied: "Yes, for several days a squirrel keeps showing up that I've never seen before."

"And what about right now?" I asked.

"It just scaled up the tree trunk."

At that moment I knew everything would fall into place and I told her: "Your plan will turn out to be a success. If not, I'll assume your debts."

Today, Sabrina is a different person. She reached break even after only three years, and she's happily married to her former investor.

All of this is dating from the very moment in which her doubts changed to faith.

Faith – that is the strength of the angels.

And that is what they give me: They give me faith so I can pass it on to other people.

The third story: My own.

Things had turned out like this for quite some time. No matter who I met in my workshops, I found a solution, an inspiration to make everything right. And it made me happy; it's wonderful to be able to help other people, a beacon of love. I gave love and in return I received love.

Nevertheless, when I came home in the evenings, nobody was there for me. It was always the same feeling. I stepped into the flat in which we had spent our time together and my energy simply dissolved like a balloon that deflates because there is a hole in it. That void – at the place where we had once shared such an abundance of happiness, joy and love – it felt like death amidst life.

My friends told me to look for another flat. 'You need to clean house, keep only a few memorabilia. You need to create a new surrounding and start a new life.' Trouble was, however, that the mere thought of doing this paralyzed me. I just didn't have the strength. Because deep inside I was convinced that nothing would ever change.

Because there was this one thing I missed so desperately: For twenty years I had shared my bed with Oliver. Except for very few nights we had spent all our nights together, embracing each other. To sleep alone felt like the second half of me had been torn out. Every single day and all night long I heard my body cry: "When will you come back? When will I touch you again?" If a baby is denied the comfort of physical contact, it will die. The same is true for adults – it just takes longer.

So, one day I had a serious conversation with archangel Michael.

"I get it," I said to him, "I understand that I'm precious because I'm delivering your message to the people. But, what's in there for me?"

Silence.

"Didn't you say I need special care?" I continued. "Where's it got to?"

I think, he understood how important that was to me. He said something like: "Here I thought you'd never ask." Of course, he didn't talk as mundane as I'm reflecting it, but that was the gist of it ...

It took some time for me to understand what he was trying to tell me. Was the meaning of his words that I should simply ask for it – so he could meet my request? Or was it maybe that it was normal – and rightly so – for me to want my share of the pie of love and success I had piled so generously onto the plates of so many others? Or was it even possible that another man might come into my life to share those things with me that I couldn't share with Oliver any longer – warmth and physical contact? Of course, I had been thinking of this possibility but couldn't imagine it to really happen.

Finally, I couldn't help laughing. The very thing I had given to all the other people – faith that their dreams could come true – I just couldn't find it in me. There wasn't the tiniest bit of faith in me that my situation would ever get better.

Heaven was very silent. I got familiar with this silence over time. It was like the very first, nearly inaudible whispering of a storm, approaching slowly but unstoppably.

No, the angels abide by their promises. It's just – sometimes, when your dreams finally come true, the outcome is very different from what you had imagined.

Some weeks after this conversation with archangel Michael I was invited to conduct a workshop in Austria at a beautiful horse farm in the Vienna Woods. I was on my way home, the hostess had dropped me at Vienna airport, and I had already passed the security check. As there was still some time left, I took a seat in a small cafeteria where I had an espresso and croissant. A man sat down on the stool next to me. I don't remember how we got into a conversation with each other. He seemed very tired, like a fallen king. His skin was very dark, almost black. He was wearing an expensive suit and a white shirt und his English was sophisticated. He asked me where I was from. I said, "From Germany."

I asked him in return where he was from and he said, "Jamaica."

Oh, the way he pronounced it. The second 'a' in the middle more like an 'e'.

And at that very moment, it hit me. That was the answer. Michael's answer.

I wasn't alone.

Jamaica
ONE LOVE - ONE HEART

Chapter 4 - Jamaica - One Love

A new morning has broken in my cottage in Te Moana. For the first time in a while my sleep has been deep and calm. I wake up feeling very at ease, a complete ease of mind. I can feel myself beyond the fear. I've dreamed of an angel who was standing next to me, taller than me. I was trying to solve some technical issue and there were people waiting for me to find the solution.

Here I am, in Ocho Rios, Jamaica, living the life of a digital nomad. Some time ago, the book by Tim Ferriss fell into my hands, "The four-hour-week", and that's when I heard that term for the first time – a 'digital nomad'. It describes someone who's able to live anywhere in the world just with a notebook and a mobile phone. Someone like me, solving issues of other people in her dreams with the help of angels.

Right now, the sun is coming forth from behind the clouds, saying hello and wishing me a good day.

The pupils of Archangel Michael seem to have a class concerning their project "Viola". That's me.

Dreams are the means of communication between the angels and me, that much I've learned by now. I feel dizzy thinking of all the ways I'm receiving and sending messages: Email, Facebook, letter mail, WhatsApp, mobile phone, dreams and the messages of angels.

True, I'm far away from basically everything here in Jamaica but I couldn't exist without all those means of communication. They are soothing my fear of being alone, replacing the physical contact I used to have with Oliver and that I miss so desperately. Yes there was the stranger I met at the Vienna airport. I will tell the story, soon.

Rennill, the gardener, is walking by, pushing a wheel-barrow. He's wearing a black and white striped shirt and dark green gumboots. "Good morning," I say. "How are you today?"

"Fine," he replies speaking with a voice that's as smooth as is his way of walking.

"What a wonderful day," I continue.

"It's supposed to rain in the afternoon," he says.

Here you are. A rainy afternoon. Even in paradise there's rain.

The next person to pass by is Marge, wearing a lemon colored dress. Marge is responsible for the rooms. She was here and made my bed, brought fresh towels and put some flowers onto the table. Marge is the kind of mama every little girl would want to have, soft and plumb, 'delicious' like a chocolate cake you'd want to drown in, so much so at peace with herself that you're absolutely sure you cannot get eaten by the wolves while she's near.

Marge spots me on the terrace and waves at me, swing-ing her arm over her head from left to right, like a watch hand, like you would wave at somebody sitting in a train, looking out of the train window while leaving the city. I beckon back with the same sweeping gesture. It's just wonderful. One moment like this can make me happy for the rest of the day.

I hear the noise of a lawn mower from the neighbouring property. The lawn of Te Moana will be cut tomorrow. They asked me if I'd prefer today or tomorrow. I said, "tomorrow, because I won't be here then." Thus, Rennil is doing it tomorrow.

That's love.

To ask me when to cut the lawn so I won't be disturbed, is love.

It is love to wave at me from a distance, wearing a lemon dress, although we've met only once so far when she brought flowers for my table.

I'm not alone. These people see me. They feel that I need their love like the air that I breathe. And, so they share it with me.

I couldn't get into contact with Sharon, my last outpost of civilisation before the prairie begins, yesterday. Because of technical issues. Sharon is not only the last bastion to prevent my mind from drowning, she is also the mama who has been taking care of my heart for many years.

Initially, when Oliver and the kids were still there, she was my teacher. I've learned very much from her about the wisdom of horses, animals and trees and how to read energy. Since the accident, she is the keeper of my heart. She is like the angels, save that she's living down on earth and I can talk to her on the phone. She's living at her ranch in Colorado, US.

Skype and Zoom didn't work because of some plug-in problem and a phone call with my mobile phone costs seven dollars a minute. Sharon said she'd get an international rate for her phone. We postponed our talk to Sunday.

I am becoming aware that writing this book is different than my other novels. I have invited the truth; invited the readers who are so very honest and reply in such honesty, confessing their own vulnerability, that I simply cannot tell some farfetched fictional story just to be a little entertaining. Doing that would be easy – I am a writer, after all. But if I did, I would deceive them, and they would know it. They would turn away from me and rightfully so. Or they would let me know that, above all, I'd deceive myself. Yes, that's just how my readers are – wonderful persons, blessing and curse. No, in fact they're pure blessing, expecting the truth from me. I love them.

Now the fat's in the fire and I'm sitting here with my truth that's waiting to be finally written down. But, I'm much too afraid. You may skip the next few sentences if you want, but I need to write them down to unburden myself a little. I just need a little self-pity right know.

Ah, Viola, you're so dumb! Why ever did you start this at all? Why couldn't you be content with just taking a vacation, doing nothing as it was planned? Just drifting through the days on beautiful Jamaica.

And why, oh why!!! couldn't the angels leave me alone? Just this once? Why did they have to spoil this holiday as well? With their *super-duper-mega-idiotic-and-daft-as-a-brush-move* two weeks before the beginning of my holiday. Just when I was back to feeling okay, they dropped a bomb. Who is the amateur responsible for that? And why didn't you watch out, Michael? Damn!

I'm going for a swim now before it starts raining. The rain won't win, and neither will the problem. Even if it's almost killing me. I'll pass the problem on to the sea. The sea won't die from it.

Two hours later:

The sea is like home, that much I can tell. It's like being embraced by something inconceivably great. I saw it from above after all, sitting in the plane that took me across the ocean for hours. I could see how vast it is. And now I'm swimming in it ... and I'm in good hands. Everything inside of me is calming down. There is nothing holding me. There is nothing letting me down. The sea is warm and calm. There are those fascinating plants, growing on the cliffs near the water, inside the caves and at the sharp edges of lava long solidified, looking like flying saucers. And again, I'm totally entranced by this beauty.

Above, a bird is circling through the sky and I remember I saw one of those for the first time when I was living with Patrick, the guy I met at Vienna airport, in Jamaica. Those birds have wings like bats, the same double curved outline, and long and pointy heads. Their silhouette is like the drawing of an artist in front of the sky.

One of them is circling above and while I'm watching it, I feel something changing inside of me. The fear will not win. Up to now it's just been a thought but now I can feel it all over my body. The ocean is my witness. Never! I will face the truth and find a way. My fear can win only if I deny the truth. No matter how frightened I might be, I will hold my ground.

Finally, I'm able to write. The words are carrying me like the sea. I'm able to write down what's scaring me so much. I'm able to write about that day, about what happened two weeks before I came here.

Two weeks before I came here, I found a letter in my letter box. Sent from Morocco. The address written in handwriting, an exotic kind of handwriting. The sender's name female. I will never forget that moment I held that letter in my hand.

This scene will always stay inside my mind: I'm holding that letter in my hands looking at the handwriting, looking at that woman's name. Adrenaline is coursing through my body. I'm all ablaze. And I just know it: The news inside this envelope will rip me to shreds, and there's nothing I can do about it. True, I could just leave it unopened, discard it. But there is that one predicament about truth: Is it more dangerous to know it or to be ignorant of it?

So, I open the letter. Inside there's a sheet of paper with that same foreign handwriting on both sides. It's from a culture unknown to me. And there's a picture. That one I put aside. Sometimes I get letters from foreign countries when someone has found me on the web and is asking for support. That's my last hope – although deep inside I know that this is not the case.

This letter is from Charifa. She's writing in English,

just a few sentences. She says that Oliver had given her my address. That she'd been thinking very long about whether she should write to me. Says that I've lost everything – everything but this: "You have a friend in Morocco. And a family."

A son. Oliver's son. I look at the picture. The boy looks half Arabian and half German. Maybe nine years old. He has Oliver's high cheekbones and his mouth and his eyes. His name is written on the back of the picture: Ismail.

I feel like I'm torn into pieces. Exactly the way I felt when that Moroccan doctor broke the news to me on the phone. I just cannot conceive what's happening to me. But I do know that I cannot deal with all of this on my own.

Three years after the accident, three years after I'd planned to jump down that high-rise, I'm back at that very point where everything began. Torn into a thousand shreds. Shortly after reading the letter, I call a friend, beg her to come over because I cannot deal with it on my own. She comes and finds the words I need to hear. She says: "That's in the past. You have a new life now. This child is not your responsibility. Don't give this room in your life."

Do I have a new life? Will I ever have one? That's what I'm afraid of: How blind have I been all those years? For I didn't realise that Oliver led a double life, had another life in Morocco, a second family. Of course, I knew he went there quite often because he was supervising the construction of several hotel complexes. But I did not know that he had a 'wife' and a child there.

So far, as I see it, I was a woman who lost her husband

and children in a tragic accident. Now I am a woman who lost her family and discovers that the happiness she took for real before the accident happened was an illusion. How twisted of a fate was that? Not only victim of fate but victim of deception too.

And there is another question even bigger than that one: Am I still blind? Will life delude me again? Am I to receive news like that again and again? And if so – how often will I be able to put the pieces together again when everything keeps falling apart?

Dear angels, at least I know now why you called me a difficult case that night on top of the high-rise. Why you said I was completely infested. I'd been living a lie and hadn't even been aware of it. But you were able to see it. You could see the things I couldn't. How can I protect myself? How can I prevent myself from experiencing such a thing again? That's the most important question of my life. How can I protect myself? What do I need to accomplish this?

I know what I need – it is always the same thing: Love. But will there be enough love? Enough for this?

I realise that love is more demanding than I thought up to now, much more.

In Jamaica they call it 'One Love'. Yes, there is only one love. The plants know it. The animals know it. The sun knows it as does the ocean.

And I need to get to know it.

Chapter 5 – Loving People

Love – the big mystery. Just like the ocean. I wake up and it just is. And it is like it must be – no questions to be asked. Not to be touched. Just this minute, while I was waking up, it was talking to me. So, I hurried and put on my clothes, got my notebook, put up some water for a coffee, prepared to write down everything it had told me. But I wasn't fast enough. It has fallen silent. No, that's not true, I just cannot hear it anymore. It ran away just like a shy horse.

Now I must not be angry like a human being or sad or fancy that I knew how I could reclaim it. I must not build a fence for this horse. And even if I did, it wouldn't make the slightest difference.

I've known horses jumping over the highest fences. And I've seen horses dying behind fences, though basically missing nothing – apart from love. I must not quarrel with love because the illusion of a fulfilled life was taken away from me. A life with a husband and two children. And an accident. Truth is, I lived an illusion. Truth is, love was to be found somewhere else. Just like this morning. Can I really quarrel with it? Can I quarrel with the sea?

This morning the sea is even more beautiful than usual, so beautiful it makes me cry. Smooth, flowing and gentle. There's a silent, so very silent rolling at the surface starting invisibly at the horizon and becoming visible at the extensions. And there was something new today, something that attracted my attention immediately after I'd pulled back the mosquito net and looked out of the window. Just a second – I'll come back to the sea in a moment. The grey bird is coming very close now, I can see its dove-colored feathers and how they harmonize with the metal blue of the ocean. It's never come so close before. Just like it wants to jump into my written text ... and it does.

What's different today? The transition of the colors where the sky meets the sea is a deep dark blue today. An almost solid bluish black getting lighter and lighter, finally fading into a silvery, almost colorless very light grey blue.

As I'm writing this, daylight is arriving making everything brighter by the moment. Michael. Your pupils. Thank you! And they're sending even more light. Thank you!

But there is more about the ocean. It's very important because that's where the love is. Not just this gradual color gradient ... there's a radiance over everything. Light. A radiance consisting of light.

No, I cannot quarrel with love. It might shatter my heart into a thousand pieces, but it won't hinder me from experiencing all this beauty for which I'll never find the proper words to praise.

Michael and his pupils are still in the act of brightening the day. All the shades of green are slowly becoming visible. Marge is passing by and again waving with her arm lifted up.

She tells me that soon Mr. Salmon will arrive. I read in the visitors' book that Mr. Salmon comes by every Saturday to sell fruit and vegetables and that he's done so since 1981. That's 37 years.

Shortly after, Mr. Salmon is standing in front of the door. His car has a truck bed which is packed with baskets filled with potatoes, carrots, papaya, melons, onions, bananas, cucumbers, cauliflower and peppers. He weighs out everything I buy and puts it into black bags. His hearing isn't all too good any longer and Marge does the talking. It's more of a communication with distinct sounds than words. When we say goodbye, I express my thanks and Mr. Salmon's wrinkled face lights up. Just a gentle touch. My skin is pale, and I come from a faraway land. But this is not about the things that make us different.

It's about love.

There's a gecko sitting on top of the balustrade. It turns around and looks at me. It also wants to be a part of this story and just like that it's in.

Can you assume why I'm writing down all of this? Because Corinna, one of my readers, mentioned yesterday in the blog that she had missed those detailed descriptions of the here and now in chapter three. I'm writing because the readers are so close to me. Their words are showing up on my monitor and touching me. Yesterday Stefanie wrote in Facebook:

"Every day I find myself waiting impatiently for the story to be continued :-) – the style is

so captivating I'm literally soaking it all in.
I always want to stop myself because I think
I should read it slooowly and thoooroughly,
but I just cannot, I'm soaking it in and
ffffffffffffftttt – it's gone, sort of inhaled :-). But
it probably gets kind of reprocessed inside of
me, digested quasi, and there are a lot of nu-
tritional components in there that are impor-
tant for me ... I'm a little surprised at myself,
at what I'm writing and all the connotations
I'm using ... anyway, the style is just awesome
and I'm looking forward to chapter five ... :-)."

I'm so happy because of comments like this one, and I can feel all the love. It's just – with the love the fear is coming back as well, the fear that everything could just vanish. The readers, their words that are affecting me so deeply, meaning so much to me, making me write. The fear that everything might collapse like a house of cards, might disintegrate just like the illusion of a great love, destroyed with one single letter.

I hear the archangel say: "Would you wish you had never loved him instead?"

"No, I wouldn't."

"You think that you've lost something?" Michael says.

Do I really think this? Have I lost something? Does a person who loves lose something because his or her lover chooses another path? Have I lost Oliver because of Charifa's letter? Have I lost one single moment that I've shared with Oliver in perfect love? Is love imperfect just because it's coming to me in an entirely different way than I would have wished for?

Evening has come. I've spent the day with John and Joy, two friends of mine who life gifted me with like precious stones smoothed by the water, selected from a large variety because of their beauty. Delroy, one of the drivers of Te Moana, took me to the Seventh Day Adventist Church in Ocho Rios.

I was welcomed at the parking lot by a young, athletic looking man with a cordial smile. "Welcome back," he said. "Sister Wray asked me to welcome you." Love. Sister Wray being Joy Wray, one of those precious, smoothed stones.

The young man led me into the church and Joy waved to me. I took a seat next to her in the wooden pew. It'd been a few months since I' seen Joy last, but immediately the warmth of our friendship was back. And immediately I was utterly happy to be in that church.

The church is under construction, its walls and floor are made of rough concrete, its roof of corrugated sheet and its windows are just holes in the walls. It's a big place with room for many people, a municipal building for the old church has become too small for the growing township. There's a stage at the front with a speaker's desk and some people were sitting behind that desk. But that's about the only thing in there that's somehow sacral.

What is sacral or holy about this church is the people.

The room was filled with people, young and old. The men were wearing suits and the women festive dresses, some of them wearing beautiful hats. I was the only white person in there.

Why am I always happy in this church? Because none of the things in my life that sometimes seem to be so vital are of any importance in there. I feel something different instead: Faith. The faith of these people is not locked up in a small space in their hearts, buried under a thick layer of whatsoever. Their faith can be felt with every breath they take. It is palpable, the whole room is suffused with it. And although it's not visible, it is so strong that I feel absolutely at home.

I can think of only one thing: This is the one place I need to be. The people here are feeling deeply – so do I. They're desperate and unrelenting – so am I. There are no boundaries for my faith or my strength. I can share the one thing with them which is most important to me.

I can be with them, hold their hands, sing and dance together with them. I'm allowed to cry, me, the only white woman, and it's utterly natural. They don't expect anything from me, they don't press me, they don't exclude me, they treat me like anybody else – with kindness, attention and warmth.

The sermon lasted for at least one and a half hours. The voice of the young man with the black suit and the flashing pink tie was loud and forceful and sometimes playful and I didn't miss a single word. Not a second was I distracted or let my mind wonder. He told the story of Moses who freed his people from captivity. He kept mentioning special passages from the bible and I kept skimming Joy's bible to find them. It's a big bible with many gossamer sheets. Sometimes, the wind breezing through the windows turned some of them, too.

The words in the bible seemed suddenly so vivid, the story one of survival under harshest conditions. The chosen people walking through the desert, finally freed from imprisonment but so very hungry and slowly losing faith, starting to complain to Moses, starting to quarrel with God. Unbelievably hard ordeals must be faced and only the ones whose believe is strongest are still standing firm.

That sermon wasn't about the Israelites; it was about every single person in that room, about the pain everyone must withstand – sometimes nearly breaking from it.

A young woman sang, accompanied by an electric piano. Her voice was so vibrant I was trembling. Haunting, yet not depressing or making you feel trapped; on the contrary, it was liberating and could be heard far beyond the interior of the church.

The people here, I thought, are just like horses.

Maybe that's the reason I came to Jamaica. These people are strong and expressive, but they don't attack. They have a distinct feeling for the things that could hurt someone else and so they don't hurt me. They're gentle.

What I'm finding here is so very rare among people: Sensing the feelings of others and showing great respect, but without creating a distance. No distance, but trust and warmth. Yes, I can find it here – in the congregation of the Seventh Day Adventists.

After the service I had lunch with John and Joy. Joy told me she will be 79 years old next Saturday. It's hard to believe. She is so petit and lively I'm feeling old next to her. Many years ago, Joy started to cook vegan, for example the typical Jamaican ackee, harvested directly from their kitchen garden. John and Joy celebrated their 50th wedding anniversary last year but when you see them together you'd assume they fell in love just recently.

John grew up in Jamaica and came to England by ship when he was 18 years old, joining some relatives who already lived there and receiving a training to become an elementary teacher.

That's also were he met Joy who originally is from Barbados, another Caribbean Island. Back then, Joy was working as a hospital nurse. 30 years later John returned to Jamaica, together with Joy, where they bought a house to call their own and have lived since then.

I came to know the two of them two years ago when I came to Jamaica for the first time. Whenever I'm back in Germany, John and me are sending funny emails back and forth. I love his distinguished British style and I always find some amusing facts to tell him. And when I'm here in Jamaica, he always finds some small presents for me, like a watch with the Jamaican flag on it, a book about the native dialects or self-made sweets. He's one of those people who like to make presents. John and Joy are my anchors in a storm, with them I find peace and quiet.

They live in this space beyond pain where I can find a home. Their kindness is pure. They never hurt me, they never turn away from me and they never use me. They just love me, and I love them.

I'm not alone.

ONE LOVE - ONE HEART

Chapter 6 – Jamaican Truth

Waking up today I'm thinking of John and Joy. Today there is a gentle feeling of happiness inside of me despite the already familiar feeling of fear. The day I spent together with them yesterday was pure happiness. It felt like I had visited my deepest wish for love, and it came true in the presence of John and Joy. To love like John and Joy is what I want for myself.

How often he calls her by her name, and how often she says his.

"Joy ..." his silky voice floats through the living room.

"John," comes her answer from the kitchen.

"What would you like to drink?"

"Plum juice," she says and continues twittering how much she likes plum juice.

But the real dialogue between them, the one between the lines, is more like: "Joy, I have no words to tell you how much I love you, and how happy I am to have been spending my days with you for more than fifty years now."

"John, my love, I know. Your telling me daily, again and again, makes me happy; so much so that I feel like I did the day we met despite the fact I'll be 79 years old soon."

"I ask you what you would like to drink because I want only the best for you, because I want to make you happy every minute of the day, because it makes me happy to see you so sweet and alive."

"I simply love plum juice, John, but I love it even more when you hand it to me. And most of all I love you."

Not once since I met John and Joy, have I heard a single harsh or critical word between them. Never a complaint or an accusation. I don't know their story, don't know much about their life. Most certainly, they had to deal with pain, had to suffer loss and disappointment, just like every single one of us. But they always maintained their conciliatory attitude. Their stories always have a happy ending – because they choose them to.

John told me about the time when he went to Great Britain as a young man. Back then there weren't as many people with dark skin as there are today; told me how they used to ask him from which African country he was when he came from Jamaica in fact. He told me that there were ethnic riots, that he was part of joint projects trying to integrate people from different cultures during the thirty years he lived there. He never complained about racist assaults or insults, there is no bitterness on his side.

Patrick, the guy from Vienna Airport, told me about those. Patrick, the Jamaican, who was born and grew up in England, who was the only Afro-Caribbean attending a "white" school. He said: "You never knew who of the whites would be kind and who of them would punch you the next moment."

I can understand that feeling, that ever-present fear John surely knows, too. That fear every person knows to some extent. And yet John decided to refuse giving in to it. He decided and keeps deciding to admit only different thoughts.

After dinner, Joy asked how the world had been treating me since we last met. It was the beginning of a profound conversation. I told her about the letter and about the feeling that my life went to pieces for a second time; about Oliver having another family and his eight years old son. She told me the most important thing was to not fill myself with bitterness.

She said, "Lay your pain down at the cross's feet. Jesus had to endure insults, humiliation and finally was murdered although he was innocent." She took me into her arms and prayed for me. Her prayers weren't just hollow words or empty phrases. I could feel her deep understanding of my pain. I started to pray as well, and we prayed together. We voiced everything that was on our minds.

Finally, she asked me what song I liked. I'm not familiar with English church songs but "Go tell it to the mountain" came to my mind. She looked it up in her service book and we sang together. We sang the complete three verses and then three verses of another song she likes. Our singing was at least as fervent as that of the young woman at the service. It might have sounded like charivari for other ears, but did that even matter? Love shows itself in an unfathomable abundance and every single variant is irresistible.

I don't know how much time Joy and I spent singing and praying. John had disappeared and I assume he might have taken a nap.

Some time later he was back, and he gave me three little presents: pictures I had sent him per email some time ago. One picture of my horse, one of an invitation I had sent to him and Joy and the augmentation of one of my business cards. All three of them lovingly furnished with a frame and a background. That's the way John is, he never ceases to find ways to say: "I love you".

I am truly not alone.

We talked about the geography of the Caribbean Islands. John took out an atlas and we looked up Barbados, where Joy was born. Barbados is 1,000 kilometers away from Jamaica, bounded by the Caribbean Sea on one and the Atlantic Ocean on the other side. Joy told us about her childhood days she'd spent on the beaches together with her siblings – on the island's Atlantic side where the waves are huge.

I thought: Grown up in paradise. And we talked some more, sharing events of our lives. Soon I could hear the first insects sing, and it was getting dark. But there's one more story I'd like to tell you: For a time, John and Joy had a visitor, a cock which had strayed to them and decided to stay in their garden. They called him "Strayer" because that's what he was. "If you got too close to him, he would run away," says John. "We always respected that boundaries. Maybe that's the reason he stayed for such a long time."

Eventually it worked out and I could finally talk to Sharon, to my shaman, my last outpost of civilization before the prairie begins. That's how I'll name her in this novel. I think she would find it amusing. Sharon managed to establish an international telephone connection. She's always there when I need her. Love.

Sharon is not an angel, she is a horse in human form, an unfaltering voice of truth. She can smell lies from ten kilometers away, especially the ones you're deceiving yourself with. What she tells me isn't always pleasant, but it surely is true. It's a truth resting in love. I need to talk to her about the letter. About the pain that's come so close again and that I cannot escape. About my life gone to pieces again and me desperately trying to pick them up.

Sharon tells me in no uncertain manner that all of this "is fine material for a novel, but it's no use clinging to this drama."

"He has a child from another woman," I say quietly although in fact I want to scream it aloud. I want everybody to know in what a mean!!!, vile and destructive way life is treating me. How I'm cheated of my happiness again and again. How it's truly!!! impossible for me to live on like this.

"You lived an illusion," she says.

That doesn't sound all too flattering, but unfortunately its's true.

"I've been blind."

"But now you see and that's good."

Everything inside me is rising up against this situation. What kind of person am I to have lived an illusion thinking it was my life? How can I live on with this knowledge?

Knowing that my life, my love, my domestic happiness – those very things that were most important in my life, all I ever wanted from life – were just an illusion?! I want to go back to this haven, into Oliver's arm, back before all of it happened. I want my children back, want to watch them grow up, want to live with them.

"For as long as I've known you, something deep inside of you has always been searching for truth. Truth is a good thing."

"Yes," I say, the word feeling heavy like a rock falling to the ground because there's no one there strong enough to hold it up any longer.

It's a devastating feeling to finally approach truth, the bubble eventually bursting. I don't know if there's someone in your life forcing you to see the truth. Maybe a horse or a dog? Those are also able to do it. And do you understand what they want to tell you? Then you know, what I'm talking about. It's devastating and disillusioning and you're spontaneously losing three kilos during the process.

I keep trying to explain to Sharon how cruel everything is, how inescapable. How it's not just me but also our children who are losing their family in retrospect. How they used to live in a blended family without knowing it. And so on and so forth. Sharon keeps reminding me that I used to live an illusion but that I finally woke up and what a good thing that is.

Little by little I begin to see that all the turmoil and the drama, all the self-pity and the hopelessness are just different ways of trying to evade truth: I was blind. I'm not just this unfortunate woman whose husband and children were killed in an accident, a situation nobody can be blamed for. I'm also a woman whose husband led a double life, a woman who lived just the illusion of a perfect family. An illusion of faith, an illusion of the one and only great romantic love.

Gone.

Forever.

Welcome to the real world.

Rarely have I felt as disillusioned as I do right now. Sharon doesn't wrap me into soft wool blankets. But I feel loved by her, nevertheless.

"Love without truth is just a lie," she says. That much I can see now.

In the afternoon I'm invited to meet Jamaica in all its truth in the guise of Johnathan Edwards. Johnathan Edwards is a Jamaican truth. He picks me up and we head to Sugar Pot Beach in Rio Nuevo. Sugar Pot Beach, just a ten-minutes ride from Ocho Rios, is an insider tip concerning Jamaica's beaches. Sugar Pot Beach is owned by Josh, an old friend of Johnathan. Although I've been to Sugar Pot Beach on several occasions, today is the first time I meet Josh in person. I've always been fascinated by people who are living their dreams. Because that's where I'm heading as well. Towards a dream completely and utterly come true.

Here's what I know about Josh: He's from Belgium, earned enough money with his business to buy that part of the beach and is living here nowadays. He's someone who cannot be overlooked. White beard, white hair tousled by the wind, weather-beaten dark skin and an inner peace like a beach on which shores the waves are washing up, retracting and washing up again – every day, every hour and every minute since time immemorial.

Josh is sitting at one of the tables in the café, his notebook in front of him. A digital nomad gone settled. Aside from the waves there are people from all over the world getting washed up here. You could possibly write a complete novel just about those women and men.

About Johnathan, for instance, the Jamaican truth. Johnathan's family owns one of the last colonial estates in Jamaica: Bromley in Walkerswood, about half an hour inland of Ocho Rios. His genealogical tree is widely ramified with his family hailing from Scotland and living throughout Jamaica nowadays. Some of his relatives are celebrities, some are very affluent, some are commanding political power. Johnathan is living at Bromley which is a complex of charismatic buildings originating from the Jamaican colonial period.

But on Sundays you'll probably meet him on Sugar Pot Beach. I met him for the first time at Bromley when I'd rented one of the guest rooms. Bromley is for sale and I was one of the last guests to stay there. That's the reason why I could enjoy Johnathan's hospitality and, while having a glass of wine in the evenings, was granted an indepth look into Jamaican lives.

Johnathan is so much more than just a perfect host.

His life is that rich you could fill volumes with it. He's travelled the whole world, established and ran a technology business in California and he's a philosopher. Was I to take three snapshots of his life, it would be the following:

Grew up in Jamaica at a place called "Heaven". Barefoot, next to a well, among the workers' children, on the beach. It's always warm, the sun always shining. When he got his first school uniform, he rolled it up and threw it into the river; never wanted to attend school; spent his childhood in paradise. And like so many Jamaicans John is radiating this gentleness. Nothing about him is hard or harsh, his character is as friendly and gentle as the nature surrounding him.

The second snapshot: Johnathan and a good friend of his, Naddy, a Rastafarian. Naddy catches a big beautiful fish; he looks at the fish and is fascinated by its beauty in such a way, he says: "I cannot kill it," and throws it back into the water. Then he looks at Johnathan and says: "Never lose your groundation." "Groundation" is the core word of Johnathan's philosophy. It means being embedded or ingrained. Since then Johnathan has been trying to remind the people of their groundation. And somehow Johnathan and I are on the same mission on that score. Even if our lives are utterly different.

The third snapshot: Johnathan Edward's car, which is 27 years old. He's not driving it because he cannot afford another one. He's driving it because it "reminds me of my socialist self". On our way back from Sugar Pot Beach this very car suffers a breakdown. In the middle of nowhere.

As Johnathan knows all the wrinkles of his car, he succeeds in patching it up and we reach the next gas station. Shortly after, Gairy shows up with a car mechanic accompanying him. The hood gets lifted, there's hissing and steaming. The insects begin their daily song and it's getting dark. Time isn't important here in Jamaica. After a while, I walk into the shop to look for some chocolate. I cannot find anything I've seen or eaten before. The young woman working the till tells me she likes my dress. I tell her how fascinating I find it that I'm not familiar with any of the sweets for sale. She thinks that's funny and disappears shortly to reemerge with a Snickers and a Milky Way in her hand. Point for her. I buy some ice cream for me and the three gentlemen trying to fix the old car.

We just stand there, three men and a woman in the dark at a gas station named *Cool Oasis*, eating ice cream next to Johnathans broken car.

Life is good.

ONE LOVE – ONE HEART

Chapter 7 – If You Follow Love

Today I love my life. It's raining, the sea is churning with the waves rushing in and breaking in white, foaming cascades, one after another, again and again. Just as life is descending upon me, as is the fear, the pain, the happiness. I didn't create the sea, didn't create the wind nor my life. But here I am.

I'm here in Jamaica living the life I've desired for such a long time. Even if my life went to pieces three years ago, even if I discovered only three weeks ago that a big part of my life was an illusion – what I'm experiencing right now is not an illusion. It's not a dream. I'm truly here even if it feels like a dream sometimes. But that's just what makes me this happy. I'm allowed to live this dream.

We all have dreams. In my business I meet many people, I learn about their dreams and my job is to encourage them to live those dreams, regardless of what they're made of.

Dreams possess a strong secret power. They tend to come true if you take action, even more so if you have faith in them.

Three years ago, I met Patrick Golding. With him I dreamed of love. It's due to him that I came to Jamaica. Life separated us again – the distance and the differences between our worlds. But the love encapsulated in my memory remained. It was bigger than Patrick and me, even if he's no longer a part of my life and the dream to live with him is gone with the wind. Even if my heart is no longer bound to him, I can see now that something much greater came into my life through our connection.

I'm here in Jamaica not because of Patrick. I'm here because love is showing me something greater. It's showing me that it can be found everywhere, I just need to follow – follow without questions. Even though my longing for the embrace of a man is not fulfilled, I feel something else: I feel the love of life itself. I feel life responding to me, tender and gentle like a lover. I feel that life loves me, in such an intimate and personal way that I can believe in it again.

Yesterday evening I had a look at flights and at my appointments as I'd like to come back in April. Just now, Jessica, the owner of Te Moana, is calling and asking if she can get me anything from the city. I tell her I'd need some eggs and some cream for the vegetable sauce. She says she's got some leftovers from hosting visitors at the weekend and asks if I would mind using those. Shortly after, she's standing in front of my door, a basket in her hands in which I find everything I need. I tell her that I'd like to come back in April. She tells me that the cottage will be available then, although I checked the booking site yesterday and it showed me something different.

I tell the angels: All the pain and fear notwithstanding, you're spilling the horn of plenty down on me. It is far more than a box of eggs and a carton of cream. It's love you're pouring on me. You never stop telling me: Follow your dreams and we will open the doors for you.

I can see that love is so much more than the physical contact between man and woman. Yes, it includes the love between man and woman but there is this much wider, greater space, it's happening on a larger scale – and only there, this love between two people will become something greater as well. I can feel that now, and I believe that life will show me how to get there.

All this beauty; the beauty of Te Moana, of a gas station called "Cool Oasis" and of a 27 years old "socialist car", waiting to be fixed; the beauty of the people whose very sight makes me happy – not because they're more beautiful than the white people in Germany, but because my soul can touch theirs; all this beauty carries this one message: Love can be found.

Love is shining on everything just like a big life-giving sun.

I'm longing for a man because I'm longing for the sun of love, which I will meet at the same time.

The one thing I must learn and that's the actual reason behind this adventure called Jamaica: To differentiate between this all-encompassing love and the longing, the desire, the daydreams and illusions leading me into blind alleys. Life has just taught me a lesson with that letter from Charifa. It revealed to me just how deeply I'm trapped in illusions and how painful it is to abandon them.

The fear of getting drawn into other illusions without being aware of it is back. After all, there is more than enough proof of my naiveté and that's scary. And of course, there is no guaranty for something like that won't happen again.

But today I can see that a dream has come true that seemed to be an illusion for such a long time. I'm here, sitting in front of my notebook, writing. This is not an illusion. Since the accident happened it had been impossible for me to write – and now I can do it again. When everything is lost you become very humble. You are grateful for your very breath.

Just like the waves in the sea there will always be waves crashing into my life. And at this very moment I'm learning to differentiate between dream and illusion. New delusions might come into my life, all my inner voices warning me might be correct, but there is this one other voice telling me that love is not an illusion. It is just a little greater than I thought it to be.

One of my readers made a comment on the chapter I wrote yesterday, the one in which I wrote what happened to me with Oliver. The illusion of a perfect love, living a perfect life in a perfect family. Thank you so much, dear reader. I won't mention your name because I don't want to invade your privacy. And as I'd like to publish your words this very day, there might not be enough time to get your approval.

Her comment:

> *"For 23 years I have worked at a machine-building company as the sole woman in a leading position. Almost every one of our field workers has had a relationship out of wedlock over the years or even got married for a sec-*

ond time. Russia, Taiwan, China, Japan – you name it. And, again and again the first family is totally unaware of it.

Men are gutless or at least they're unable to live monogamously. And only if chance intervenes, they stop living with their first family. There was this one issue, for instance, when truth was revealed because of the First Communion of a child in Mexico.

The long stays abroad play a huge part in this, of course. The new lover is exotic, has had a completely different upbringing, looks up to them and makes life very comfortable.

For her it's often the only chance for social advancement. For him it's the chance to be treated like a prince and he loves her admiration.

Please forgive me my very sober way of writing this. If you're not directly involved, it's simply an observation of life.

None of the executives we've sent to China over the last 15 years is still living together with his former life partner from Germany – not a single one.

Of course, the involved persons surely think it's love – and maybe it is.

I really like chapter seven – I would have given similar feedback as the spiritual com-

panion of Viola, but I didn't dare because I wouldn't want to offend anybody."

Dear reader, thank you so much.

Love or illusion? What are our motives – women's and men's? We want to feel like princes and princesses, want to be admired, to be noticed, to be treasured. We're searching for someone who's looking up to us and is making our life comfortable. And we're not brave enough to admit that we've found that someone somewhere else than we originally thought. We're worried we might disappoint someone else. We're afraid, and rightfully so, of the consequences. We're afraid to say aloud that he or she has lived an illusion or that a love, which once was real, has become a mere nothing.

Presumably that's the price we pay if we follow the true dreams of love: Getting the opportunity to discover a new dream every day and having to disappoint others simultaneously. And, of course, the other way around – getting disappointed by others who are discovering their dreams. A fence built to lock out disappointment will also lock out love. If we stop dreaming, we stop living.

Do women love men because they make it possible for them to advance socially? Do men love women because they make their lives more comfortable? And what about those women who are stronger financially as well as job-related? What about those women whose power of love is greater than the one of men? What about those men who search for a woman who wants to be with them regardless of money and a nice house? Who want to be loved for their own sake?

I believe I will learn to differentiate between the illusion of love and true love. And I also believe this to be the meaning of my story and that I'm learning by living through the pain and the fear. Because fear can be real or an illusion as well.

It's not easy to learn this, not at all. But it's worth it. Nothing is more important than to perceive love.

Last night, I translated the text about Johnathan into English and sent it to him. This morning he answered: "There is a yin and a yang in everything. You haven't met the other side of me so far." He also wrote he would get his car from the shop and pick me up to drive to Bromley where we could have dinner together. I should bring my toothbrush so I could stay the night and he would take me back home the next morning.

I asked Johnathan yesterday if he'd give me his permission to post our adventure in my blog; told him I'd only write pleasant things. He just said: "Write the truth."

It's been raining all day today, nevertheless, it's bright. The leaves and roots of the trees are shining all over. Every time the sun peeks through the clouds, like it does just now, everything is dotted with lights, the reflections of sunlight on wet leaves. In the distance I hear the honking of a car horn. And it's back again – the real dream.

Life is developing faster than my novel, or it's the angels who are faster than me. They thought about something special for me. A broken-down vehicle plays a role in it as does Bromley, the colonial building amidst the hills of Jamaica, a place centuries-old and filled with wonderful stories.

I won't ask.

I'm just going to have faith.

Chapter 8 – The Rock

It's raining. And if it rains in Jamaica, it pours. It's a deafening, pelting rain. The sea is churning, waves are crashing in, one after another, like an atmospheric discharge.

I didn't go to Bromley yesterday. Johnathan had to cancel our date because his coughing got worse. I swam in the ocean for quite some time. First, I was afraid to go in because of the heavy swell. I tried to cling to the cliffs because my feet couldn't touch the ground.

But after a while I just let go and I didn't sink but floated on the surface. When I'm in the water, my thoughts and feelings become liquid. When I'm in the water, I can feel my story without hurting because it's encased by something greater. I start telling it, little by little; telling it to the water, word for word. And while I'm telling it, it's changing and becoming something good.

I come to understand that this is just how my character is: My soul is constantly seeking a connection, no matter where I am. Amongst people, amongst horses, under trees or in the water – in this connection I find myself.

Whenever I let go of everything, my soul takes off and begins to search for connection. It's then that I discover a whole network of connections. It's also then that the ones I think of just know that I do; and respond to it. Often I'll receive an email or another sign shortly after.

When I'm in the water, I realise that those connections are moving just like the water, that I'm just a small human being in the middle of this huge ocean of connections and yet I'm able to connect with it.

When I was a child that longing for love was always on my mind. All I dreamed of was to have a family one day.

And because I wanted it so much, I couldn't sense that Oliver, my husband, had given his heart to another woman. Or maybe I did sense it, but that desperate longing for love, that fear of being alone, didn't allow me to see the truth. We'd made a promise after all: " ... in good times as in bad. Till death do us part." Back then, I'd felt so certain that everything would be alright. That I would never be alone again. I couldn't see the truth. I was blind.

The gray bird is back. It's striding across the lawn, not minding the rain. John and Joy call. We're going to meet this evening, I invited them for dinner to the "Hermosa Cove" in Ocho Rios. John asks if we still have a date. Of course, we do. To hear his voice and talk about the plan to pick them up later makes me happy immediately. Joy joins our conversation and it's so good to hear her voice. John and Joy are like me. They feel the same joy in being together than I do. No rules of the game. You do it, simply because it makes you happy.

Suddenly I remember that I mentioned the wrong time. I told them I'd pick them up at half past six, but I mixed that up. The driver will pick me up at half past six, so we will be at their place at a quarter to seven. I don't want them to wait without knowing why, so I call them and leave a message on the answering machine. Shortly after, John calls me back. Again, I hear his voice and again it makes me happy. I explain my mistake concerning the pickup time. He talks about the rain and I know he feels bad for me because it's rainy instead of sunny during my holidays in Jamaica. But I don't mind the rain.

I can write. I'm in Jamaica. I love Jamaica – with or without rain. I hear him laughing. He says: "You have to circumvent the challenges." Here it is – "circumvent". John loves words. He knows that I love them and that's the reason why he chooses those very expressive ones. I delight in this word "circumvent". Circumvent – to negotiate an obstacle, to avoid the pitfalls, to find a way around the challenges of the rain, a way that'll keep you dry. That's John. He has a plethora of phrasings concerning the challenges of life.

I remember writing to him last summer. I was quite upset because of a business situation that made me feel cheated. And he sent me his words: "Move on to better places." That phrase is my inner Sunday since then. Whenever dirt spills into my life. I move on to better places and better people.

That's Jamaica. That's Bob Marley, one of the most influential musicians worldwide. Wisdom born from pain. Plain wisdom every person knows in their heart. Because we all are searching for love and all our hearts get broken again and again. Because our hearts seek a way to some better place, as does the smallest insect. A place where there's love without rules, only the desire for love and to experience it, par for par.

Donald Trump called countries like Jamaica "shit holes".

During the service on Sunday the preacher spoke of those voices, coming from the US, talking about corruption and crime in Jamaica. He said: "All the more, we need the power of faith." And every single person inside that church knew what he was talking about. It's about faith being stronger than money or power. It's about love being our strongest power by far.

I do find this love and power of faith also in Germany. But it's not as unmediated as it is here. Here it's like that because there is less safety. Faith comes when the outer hull is broken.

Johnathan told me that Jamaica is the country with the third largest national debt worldwide. There is no money for schools or infrastructure because the whole revenues of the state are needed to pay of the debts. The streets throughout the residential districts and on the countryside aren't getting repaired because there simply is no money for it.

Many of the cars driving around here are imported from Japan, used cars that would be unsaleable there. I marvel at the sturdiness of the underbodies of those cars. That they can withstand these streets full of holes is a miracle in itself. There are import taxes as high as the prices of the cars themselves. To be a taxi driver is one of most popular jobs here and the cars are that old I'm astounded (coming from Stuttgart, the city of cars) they are still moving at all.

Gairy, the driver who's chauffeured me around quite

often, tells me he's a trained plumber but that there are no jobs for craftsmen. Many of his relatives have moved to Canada where workers are still needed. His daughter is studying in Florida. She's that intelligent and diligent that she was granted a stipend. Many people I meet here have relatives living in countries like Canada or Great Britain. The families are separated with the children and some-times the spouses staying abroad – lots of eventualities for becoming scared, hurt or sad.

Another reason why I feel connected with Jamaica is the fact that my pain needs a lot of power of faith in order to wear off and that I'm sharing that need with the people here. I'm realising that now. My soul is searching for a cure.

In Europe I have self-confidence and live my habits. In JA (nickname for Jamaica) I feel rather self-conscious and frightened, I'm not familiar with my surroundings but my soul feels safe.

That's a gift from Jamaica. Me finding something that's healing me. Theoretically, there is no good reason for me to be here at all. But there is one reason outweighing everything. My soul needs to be cured. I don't know how to accomplish this so I can only try to listen to it and to listen to the angels like I did that night on top of the high-rise; try to learn to differentiate between a real inner voice and an illusion.

It stopped raining and the sun is back. Today I can feel with absolute certainty that it was the angels who made me come here; that it wasn't self-paced but caused by a power secretly dwelling within my soul. That this power is with me not because I'm an educated woman from Europe but because I've been touched by something way greater than me. It's the sea, the trees, the plants, the humming-birds, so tiny and agile, the gray bird, people like John and Joy and Patrick. They've touched me as I've touched them in this space that's all encompassing and where we've met like you meet a drop in the ocean. We cannot influence it, we cannot initiate it; it's not a reward for something we accomplished, it's a gift. We ourselves are this gift.

I'm thinking about my children who I've lost. I would've loved to pass this knowledge on to them. Then again, they're presumably much wiser souls now than me. I cannot give to them what a mother would. So, I give it to everyone else who affects me.

I know that I'm going to cry a lot of tears in the time to come. They're the water showing the way. And again, I can hear Jamaica calling me to return. I'll be here for the next three weeks. And I will be back. I must come back because my soul is healing here.

This is just the beginning. I never want to forget that what other people call a "shit hole" is beauty and love for me. I don't want to cling to a surety promised by marriage or to an ideal like fidelity. To be loyal is my second nature because I'm loyal to love – not to a single person or even to myself – but to love. I'm loyal to what the angels have contrived for me. Because they are love. Because God is love.

When I'm here, I can be at peace with what happened. I can say that Oliver remained faithful to his heart. He didn't tell me because he was afraid to hurt me. Death took this from him. Death let him appear innocent. And then, Charifa decided that the truth is more powerful than a lie, even if it hurts. She didn't want to hurt me either. She wanted to render a service to truth.

Can I put my trust in the fact that this too was the angel's will? To receive this letter, to wake up and see?

The love I shared with Oliver was a love that allowed him to travel freely and to discover new worlds just like I'm doing now. It was a love with me trusting without knowing. I gave my love and it was betrayed. Love tore me into pieces. And it demolished the house I used to live in. I cannot go back to this house.

But there is a bigger house, one that cannot be destroyed. I am safe.

I am not alone.

Chapter 9 – An Unexpected European Hummingbird

The next morning, I have a conversation with the hummingbird in the garden of Te Moana. It starts with me watching it and pondering why it is the heraldic animal of Jamaica greeting you everywhere at the airport from big advertisement boards and monitors.

The hummingbird living in this garden is that tiny I thought it to be a somewhat big bee at first.

Wikipedia tells me that there is in fact a certain kind of hummingbird that's called "bee hummingbird". The German name is "Bienenelfe", literally translating into "bee elf", which I find even more appropriate and I assume that the ornithologists (I love this word) who came up with that name must have been poets. Because a bee elf is bustling about the garden. A bee like an elf – bustling and humming and glittering. It's not for nothing that this animal is called a hummingbird – a bird that's humming.

Marge just came by to change the bedclothes and I ask her if a hummingbird literally makes some noise like trilling or singing. Marge thinks about it and finally answers, "I doubt it does. And if so, then very, very quietly."

Maybe it is called hummingbird because of its incredibly fast flapping? Between 40 and 50 wing beats per second, as Wikipedia informs me. I try to imagine that: In the same time it takes for me to pronounce "twenty-one" the hummingbird beats its wings 50 times. That's almost unimaginable. Flying forward at top speed the humming-bird is able to cover a distance of 385 times its own length per second. A jet fighter is quite lame compared to that, reaching only 40 times its own length. And yet the hummingbird moves more elegantly.

I'm telling myself that a bee isn't singing or humming neither and yet there is this German nursery rhyme of the humming bee. "Sum, sum, Bienchen sum ... (hum, hum, little bee, hum along ...)".

The hummingbird is beautiful and fast and viable all at once. It feeds on the nectar of the flowers, a high-energy nourishment. And it loves beauty, preferring the red and orange blossoms. In Jamaica there're plenty of those.

And I find another surprising detail: The humming-bird is native to the continent of America and cannot be found in Europe – currently, that is.

Because once upon a time – about 30 million years ago – it used to live in Europe as well. Gerald Mayr, a German paleornithologist, discovered one in a city called Frauen-weiler in Baden-Wuerttemberg, which is not far from the place I come from. He named it "Eurotrochilus inexpecta-tus – unexpected European hummingbird."

Knowing this – what else could I believe than the fact that everything on planet earth was created in perfect harmony millions of years ago? The European humming-bird and the fact that I'm meeting the Jamaican hum-mingbird this morning?

I'm watching it and I read about it and I have the dis-tinct feeling that it's aware of all of this. I know that feeling, it happens quite often with animals, no matter where. Now the gray bird is here, it stops in front of my porch and looks at me. Then it starts dancing. Like a stage actor, it dances through the garden until it disappears behind a bush. A gecko shinnies up the wooden beam of the banister. Then it jumps elegantly onto the next brace 20 centimeters away. I'm astonished – I didn't know geckos can jump!

Farther back in the garden there's a commotion, something causing some big leaves to rustle. Several of them are swaying and clashing, it sounds as if they're getting torn. Two big black birds appear, one chasing the other, and fly away.

The wildlife in the garden feels addressed and joins the conversation. I'm amazed.

I need to talk to the hummingbird. I have one question I need to ask. It's been playing on my mind and since yesterday it's grown even more important. Yesterday I skyped with two dear colleagues from Germany. We know each other because we're participating together in an online-class to learn exactly this – how to create online-classes.

Online-classes are the marketplace and working place of digital nomads like me, those people living and working at no specific place. Claudia shared her dream with us. She wants to be free, travel to and live in various countries and to stay just as long as it feels right. That's the freedom a digital nomad can enjoy.

And that's exactly the question I need to ask: When will my story connected to Jamaica end? When I go back to

Germany in February? Will I go on and discover another country for me this year? Or will I return to Jamaica? I chose a date for my next journey to Jamaica, I found a flight, Jessica blocked the cottage for me – and yet I haven't made the bookings yet. The question has become more urgent, much more important.

It's become a fundamental question concerning my whole life. A question we all ask ourselves over and over again. What is the right place for me to live? The right life? The right people? The right work? Why am I here on earth, at all?

Since the accident, that completely shattered the life I used to know, I've kept asking myself this very question. Since then, that feeling of rootlessness, of searching restlessly but never arriving anywhere, has constantly been present.

I try to listen to my inner guidance to understand the plan the angels and God have made for me. Until today I've always found the answer in natural surroundings. The trees talk to me, as do the horses and the spirits. Today it's the hummingbird, I can sense it very clearly. It seems to know that this question is burning me up and it's there to help me.

So, I tell the hummingbird, "I need a kind of safety that's not just based on myself but on something greater than me." I take a deep breath.

At this moment Marge is passing by with a bunch of flowers in her hands that she picked especially for me ... In the sea, which is very calm today, three waves break.

"Where do I belong?"

This question is deeply affecting me. "For years I've been travelling around the world, discovering many beautiful places, many paradises. But where is my home? I'm longing for a home, I just can't find one."

I watch the hummingbird buzzing from one flower to the next. I can feel that it can hear me, and I can feel as well that it can't give me an answer because I'm not yet there. I'm not yet where it is, beating its wings 50 times a second. I'm too slow. My human mind, needing to illuminate things from each side, needs time. I know there is an answer, but it takes time to get close to it. Human beings need time, and that time cannot be cut short. What else do I need to tell the hummingbird until it's able to hear me?

Suddenly, there it is – the buzzing. I feel it all over my body. 50 wing beats per seconds, it's unbelievable. Never before have I connected with such an animal. My horse taught me many years ago how to do it – how to talk with animals. I'm sensing the vibration of the animal inside my body, resonating with its energy, just like a chord is resonating with the desired note when struck. From there the energy is translated into thoughts and feelings. I've talked to many horses and a lot of other animals all over the world, but never to a hummingbird. It's just crazy!

It's an unbelievably fast vibration. So, this is how it feels when a hummingbird is hovering in front of a flower sucking nectar with its beak – seemingly motionless, but in fact moving from one flower to the next quick as lightning.

The only thing left to do is to listen to its thoughts and feelings to understand what it's trying to tell me. I mustn't lose this "user-to-user connection" now, it says. And there it is – the answer of the hummingbird: "You must come, regardless of the costs. – Come at all costs."

And then – silence.

I've lost the frequency. Oh boy! This hummingbird is that delicate and fast that my human frequency is failing to keep up. So, I try to calm down and open my mind completely. And I can hear it again: "Go for the soul. – Go for the soul." This is like a spring tide to me. Because those four words mean so much more: "You will find the soul in Jamaica. That's what this is all about – to follow the soul. You're not talking to me right now – you're talking to God. God made you come here. Don't ask questions. God is so much greater than you could possibly know. 30 million years ago He created a hummingbird and today – this very day – He's giving this message to you: It's you who this is all about – you are the unexpected European hummingbird. Stop questioning everything. You will find all your answers here in Jamaica if you stop asking. God can do so much more. But you will never know if you don't stop asking so many questions."

Hm, but there is one question I need to ask, nevertheless: "Is Jamaica the home I'm looking for? Delroy, the driver who took me to the restaurant yesterday, told me about a Swiss woman who came to Jamaica 13 times in seven years and finally stayed. Okay, okay, I get it ... I stop asking. 30 million years is really a lot of time. And all this time ago hummingbirds already existed. Who am I compared to this? An Unexpected European hummingbird; I just can't help laughing. I bet this idea of a fossil hummingbird in Frauenweiler, Baden-Wuerttemberg, was from Michael or one of his trainees who has a special kind of humor. Never mind, I like it. 30 million years. Says Wikipedia: "The skeletons have a length of four centimeters, a beak to suck nectar and wings that enable to hover in place. Thus, they expose the typical features of hummingbirds of today."

Nope, even a writer like Viola Messerschmidt cannot make up something like that!

It's the angels, dribbling their messages into our reality like espresso gets dribbled into frothed up milk.

The hummingbird in the garden of Te Moana is flying away – at a speed incredible. Ten times faster than a jet fighter, e.g. the MiG-25 (a jet fighter reaching three times the speed of sound, and a great abbreviation by the way! – MiG being the initials of „Mikojan und Gurewitsch", the inventors, and at the same time an acronym of the Russian word for moment or blink of an eye – dig it!) and much more elegantly.

I go for a swim to assimilate all of this. Initially, I came to Jamaica two Years ago because of Patrick Golding, who was angel-sent, too, by the way. Quasi a similar espresso-dribbled-into-frothed-milk-message as a 30 million years old fossil ... I'm writing this, just to be fair. They're not just sending hummingbirds to look at, but also a man of flesh and blood when necessary.

But now, I'm not here because of Patrick, but for some other reason. I cannot change the fact that he is gone (not dead, just gone). And as I'm not allowed to ask, I can merely observe. Patrick is gone and has been replaced by something else – even if it's hard to grasp.

I'm swimming for ages. It's this wonderful and warm today that I'm not willing to leave the water. Everything is adjusting and answers are arising without me having asked questions. It's getting more difficult as soon as I start asking again. So, I surrender.

I give up trying to understand everything or anything at once. I have a contract with the angels. I do what they tell me to. Their messages are picking their way to me. I carry out their instructions, that's all.

Today it's the hummingbird telling me that I must return at any cost. I need to come back for the soul. To put a stamp on it: God created a hummingbird 30 million years ago, and He made sure the fossilised skeleton was discovered from a German scientist right in front of my door. And He made sure I received that information. Do you still think that something on this planet or in your life could happen by circumstance? Or that there could be anything impossible for Him? Nothing in your life happens without reason, and that reason dwarfs any jet fighter and even the curiosity of Viola Messerschmidt.

True, I would have liked to ask why Patrick had to disappear from my life and if he might come back, nevertheless. But then I drifted into that perfect inner calm and found that wonderful inner peace while I was floating in the Caribbean Sea surrounded by the rocky shore and the fairy tale plants growing there.

I walk back to my cottage and lay down on the sofa. I feel tired. More tired than I've felt for a long time. All the strain seems to be melting away. All the whitewater paddling I had to do in the years past to survive, to find a new home, to find love and a reason to live – it's over. I stopp paddling. I won't do it any longer.

I hear the singing of the first insects and see that dusk has arrived.

I'm happy.

No more questions, Your Honor.

One hour later I book the flight to Montego Bay in April.

A special offer appears on the screen showing a price 300 Euros lower than usual.

I can hear the rustling of white wings and one of the pupils of archangel Michael is surely drawing praise for opening the right door and nudging me to walk through it.

The angel who desperately tried to convince me to sign the contract on top of the high-rise, back then when I couldn't have cared less about angels, says: "I told you she's a difficult case."

Michael replies: "Yes, we can handle even the difficult ones. 30 million years and the *Unexpected European Hummingbird* finally floored her."

I think: Maybe the angels allow themselves a beer tonight.

ONE LOVE - ONE HEART

Chapter 10 – It's So Nice Talking to You

This morning I feel like I'm on the verge of falling back into it – into the sea. Last night, everything was just fine. I felt at peace and it seemed to last. I even assumed the novel might be finished. There's nothing left to write, after all. True, I could write about Patrick and it would be a beautiful, romantic story, but there isn't a reason to write any longer, basically. I've arrived. I leave everything to God and the angels. God's creation is perfect. Just now, the hummingbird is passing by.

Johnathan had picked me up to have breakfast in his favorite café at the entrance to Ocho Rios. I haven't met many people in the days past and when I'm amongst them again ... it's different here in Jamaica than it is in Europe. The café we went to isn't like Starbucks, it's just a plain room with a roughcast made of clay. The waitress' smile was utterly gentle. The way she put the cup of coffee in front of me you could think I was her sister. I wasn't allotted a certain role as 'the guest' or as 'the woman with fair skin who accompanies Johnathan', who is known all over town.

Maybe that's the reason why I'm so happy to be here. Because no judgement but embrace. At the service, on Sugar Pot Beach, in the garden of Te Moana – my system keeps trying to align to something that's probably expected from me. I keep trying to read the people around me and find out what they see in me and behave accordingly. But, as a matter of fact, the people here don't see anything special in me; I really don't get the feeling that they do. They don't ignore me, either. They're affecting me and I'm affecting them – and that's also not surprising. I feel like I'm coming from a world in which I usually walk around frozen inside a block of ice surrounded by others blocks of ice. Here, I don't feel icebound. And no one else is.

Once again, I feel that I want to drop everything I carry along with me. There are huge waves in the ocean today and that's just how I feel – like waves crashing down on me but I don't fight against them. Today I let myself sink.

I dreamed of Oliver last night. He started to quarrel with a waitress, and I felt ashamed standing next to him because he accused her of being lazy and that was unfair.

After breakfast, Johnathan took me home. I was in a very good mood because our conversation had been inspiring, as usual. I'd told him about my experience with the hummingbird and he was fascinated. Johnathan, who founded a technology business in California, who travelled the world, who knows important people everywhere and knows more about German politics then I do – a man like him understands what I'm talking about, what's important to me, understands my vision to re-connect human beings with nature.

He understands and accepts that I'm able to talk to a hummingbird. Men with a background like his normally smile at me condescendingly. They find me amusing and unimportant at the same time. Johnathan on the other hand has been pondering similar questions and drawing similar conclusions for many years. He told me he visits the Bushmen to find his soul again. That's the reason both of us like our conversations that much. It's a great gift to meet such a person. The angels just earned some more Brownie points.

Now I'm back in my little cottage, and while I'm reading emails, I realise it's coming back again. It starts with a void. Everything I considered sacred yesterday becomes meaningless. I feel numb. Or rather I can't feel myself at all anymore. I think I'm not able to write a single word today just like I couldn't write over the last years. I think I must be crazy to expose so many details of my life in this blog and that the people are going to blow me apart – and that everything will get even worse. Then, the fear will have won once and for all. But I won't even care about that anymore.

I receive very private emails, some of them telling tragic fates – about people who had to suffer the same or even worse. It hurts me to read them. I can see how these people are suffering and how much healing is needed.

And that's the moment when I fall into a deep dark hole. There is no concrete and no indifference but a blazing fire and pain, crashing like the waves onto the beach, again and again, until the wind finally abates, and it gets calm again. There are so many dreams there – and each time I'm afraid they might shatter forever.

I think about Joy who told me to "lay your pain down at the cross's feet." That's exactly what I do. It's her birthday on Saturday. I asked her if she had any plans for that day and told her that I'd like to go to the service. She said, "As usual. You come with us to have lunch together."

"As usual." How often have I been to lunch with her and John? Four times in the last two years. And she says: "As usual." This means the world to me. It's incredibly important to me. It means to lay my pain down at the cross's feet – to feel how much their invitation means to me, to know that I have a home there. In a foreign country. Because I cannot find one at the place I once called home; because I'm too afraid when I'm there, I will lose it again.

I can feel it now. My greatest wish to find a home I can always come back to. For a second I feel it not paralysed with fear. I feel it here, in Jamaica. I don't feel it in Germany, never.

This seems to be the distance I need: 5,000 kilometers, ten flight hours and a huge ocean. And the warmth and love of John and Joy, the groundation of Johnathan, the profound faith of the church, the humming bird, life reaching out its hands to me.

Slowly, I begin to see that my fate, the accident my family died in, was the break that had been on the horizon for a long time, that there had been many small cracks, that I did everything to avoid seeing those cracks, that I was too afraid to look at them and that I'm learning just now not to cover them anymore ... I'm so very tired. I have no strength left, cannot hinder the waves from breaking, one after another. It's beyond my power to tame the sea.

I feel at home with God, in His Creation filled with wonder and beauty 30 million years old, in this ancient house of truth. It's washed up to the shore. And I'm learning to trust that I won't drown, that it's okay if I need to travel several thousand kilometers to gain enough surety to face the truth, that the angels brought me to Jamaica to show me it's possible. Here on earth. I don't need to leave earth. There is a way to meet life without drowning.

Marge passed by and waved to me. It's as if she knows that it means the world to me: Her genial waving. And even Rennil, the gardener, who is not very talkative by nature, did talk to me at length today – about the weather and the ocean. But the actual content of our conversation was a different one: "It's so nice talking to you." – "Yes, likewise." – "I'm blessed to see you that happy just because we're talking to each other." – "Yes, likewise." – "I only wish for you to be happy." – "Yes, I wish the same for you."

That's enough. A short communication like that is enough for my heart to trust it's possible to heal. Several thousand kilometers from home. I'm safe.

I think of my readers and of all the people who leave comments in the blog or write to me in private. Their wisdom and the ways they discovered are amazing and they make me feel that I'm not alone. What I write in my daily chapters are answers to their comments. We are creating this novel together. It's the pain all human beings have in common – and that could never heal if we couldn't share it.

I learned one thing today: That thing about the ice. That

I'm walking through my life like a block of ice. Sometimes people tell me that I'm unapproachable, unreachable. It hurts because I know it's true, but I'm unable to change it. My soul is in denial in moments like those, unable to interact with others. That again causes the people around me to draw back and as a result my soul gets even colder and cries like a little child.

But there are people who're able to see this. They see that my soul reacts like that because it's scared. It's scared because it might get hurt. But deep inside it wants to be found. There are a few people who can feel this. Those people don't turn away from the blocks of ice but know that they need to approach them all the more – to give them warmth until the ice starts to melt. It takes a lot of love, pure love. And sometimes it takes a lot of persistence. I am such a case.

A difficult case, as the angels say. But they have something for me in stock, of course. A 30 million years old unexpected European hummingbird. Difficult case. It doesn't matter. Love will make everything alright.

Love as people like Joy possess. They look behind the wall. This morning I wrapped up a gift for Joy's birthday with paper white as snow and a white ribbon. It's a small book to take some notes if she likes to – that kind of gift you tend to get from a writer. It made me happy to prepare this gift for Joy. I felt again how happy I'd been when she'd looked behind my personal wall to find out what I need. And she's given it to me: Her love.

Some people tell me to tear down that wall, but that's

not possible. On the contrary – it even gets higher in moments like that. The wall will tumble down by itself when the love is great enough. But first my soul needs a little more nourishing. Safety. An "as usual".

That is presumably the most important thing I'm learning on my way: How important it is to look behind those walls, that we need to learn to see what's hidden from our sight, that we mustn't abuse or hurt it, but provide it with what it needs, this desperate being.

No, I'm not any longer one of those achievement-oriented people who want to do everything right. The Viola who always did everything right doesn't exist anymore. She gave herself to the sea. Now I'm lazing on my sofa doing nothing right anymore. Period.

I know how it feels to become a block of ice. There is little you can do about it when you're just human. But the angels – they can do a lot. The angels understand. That's why they brought me to Jamaica where you can meet those waitresses who treat you like a sister, the gardeners who cut the garden at a time when it won't disturb you. To affect each other and the being behind the wall.

The angels are very good in doing this. They understand. Today they riled up the sea quite a bit.

But I went swimming anyway. And I saw them in the white crests of the waves where they were dancing. And they were singing: "As usual." – "As usual."

Jamaica
ONE LOVE – ONE HEART

Chapter 11 – Goodbye, Te Moana

Today is my last day in paradise. I can hear Rennil, the noise of his besom scraping in the driveway. Rennil is very gentle and loves the trees, the bushes, the flowers and blossoms. He spends his days in this garden, nourishing and cherishing it. He loves it in a gentle way. He don't change it, but brings forth its beauty by just being there, picking up some leaves here and there. By looking at it, he makes it beautiful.

The paradise of Te Moana is inhabited by people who love. It's a place where love, usually invisible, becomes apparent. You can feel it and you can see it. It's apparent in each leave, each gecko climbing up a wall and in the sea swashing onto the rocky shore. Every being coming in touch with this place surrenders to this love and becomes a part of it.

Paradise.

Here, I find the love I thought I'd lost. I can completely and utterly feel it. It's not an illusion, it's real and it brings forth beauty. A tree might shed its leaves, a gecko might die, a blossom might wither. But the love remains. It's older than 30 million years. It's endless and yet alive in every single leave.

I can see now that my story is embedded into this love, that the pain, the fear and the sadness are a part of its beauty.

I can see that the almighty love has guided me to this place for me to see. And I do see it now, completely and utterly.

I can see that love brings forth my beauty. I'm at a place here that was created by artists. I wasn't aware of this fact when I booked the cottage last summer – on a day I was very exhausted and my longing for love was that great I was looking for a straw to clutch at. I found it in a sleepless night while I was surfing the web. I saw it, just a few words and a few pictures on Airbnb, and suddenly was very calm.

Now, half a year later, I'm here. Yesterday, Jessica, the hostess, thrust a catalogue about an exhibition in her mother's art gallery, which is not very far from Te Moana, into my hands. Harmony Hall.

I visited Harmony Hall two years ago together with Patrick. At that time, I didn't know about Te Moana. In Harmony Hall Annabella Proudlock and her husband Peter created a place where the most talented local artists can find a home for their pictures and sculptures. I also met the curator of Harmony Hall yesterday, a person as delighted as I am where art is concerned. He visited Te Moana.

I told him how much I loved the beauty there and he said, "Yes, I'm here solely because of the beauty of Te Moana. I live in Kingston and I drive the long way just for the sake of being here. There is no other reason. What's there to talk about could easily be dealt with on the phone." He told me there used to be a constant coming and going of artists in times past.

Today is the last day I'm spending here but I will come back soon because I find everything I need here. I find something I never thought I would: I can stand being alone here. I can allow my fear to come to the surface and I'm not drowning. I can feel my pain and share it with others without being ashamed because of it. And I can write. This is love. Greater than the love between man and woman, greater than the love of myself. It's a love that encompasses everything and that allows everything to partake.

Tomorrow I will set out to Annandale, another paradise. It's farther out in the open countryside, in the wild. I don't know if I'll be able to write there or if I'll have access to the internet. I don't know what awaits me there. I cannot know it and I cannot ask. But today I want to tell you another story that will make you understand why I cannot know or ask.

When I met Patrick at Vienna airport that summer two years ago, I stepped through a door into another world, another life. First, I didn't notice it as my life didn't change obviously. Patrick had handed me his business card and I dropped him a few lines, mainly because I was curious if he would answer at all. That picture of him, sitting there in that nearly tangible silence, wearing that white shirt, kept appearing inside my mind. Something deep inside of me responded to that silence, a silence I remembered from my childhood when I was alone. And I was alone very often. Today, there is a lot of silence in my life as well because I work with animals. But the silence I experience when working with horses is rarely to be found with people, least of all with men.

I wrote to him and he answered – in a very polite, very unobtrusive and likewise curious way. We discovered that we have a lot of things in common and quite a lot of them made us sit up and notice. Our mothers' birthday is on the same date, he's got a cousin with the same name than a cousin of mine, we've read the same books, watched the same movies and feel the same way about those. But the best thing of all: We visited the Taj Mahal in India on the very same day. Back then we both were still married.

It was the coincidence about the Taj Mahal which affected me the most. I could feel a door opening for me, in fact. We agreed on meeting in Vienna. Patrick had booked a hotel room and we spent the night together. During that night, something came into my life that changed everything – not because of me or because of Patrick, but we both were part of it. It was a wonderful night, gentle, a sensual touch between man and woman that made us both happy.

I kept waking up and falling asleep again, drunken with happiness. At first light I woke up because my mind was riveted by something special.

Completely unable to resist, half awake and half asleep, I saw a picture with my mind's eye. It was a very distinct picture and one I'd never seen before. It was the face of a man of African origin. I could see his facial features that were very archaic. They radiated that silence which I had also found in Patrick and which I could find in myself through him. The face was surrounded by a circle, making it look like a medal and because of that there was something symbolic about it. It was a picture beyond day to day reality. And yet it wasn't a lifeless picture or a lifeless symbol – on the contrary, it was very much alive. Rendered to fit our western conception of the world I'd call it a manifestation.

I was already familiar with intuitive pictures like that one because that's the language I share with animals. But that one wasn't just a picture – it was a being manifesting. I'm used to manifestations of various beings. They always come with good intentions and want to help, like the angels on top of the high-rise. Mostly they're friendly and tangible, sometimes they're austere. They're teachers and protectors and normally I'm able to summon them to ask for advice or for help.

That spirit was different.

I told Patrick about it, but he didn't offer much feedback. He was a gentleman, and he reminded me of the things I'd missed in my life since I'd lost Oliver. I felt like I could find them again in Patrick, felt that life was smiling on me again and presented me with a gift called Patrick. I realised that this was what I was searching for, what I needed: A man with whom I could feel at home. Chaste touches and closeness.

He felt the same. He was divorced and was afflicted with loneliness. Both of us were life-experienced, self-confident and well educated. We had long conversations that never got boring. We liked the same things and the physical attraction between us made us feel fulfilled. We spent three happy days in Vienna, strolling through the City, visiting the St. Stephens' Cathedral (the Stephansdom), the "Café Landtmann", studying the city's history, talking about its famous visitors Sigmund Freud, Marlene Dietrich and Hilary Clinton.

Patrick has great knowledge about politics, and I know a lot about art history. We said goodbye at the airport, and the parting was easy. The wish to meet again without commitments was there, but we both led our lives with occupational obligations. Summer is the time of year when I travel and hold many workshops, so our contact was limited to emails and phone calls. Nevertheless, we got to know each other better and the things we discovered made us happy.

During all that time the feeling that our connection was part of something greater never left me.

From time to time, whenever I could find some silence, I thought about the spirit I had seen. I tried to find him again, to talk to him like I was used to with other spirits. I wanted to learn more about him. I wanted to find out why he had appeared.

I've learned that you need to be careful and to show respect when you approach a spirit. Spirits are ethereal beings. The distance between our reality and theirs is immense. And of course, you need to get to know them because every single one is unique. Finally, I did find the spirit from that night, but he was quite aloof. No matter in what way I talked to him, he just ordered me to keep silent and showed me very clearly where my place was. I'd never experienced something like that before. I was used to being allowed to ask and to talk about things. To get answers. That was what gave me surety, and surety I needed most. To be sure that something like the accident would happen never again. My whole life had become about that. The spirit told me he would take care about that but first I needed to trust him.

Back then on top of the high-rise I stepped into that other plane of existence. There is the contract with the angels and there is the spirit, who I named "Grandpa". The angels are gentle beings and they serve me like I serve them.

Grandpa is not gentle. It seems to me he's coming from a very old world. Maybe from a time when the first human being came to be? Or from an ancient time in Africa? Grandpa is strict and clear, but he has as much love to give as the angels do. He brought astonishing things to my life. And he's showing it to me. Showing me my way. It's not as easy to serve him as it is to serve the angels. He demands going back, beyond my culture, beyond human civilisation, demands that I don't act on my own authority, demands to accept things that are hard to acknowledge. He demands that I let go of everything my culture pro-vided me with, faith instead of knowledge. Even if faith demands something that is utterly contrary to the mind. Even if it demands somethings that is utterly contrary to my wishes and longings.

Here in Te Moana Grandpa showed himself in shape of

the hummingbird. I know this because of what it told me: "Go for the soul." And I'd find all the answers if I stopped asking. The hummingbird also said that I need to come back, said it with this insistence I know from Grandpa, with this unfaltering clarity.

The same clarity I felt after I became acquainted to him a little better. I learned that Grandpa isn't talking with words but in a different way. A wish kind of materialises inside of me and I know it was Grandpa who sent this wish to me. When I visit Grandpa subsequently, respectfully asking him about that wish, he confirms it and I can feel if he approves of it.

That's how I learned that I needed to come to Jamaica, that I needed to go without asking why.

Patrick owns a house by the sea, and he invited me to spend the winter there. I went there – to a foreign land and with a man I hardly knew. But I went with a feeling of confidence and it was given to me by Grandpa. He let me know that nothing bad could happen to me, that I was protected. Already before I arrived, I could see that place and I knew that he would be there as well, could see he was there to protect me. It had taken quite some time to get to know him but finally I trusted him. He protected me like a benevolent older man holding an insecure child.

Tomorrow I'm leaving for the farm of Monika Maitland-Walker, who I met in spring. We had breakfast back then, sitting on the terrace of the mansion. Two earthen pots were standing there that showed faces within a circle, just like the image I had seen in that night with Patrick. I saw them and thought: Grandpa is here. The next day, one of the pots was broken, knocked over and destroyed by the storm during the night.

The mind says things like this are just imagination. But it's not important what the mind is saying. Grandpa gives me the feeling of surety that I so desperately need, that is so much bigger than any surety the mind could give. The mind can provide criteria, but the spirit offers a silence in which I can rest. There is trust there and I can sense this trust as a deep inner calm within my body. There is protection and I can sense this protection surrounding me like a shield covering my body. Whenever I follow the way that's in harmony with Grandpa's way, I feel this protection.

This is love.

So, today I'm leaving Te Moana.

I don't know when I'll be able to write again. I cannot know and I cannot ask. I hope, dear reader, you understand and have trust in me.

And I believe that you will just know and will keep me company.

It was wonderful to spend this time with you and I thank you wholeheartedly. You are a part of this story, no matter if you wrote to me or accompanied me with your heart. We created this story as it is now.

We are not alone, and love is great.

Jamaica
ONE LOVE - ONE HEART

Chapter 12 – Are You Ready to Love Unconditionally?

I'm back. Back in Te Moana. Don't ask me how much time has passed – it felt endless. Three months.

I'm back in Te Moana in Annabellas' cottage, but my life is different. I am different. I wanted to come back to write again and I really want to write but life is taking my breath away.

Three months have passed between chapter eleven, which was the last one I wrote back then and chapter twelve, which I'm writing now. I don't recognise myself anymore.

I didn't stay in Germany for long, instead I returned to Jamaica very soon. In March, to be precise and now it's April. In March I couldn't write.

I'd planned to write about Patrick, a wonderfully wistful romance an angel had contrived for me – but now I'm in doubt if I'll be able to find the time. The story has become more than just that – it's come to be my life. Sometime around the end of February my telephone rang. I'd dreamed about that phone call more than a year ago. Yes, that's just the way it is when dealing with angels. They're sending me dreams, way ahead but I need time to grow into them in order for them to happen.

I'd dreamed about hearing Patrick. Just his voice, there were no comprehensible words. Something very unconditional resonated in this voice, something that made me tremble in every limb. I still start trembling just thinking of it. I desperately tried to talk to him but there was a hissing in the line and our connection kept being severed. I wanted to get through to him at any cost, no matter what the cost.

For one year I'd tried to talk to him, that man demanding something unconditional from me, after we'd met the last time two years ago. I'd spent a winter with Patrick in Jamaica and afterwards he'd simply disappeared. He didn't respond to my messages. He couldn't be contacted by phone. Gone. He'd vanished as if he'd never existed at all.

And then I had that dream. I'd come back to Jamaica because of it, returned without knowing if I'd meet Patrick. I'd visited him at his house, and he'd slammed the door in my face. After he wouldn't let me in, I started to write to him.

It was my hunger for love – this hunger that is insatiable. It was my deepest self that started to talk and to demand. This hunger for love I'm feeling that can never be appeased. I'd finally arrived at the bottom. And Grandpa, the spirit, appeared next to me and said, "This is you. Look!" He seemed content.

Patrick never got in touch with me. I never received an answer from Patrick. But finally, it happened. The phone call, his voice. Just like in my dream. The connection was so bad I could only hear his voice but couldn't make out any words. But I could hear and understand the unquestioning nature of it. The trembling and then the words: "If you really mean it, come to Jamaica on Sunday." After that the connection was severed. That was in March. Wednesday.

My whole body was shaking. I laid down and my body didn't stop shaking. I couldn't think straight and couldn't stop thinking about things that needed to get done and be considered – there were no flights with Condor except for Wednesdays and Saturdays, and I had to spend a night at Montego Bay, or ... I went through a variety of possibilities and then thought about some other facts: That I would need a driver, that I needed to reschedule my appointments at the hairdresser, that I needed to do my advance turnover tax return before I left because after all I didn't know when I would be back. I did NOT think about one possibility: To just forget about the call and live my life as if it hadn't happened.

The book you're reading right at this moment and that I started to write in January: I named it "Jamaica – How I found love". This story has turned out to be my life. It has become this strong I can hardly find the time to write everything down. And to be honest – I don't know if I'll find the strength to write for two weeks on end like I intended to do and like I promised to my readers. I really would like to, but love is powerful. The angels are powerful. I'm not in control of the situation. I'm just following this unquestioning nature which we all are promised to. And I hope you can appreciate this. If you're following it as well, I know you can. Because if you do, you know that you always do your best to keep your promises, but there are times when something happens that's greater than you. Something you must follow. And sometimes the price you pay for it is high.

I was there on that Sunday in March. I met Patrick. And he asked me: "Are you ready? Are you?" Everything inside of me wanted to say "Yes". Everything inside of me had waited and lived for this moment. But my "Yes" was not unconditional. And he knew it.

Where am I now? Where is my unquestioning nature? Where is the one percent of my love that's suddenly missing? I can no longer find the one hundred percent of my love for Patrick. Now that everything could have been fine. I must continue my search. That was in March, now April has come.

Just now I'm coming back from Ocho Rios, were I visited some friends. There I met Richard and learned the story of his unconditional life. He used to be a taxi driver until he was robbed one day. His car was stolen, and he was shot in the head. Now he cannot walk properly anymore and to drive a cab has become impossible. He was supposed to get married but shortly after the mugging his future wife left him. The bullet is still in his head. It could be removed with a fifty-fifty chance of being healed afterwards. Or dead. His heart is broken. I can understand his feelings. A broken heart and the question: Where will I find love, after all?

I need to understand what happened between Patrick and me. The way I followed love unconditionally has changed me, even if I cannot say exactly how. The angels keep telling me to stop asking, to have faith instead. Faith in mercy and in love.

Chapter 13 – No Questions

Now that I'm back in JA I'm feeling exposed again. A state of emergency has been declared for Montego Bay as the crime in the city is out of control. I'm safe in Te Moana that's protected by four big dogs, but I feel the vulnerability nevertheless, it's affecting me.

The meeting with Patrick in March is on replay inside my head: The villa, the white furniture, the vase with the red flowers.

One month ago: His driver has just dropped me off and taken my suitcase out of the trunk and here I am. I replaced my cotton dress with a light blue summer dress at the airport. My perfume is "La petite robe noir" by Guerlain. My heart is beating like a drum and I just hope it can handle all the excitement.

It had been so easy to long for love, I had been safe and protected to be longing, but the real thing is something different ...

I hadn't remembered him being so tall. His aura feels even more silent then I recalled and right now it's exhausting. I don't know what to do or say, anymore.

I look into his eyes only for a short moment, then I drop my eyes to the floor for I cannot hold his gaze.

I feel his hand at my temple, brushing my hair away. I know he likes my hair, straight and harmonising with my fair skin. The moment is indescribably intimate and my whole body begins to shake.

Never before have I felt this overwhelmed by a man. I'm shaking with fear, but at the same time I know for sure that nothing bad will happen to me, that I'm safe with Patrick – well, maybe not my heart, but the woman inside of me.

Patrick responds to me as a man. More than being individual persons with own personalities we are first and foremost man and woman. We cannot influence the way we respond to each other. We are part of a story between men and women millenniums old.

"How was your flight?" he asks.

He takes the brown leather bag out of my hands. The driver puts the suitcase into the hallway and leaves. Patrick closes the door.

"Would you like something to drink?"

I don't know what I want anymore. My stomach is in a state of emergency just like Montego Bay.

"No alcohol," I reply. I've completely lost control of the situation and I don't know what might happen if I took just one single sip.

Patrick smiles at me, re-recognising me.

I feel like an intruder in his world, a stranger.

The athletic, silent man hands me a glass of soursap juice, made from a sweet and sour Jamaican fruit, and takes a glass of water for himself.

"Are you tired?" he asks.

If I had the chance to be myself just for a single moment,

I would surely feel bone-tired because my internal clock tells me it's three p.m. But since Patrick lured my heart to come to him, across an ocean 5,000 miles wide, I'm not willing to sleep at any costs. What shall I reply?

I look at the bookshelf. There aren't many books in Patrick's house, even if he's a well-read man. Everything here follows the purity of the colors and shapes, the purity of the message and this message being: pure.

Books are like hurricanes under the Caribbean omnipotence of the sun. You don't want to have something like that in your living room. Hurricanes are the natural enemies of Jamaica. The Caribbean soul is longing for freedom and vitality, it wants to indulge in the silence of the sun. But my thoughts are drifting yet again. I need to answer Patrick's question.

Patrick sits down next to me on the sofa. Suddenly his nearness is threatening. My heart has leapt out of my chest and is dancing on the table in front of us. It's hard beyond measure only to simply stay and keep functioning. I know that as soon as I'm back to being myself something inside of me will demand to return to this liquid state. But right now, right in the middle of it, I feel utterly lost.

„Do you still love me?", he says.

I hear myself answering – in a very clear and very determined voice – hear myself saying, "Yes, I do."

My mind is satisfied with this. It nods in approval and repeats, just to do it properly and stress the importance: "Yes, I really do."

My heart on the other side is chiding me: "You're a complete moron. Yet again you gave birth to a huge sentence of lies." And I'm so scared. There's nothing but fear.

I feel Patrick's arms, strong muscled arms able to hold and protect me. With muscles he trains every day to be able to hold his ground in a world full of enemies. He lifts me up with these muscled arms and places me onto his lap. His hand is wandering under my skirt. He knows what I like. All the fear is gone. My body stops shaking and my heart beats slowly and peacefully. I'm at home, at home in Patrick's arms.

He carries me into the bedroom and lays me down on the pristine white bed. The cooling draught generated by the fan feels good on my skin that is covered with beads of sweat. Patrick strips me of my shoes, one after another. He turns me around onto my stomach and opens the zipper of my dress. I don't need to do anything. It's his pleasure to be allowed to do what we both enjoy.

He opens my bra and pulls my panties down my hips. Each touch makes my body shiver and I sigh with pleasure. My limbs move like the leaves of a mimosa touched by his fingers.

This is his pleasure: To touch me, touch the heart of my being in a very gentle and effortless way. Now I'm utterly present and completely calm, utterly lost and completely here. In this moment, yes, I love him.

We're sitting on the patio and I'm looking at the sea. The smell of the flowers is wafting up from the garden below, carried by the cool evening breeze. Down at the jetty I can see two lamps, their lights reflected by the dark, soft waves. The ocean is lying in front of us like a black liquid full of secrets. Like a single huge secret stretching into infinity.

Patrick tells me what happened in his life since the time we last met. That was two years ago. He's been working. Building his life, he says. He tells me all sorts of things I don't really understand, but I get that he's accepted a lot of responsibility: an important political project in Jamaica, implementing an administration, leadership. That's his mission.

I know that's just the thing he'd been looking for, that suits him. I get that's the reason why he wasn't heard from again for two years. Because he feels obliged to this task. I really get it. That's just the way he is. – Silent. – Following his own way.

"I'm tired," he says. I can see the weariness in his eyes – and the sadness. I've always been touched by it. That sadness beyond the appearance of the strong and charismatic man. The sadness of a warrior whose fight can never be won.

"Never before have I been felt so much longing in a woman," he says, and a long silence follows these words. I know: my hunger for love. My longing.

I'm moved by his words. I feel that everything's here, after all. I feel his warmth within me, now, that we've met again. Nothing is lost, our mutual attraction is unabated.

"I need a woman by my side," he says. "I cannot manage alone."

I'm sitting on the patio next to Patrick, sitting in this beautiful house next to the man who's ignited a longing so fierce that I came to Jamaica. My heart is talking to him with every breath I take. He's inviting me into his life, he offers a new home. Everything I wished for.

That's the very moment when I feel a crack in the story.

"Would you like to be that woman?" Patrick asks and I feel the deep seriousness of his question.

YES. Again, I hear this strong and self-confident voice, my voice, saying "Yes" fervently.

And at the very same moment I can feel this part of me, the one that's talking, breaking loose like a behemoth tumbling into the ocean. Sinking.

What's left is a gentle and frightened part of me, like a child searching the protection of its mother. Patrick cannot see this side of me. He sees the strong woman. I look at him and see the warrior, the leader, see the sad man walking a lonely road. And I feel that unfathomable love he is awaking inside of me.

But, I realise that something happened to me during my search for love over the past two years. I'm an author again. Life had broken me in such a way that I hadn't been able to write anymore.

But now I can do it again, I can write. Not just love letters to the man I desire, but I can write for readers. I can feel their love and it's not just a mirage.

I've become more than a woman longing for the love of a man. I've become more than a story of death and betrayal. It's me. I can feel my truth, I can feel God, I can feel the language again, the beauty of the words, I can feel their touch. It's not an illusion, not at all.

I'm not content any longer with being the woman in the life of a man. I'm independent now.

Suddenly I sense a distance between Patrick and me that wasn't there before. He senses it, too.

There is this one question: "Would you like to be that woman?". And there is my answer: "Yes." But there is something else, too, even if I don't know yet what this something might be.

I think of the novel I have started writing two months ago. "Jamaica – How I found love". Where is it –this love?

I smile.

"Why are you smiling?"

"It's Jamaica," I reply. "Everything is a great adventure in Jamaica."

That again makes him smile.

And just at that moment I realise what's causing the crack:

At that very moment I'm thinking about another man. At that very moment something happens that I promised to Patrick in my love letters never would: There is another man in my life.

This other man – I met him in January shortly after I'd left Te Moana to go to Annandale, to the farm.

That other man would kiss me right now. We would exchange a few words, just like Patrick and I did, – and then he would kiss me. He would cover my whole face with kisses out of sheer joy, craziness and infatuation and

I would burst into loud, happy laughter and he would kiss me even more like crazy and I would laugh even more.

Patrick has never kissed me. And I don't know if he ever will. It's just not him.

So, at that very moment I realise it.

Two years of being certain of who I am and what I want – disappearing into thin air. Just because of a few kisses on a farm. That's Jamaica.

It's not only dangerous to walk the streets of Jamaica. Your heart is in danger as well. A bullet hits you, an arrow goes straight through your heart and everything changes.

Jamaica – One Love. What was it the angels told me? Don't ask questions. Just follow me.

ONE LOVE – ONE HEART

Chapter 14 – Daniel – The Other Man

January 2018. Annandale, Jamaica. The driveway leading to the farmhouse is about two kilometers long, it's a stony cart track.

A few days have passed already since I arrived at the farm, Annandale. I can feel myself immersing into a substance that infuses everything, seeping into my body bone deep. I followed Grandpa's instructions and they led me to this place, into the green.

I came to Annandale for the first time nine month ago. I had asked Johnathan where I could find horses in Jamaica, and he had answered, "You need to meet Monika."

I ask myself frequently how oneself could know that it's God or the angels speaking as there is no evidence for it after all. One of the indicators is a feeling I would describe like this: Your breathing gets very calm and deep, you feel like it's expanding into infinity, your heart beats like the one of a young bird leaving the nest for the very first time and your mind falls silent.

And I, having looked at the world through a small opening in a box so far, am suddenly standing right in the middle of everything. There are no boundaries anymore. That is how I felt when I went along the driveway to Annandale for the first time.

I came to a place of infinity. There is this distinct interaction between the inside and the outside and sometimes the outside is that threatening or overwhelming that the inside shuts itself away. But there are also times when the outside is that beautiful that the inside opens like a burgeoning flower – you can even smell its fragrance when it does.

Sometimes the angels push open a gate and the driveway to Annandale is such a gate.

I say hello to Monika, owner of Annandale, who is just treating an injured horse, a young chestnut mare called Orchid whose knee joint is hurt. I hold the horse while Monika tends to the wound. She invites me to the mansion to have a cup of coffee. For about 180 years Annandale was owned by the family of Rocksborough. The very first Rocksborough moving in was a son of King Edward. Pictures of the Royal Family, Queen Elisabeth's mother and the Duke and Duchess of York among them, are covering the walls of the house, they're in the hallway and up along the stairways. The house's furniture consists of antiques, you feel like you just entered a novel of Jane Austen.

It was here on this farm where I met Daniel. He was walking up the long driveway towards the house and the first thing I noticed was his distinct way of moving. Slowly, his upper body swaying with the rhythm of his steps. I was fascinated, unable to look away – but then forced myself to and suddenly he stood right in front of me and looked at me. I felt utterly calm. I didn't need to get calm, his presence brought my inner calm to light, my essence. It was a very peculiar feeling as I didn't feel it about him but inside of my very being. And yet, at the same time, I knew that it was caused by him. In contrast to Patrick, whose silence intimidated me, Daniel's inner calm let me find myself.

I could hear the shouting of the geese, could hear the rustling of the wind in the trees. I could smell the rocks heated by the sun. I was perceiving everything very clearly.

"I'm Daniel," he said.

And I said, "I'm Viola."

He held a halter in his hands and asked me: "Are you working with the horses?"

He smiled. His smile was very fine, innocent like a child's. And again, I felt everything that is within myself. I smiled as well. And just by standing there, he and I became one – it simply happened.

"I was planning to go to the horses," I said. "Can you show me the way?"

So, we walked together. The ways at this farm are long and time doesn't matter. We didn't talk much, but that wasn't necessary anyway. I could hear the crunching of his steps on the stony ground. I could feel his steps while he was walking next to me. It felt exactly the way it does when I walk next to a horse. He felt my presence and I felt his. It was something natural. I know this feeling very well as it's normal and natural for me where horses are concerned, but it's a rare thing with human beings. It felt so very comfortable that there was no need to talk. Just walking side by side was enough.

He opened the fence to a wide area where a group of horses was grazing further down the valley. I don't recall how he did it, if the movement was deft or clumsy. Usually, when I meet someone new, I notice many details of his or her movements. With Daniel I noticed but one thing: All his movements were flowing in a certain manner that made me flow with him.

When you meet someone for the first time there is usually some kind of unfamiliarity. It takes a little time until you get familiar with one another and can move along freely. With Daniel I felt at home from the very first moment, more so than with many people I've known for quite some time.

We walked down the hill into that vastness that is so characteristic for and dominates everything at Annandale and came to a weathered gate at last. He opened it and we stepped into the corral the horses were in.

A greyish brown colored mare caught my eye right away. While the other horses lifted their heads just briefly, she looked at us alertly, her attentive gaze following us. Her body was tense, seemingly ready to run. And yet there was no fear. I've seen a lot of scared horses but those in front of us weren't, they were just alert.

She kept watching us curiously, seemed to absorb everything she looked at. It felt like an examination. I felt myself tensing and wondering if I would pass this test, if she would approve of me.

Daniel approached her and petted her neck. She allowed it. I was quite astonished because she didn't make the impression as if she liked being touched.

That was the moment when something inside of me

shifted. It felt like I was about to forget anything and everything I knew about horses – forget for good.

I looked around and saw a drystone wall covered in moss, huge bamboo swaying and grating in the wind right behind it, a fence consisting of iron rods partly rusty and a herd of horses exposed to that frightening noise and radiating utter calm. I realised then that everything I used to know, not only concerning horses but also life itself, couldn't be applied here.

What I used to think to be my life and my reality was just a tiny snippet compared to what I encountered right now. It was a calm and a naturalness in which boundaries had no room. And I felt like my whole life had been an illusion up to that point.

Not only my marriage to a man who had led a double life, but my whole life.

Suddenly I was naked. Much more so than I could ever be simply without clothes. And that mare in front of me just knew it. If I tried to touch her, she wouldn't allow it. I was certain of that.

Daniel put the halter on her, not too early and not too late he sensed the right moment and she allowed it. I could see in her eyes that she relished that unknown experience.

Then he led her away, just some steps. I could see that she wasn't used to something like this. Her steps were a little stiff-legged as if she wasn't quite sure what to think.

But all this time Daniel's behavior was so transparent, calm and clear that she stopped resisting and followed him despite her uncertainty.

And my old "Me", the one that had just vanished, was thoroughly astounded. It gave one last sign of life, then was swallowed completely.

Daniel had passed me a second halter and I put it on a chestnut mare in order to become familiar with her.

I worked with her, lunging her in an adjunct round pen while Daniel worked with the greyish-brown mare. He never once looked my way, didn't even think about checking or judging my way of approaching the horse. For him it was a matter of fact that this was just between the horse and me.

That was in January after I had moved from Te Moana to Annandale. In March I had met Patrick for a brief encounter of one week.

Now April has come and I'm back in Te Moana. And Patrick's question is still hovering above me: "Do you want to be that woman?"

Did I want to? Was I willing to live a life on Patrick's side? A new life with a new man in a country far away. After I'd met Patrick in March I'd returned to Germany. I'd said Yes and now I was waiting for him to make his next step.

Daniel and I had come to know each other better during my stay at Annandale in January. It hadn't been all too hard. I'd simply followed his steps. He never told me no. Took me to his village and just told me to "stay by my side and you will be safe."

We sat together with his friends on a patio, eating

chicken they'd roasted over an open fire pit. They talked to each other in Patois, their local language, and I could understand only fragments, but I liked the sound of it.

Later that day Daniel told me he wanted to show me a piece of land he wanted to build a house on. I went with him. We disappeared behind some high brushes and palm trees and a thicket that obscured the view. He showed me the area in question and opened a coconut for me so I could drink the coconut water. Then he kissed me. His kiss was so gentle. Completely different to what I'd expected. He, being so clear and unambiguous when working with horses, was suddenly as playful and dreamy as a child. He kissed me with a childlike curiosity, as curious as the mare had been when being led by a halter for the very first time.

I was baffled and confused. And again, I felt like he was my mirror image because I own those two sides as well: The clearness and ambiguity with horses on one side and the playfulness and dreaminess on the other side. I'd used to think that those two parts weren't compatible, that it's impossible to be clear and brave and yet playful and childlike. I'd used to think that people wouldn't trust me if I allowed my playful side to come forth.

That evening I felt like stepping into a magic garden, together with Daniel, playing like two children.

Later we returned to the village and went to a small bar with the name "Pit hole". We drank beer and rum and they explained to me that Jamaica is the county with the highest per-capita number of bars and the highest per-capita number of churches. Every small village has several bars and several churches of different denominations.

I felt utterly happy.

Then, suddenly, we heard a shot. Daniel threw himself atop of me to protect me.

Someone screamed, a scream that cut through the reggae music like a knife. The music went on, but everybody stopped to talk. For a moment time seemed to stand still, like a frozen screen.

At first, I'd stayed very calm, I was fine. But then I could see the body of a young man lying on the ground farther away. The people flocked around him and after a while carried him away. All of this felt as unreal to me as the time together with Daniel in the magic garden.

For the second time in close succession the reality I knew was shattered to pieces. Three years ago, I'd intended to end my life because I felt lonely and hopeless. Me, a woman living in prosperity, knowing nothing of hunger, violence or poverty. And here somebody had to die who undoubtedly would've wanted to live. Nobody was willing to tell me what exactly had happened. And nobody called the police.

Daniel, too, refused to tell me. Finally, I learned it from the taxi driver who took me home. The young man had been gay, and somebody had seen him with another man. The other man had been able to escape. The police wouldn't do anything to clear the crime and neither would the people of the village.

I learned that this world was very different from the

one I come from and that Daniel was part of it. And I realised that it was not my right to judge any of this.

But I was afraid, and I didn't want to see Daniel again. It felt too threatening. Whenever I thought about him, the murder I'd witnessed also surfaced and I felt nothing but pure fear.

Until that evening when Patrick asked me if I was willing to share my life with him. That evening when I thought my greatest dream was coming true. That was the moment I remembered Daniel's kiss.

Here I am. I – my world, my life, my love – seem to be split into two incongruous halves. Who am I? The well-educated, sophisticated woman living her life with an affluent and powerful man, or the dreamy, naïve woman living in a world where dreams are paid for with your life? Or the writer who makes a story out of it and moves on to better places?

Jamaica – One Love. Where is the love?

ONE LOVE - ONE HEART

Chapter 15 – Why Me?

I started writing when I was eleven years old and it has been a long journey ever since. My way as an author may well be compared with my way concerning love. After all, you cannot just love and write genuinely and whole-heartedly and everything's fine. I've always written and loved like I do today, but I've never had readers or lovers who responded to it like they do now. I've learned that much: Everything depends on the people, and on my courage.

Of course, people have always responded to me. But their answers used to be short, and that small remnant of longing was always present. I adapted to their wishes. I developed a certain pride in being able to adapt. For many years I'd adapted to what my readers presumably wanted to read or to the wishes of my literary agents, publishers or producers, because they knew what would sell. I don't have a literary agent any longer, I incorporated my own publishing house and, like now, I publish online. I don't base my decisions on what to write on the question if it will sell.

I no longer feel the need to adapt because I no longer feel the need to survive.

I live because the angels bestowed me with this life. So, what's the actual state of my, Viola's, quest for love – now, today?

My dear friend John gave a book to me during my last stay, a book about the Rastafarian religion. "One Love" is the philosophy the Rastafarians live by. Everything is connected, all is one.

I found two answers in that book to the question concerning love. Answers Jamaica is throwing before my feet.

Why can you find such a variety of denominations here? The Church of the Pentecostalism, the Church of God, the Apostolic Church, the Seventh-day Adventist Church – every single one of them spit out by the mainstream of the American Christian Church. All of them denominations in which the longing for faith is pure, in which they sing and dance, beat the drums and speak their mother tongue. The Anglican Church of the white plantation owners forbade the slaves to attend the Christian service. They worried that the idea of all human beings loved by God unconditionally might cause revolts. They thought that the Anglican Church was too sophisticated for the uneducated slaves. And what about me? What do I think? Is faith related to education? Is love related to education? What's the virtue of faith when there is no truth? The one truth that God loves all his creatures unconditionally.

Later, the Christian cults came in from the US, radical in their spirituality and in their concepts of enemies. Did they bring homophobia to Jamaica? A history of oppression, exploitation and abuse – culminating in the murder of the young man I had to witness? Lately I heard another story: The white people used to breed the slaves, deciding who would mate with who. For the ones that refused, the punishment was to have sex with a white man. Homosexuality was equivalent with humiliation.

The book about the Rastafarians also tells me that the slaves never abandoned their African religions, the connection to their ancestors being the heart of it. I think of the spirit who came to me in that very first night I spent with Patrick: Grandpa. The African spirit who told me to go to Jamaica – is that where he comes from?

The night before yesterday Patrick called me out of the blue. It was the first time since we had met in March. He mumbled something that sounded like 'urgent' and 'business' before the line went dead. He called again the next morning to invite me for dinner in an expensive French restaurant near Runaway Bay, the "Escargot". His shirt pristine white, his golden watch by Cartier and his eyes full of dedication – that's how he looked like when he picked me up at Te Moana.

I'd noticed that look in his eyes for the first time when I'd visited him in Jamaica. It was the look of a young man who knew nothing about career, business or manners, a young man full of a desire descending upon me like a huge wave. Never before had I felt this desired.

And yesterday evening, when I got into his black car, that very look in his eyes was back. I remembered why I'd been yearning for this man for two years.

During our dinner, right after we'd eaten the escargots, the Filet Mignon medium rare just being served, he said, "Last time we met I asked you if you are willing to spend your life with me. You said yes but you seemed a little uncertain. Did you think it over again in the mean-time?"

The owner of the restaurant came to our table to greet us. The "Escargot" is furnished like an original French Restaurant with a counter, bar stools, shelves filled with expensive French wines, the tables covered with pristine white linen long enough to nearly touch the ground. On the tables pleated napkins looking like swans are placed next to the wineglasses. A voice sounding from the speakers was singing "Rien, rien de rien".

When the owner learned that I'm German, he continued talking to me in almost accent-free German. At first, I was baffled, but then he told me that he'd lived in Munich for 27 years. He was around sixty years old and there was a sadness about him that touched me. But what impressed me most was when he told me that he was born in Jamaica. His complexion was dark but his poise, his gestures and facial expression were that of an elegant European. He held two identities.

The Filet Mignon tasted excellent. While I cut it with the meat knife I thought about Patrick's question. There was only fog inside my head. All I could feel was this enormous sex appeal Patrick exuded. And something else, something vague. All the stories I'd heard about Jamaica. The picture of Jamaica growing more mysterious, more appealing, more dangerous and impenetrable by the minute. And the distinct feeling that the "Me" that had once existed wasn't there any longer.

Patrick looked at me and spoke very softly, "You know,

there are many white women who come here – from America mostly, not so many from Europe. They're looking for a Jamaican man because those are the best lovers."

As if he could read my mind. Those were not the thoughts I had on my mind at that moment but thoughts I did ponder when I slept fitfully. Am I one of these women looking for a man here just like German men are looking for a Thai woman because they are foreign and exotic? And if so, is it unethical? Am I part of a system that has been exploiting people for centuries? Patrick wasn't a man I could buy. He was much wealthier than me. But he was the embodiment of something I yearned for. Something that attracted me without knowing what exactly it was. Was it love? Were we free of the history of our cultures or was it this very history searching for a new chapter and we had just become figures in it?

And again, I thought about his question. Was I willing to live my life with him? There was no simple answer to it. It was me setting off into the unknown, the beginning of it the moment I saw Patrick for the first time at Vienna airport. Thinking about it: Just one moment, a short encounter with a dark-skinned foreigner. And now, that I'm following that foreign attraction, I'm discovering a mysterious world, that is getting more mysterious by the hour.

Where is the love I'm searching for?

"Why," I ask Patrick and put my wineglass to my lips in a gesture that is unintentionally European. "Why me?"

ONE LOVE – ONE HEART

Chapter 16 – Shall I Allow It?

This morning, the day after I had dinner with Patrick in the French restaurant, I wake up feeling utterly romantic, the feeling cursing through my veins like honey. I have a certain song on my mind. A song I heard when Daniel took me to the farm with his weathered, old jeep.

He'd said, "This song's for you."

And at that moment I heard the lyrics, "I long to see the sunlight in your hair".

The sun was setting, that evening when he played that song, the sky sporting a ribbon of red light and the wind was blowing in through the open window and through my hair. That color, a slightly blueish red in front of the still intense blue sky touched my soul so deeply that it made me cry.

Daniel took my hand, his skin so rough but his touch so gentle.

My fear was gone, the fear that resided inside me since the shooting. At that very moment there was nothing but the beauty of the last sun rays and the colours they created – and Daniel's touch.

That was three months ago, in January.

This morning, the memory of that day is very clear. I'm lying in my bed no longer thinking about Patrick's question. I remember how Daniel has touched the mare, can see in my mind's eye how her eyes became drowsy and her body relented, how she leans into his touch. And that's exactly how I feel now.

I can hear my heartbeat loud and clear. I see the light of the dusk from that evening, the blueish red ribbon, the translucent pale blue, I smell the musty smell of the humidity, feel the warmth of Daniel's hand and the jolting of the jeep on the ground interspersed with loopholes. I can feel that evening's sky within my body, in my heart and in my hand.

Now. I think back to my conversation with Patrick in the "Escargot" yesterday evening.

"I love Jamaica so much," I said.

"Life is dangerous here," he answered. "Just this month 40 people were murdered, 200 since the beginning of the year. The police cannot protect you. The island is glutted with weapons. And you say you love Jamaica?"

I know Patrick didn't tell me those facts to scare me. It is simply his task to find political solutions for the problem concerning the weapons. He explained to me that the crime here results from social injustice. That people who have no access to education, who earn so little for working so hard, who earn not enough to feed themselves, much less their children – that the smarter among them buy weapons and deal with drugs and live by the motto: Whoever shoots first survives.

I guess that communication and the fear it awoke inside of me caused a reaction of my body while I was sleeping. My body found something within its own system, within its own memories, that's stronger than the fear. The happiness, the beauty of the evening sky, the touch of Daniel's hand, the feeling of being close to the sky – all those things my body brought forth to fight the fear.

Maybe that's the reason why I'm attracted to Jamaica in such a way: The fact that violence and fear create a medicine, an antidote; that despite crime and poverty something else is winning – not because there's a law for it or because people learn it at school, but because their body and their soul bring it forth.

I want to meet Daniel again. The love I once was looking for doesn't exist any longer. Or it still does but in another form.

I don't have Daniel's phone number. I know that he owns a mobile phone because I saw it. How to find out? I don't want anyone to know that I'm interested in him.

I decide to call Monika, the owner of the farm and Daniel's employer. She is from Austria and has lived in Jamaica for 40 years. Maybe she'll warn me, but she surely won't judge me. And that's exactly how it goes – she provides me with his number and tells me, "Be careful. Jamaican men tend to have many women."

I read on Wikipedia under the heading of "HIV/Jamaica" that 1,7% of the citizens suffer from AIDS. An international comparison shows France with a percentage of 0,4.

And there is another interesting number to be found there. According to a behavioral study 56% of the men and 16% of the women in Jamaica tend to have more than one sex partner in one year. I guess that's what Monika was talking about. I'm feeling very unromantic and almost like an intruder into the bedrooms of the local people while reading. And I wonder: Is it considered basic knowledge when having a multicultural relationship – to read the sex statistics of a foreign country? Or am I just trying to protect myself? Can I even protect myself? The probability of getting infected with AIDS is what – 1,3% higher with a Jamaican than with a French man?

Would it be more likely to catch the disease when being with Daniel or with Patrick?

Patrick told me I'm the first woman within five years he slept with. I know for sure that I'm not infectious because I had myself tested. But would I ask Daniel if we got closer? Or was this the time to get some condoms?

I dial Daniel's number having no idea what to say.

There is a brief "Hello."

"It's me," I say and launch into explaining who I am. "The woman from Germany …"

"I know … How are you?" he interrupts me. He's speaking English with me although his mother tongue is Patois and he would ask "Wah Gwaan" instead of "How are you" when talking to a local.

"Can we meet?" I ask.

"When?"

"Now."

I hear him laughing, then silence.

"Where are you?" he asks.

I explain where exactly Te Moana is in Ocho Rios.

"Do you have a car?" he asks.

"No, but I can find a driver."

"Okay."

"Are you at home?" I ask.

"You haven't seen my home."

"Okay."

"The house where we had the chicken isn't my house."

"Where is your house?" I wonder if his wife and children live there as well.

Silence.

What on earth am I doing here, I ask myself.

"You sleep with another man," he says. "So, what do you want from me?"

I'm baffled. How does he know? Or was this just a test, a bluff? Doesn't matter because he literally caught me with my pants down. I feel bad. I'm doing online researches, assuming all Jamaican men are polygamous, and yet here I am – just alike, I had several sex partners in the twelve months past.

Where did the mood I was in this morning vanish to? The evening sky, the sky in my heart? I just cannot find the right words to say. Then I ask myself: Do I always have to answer immediately? If it's important to him, he will ask again. After all, I just want to meet him, not marry him.

"I'd like to get to know you better," I say.

"Come to Annandale. I'm free tomorrow evening."

"Okay."

"Later," he says – that's like the 'Ciao' we use in Germany.

I lay back on my bed feeling simply happy.

I remember a reggae song by Taurus Riley: "She's Royal." It contains the lyrics "And when they ask what a good woman's made of – She's not afraid and ashamed of who she is."

Maybe that's my answer to love: I feel what I feel, be it happiness or divineness or fear, be it in Jamaica or in Germany or at any other place on this world.

And now I'm here. And I realise that it's plain and simple allowed to feel what I feel.

Jamaica – One Love ... I'm a part of it.

Chapter 17 – No Problem

I decide to go to Annandale in the morning. The drivers aren't feeling all too enthusiastically about that way – the driveway to the farm, two kilometers long and very rocky, ruining the underbodies of their cars. But Mr. Johnson is taking me there, nevertheless. I ask him and he just says, "No Problem."

Just like New York is known as "the city that never sleeps", Jamaica is the island of "no problem". A solid businessman from Germany told me once, "They must be dreaming."

I think about Patrick for a little while. He hasn't contacted me after our dinner at the "Escargot". I really get it by now that it's nothing personal, that he's simply always busy. In fact, I think this is quite enjoyable because should I really became a part of his life, there would be a lot of free time for me to pursue my own interests. That is … that's what my prudent part tells me.

The romantic part of me, on the other side, is of another opinion: If you love somebody, you want to spend all your time with him or her. Maybe that's unrealistic. Maybe I need to be honest with myself.

The drive towards the farmhouse of Annandale makes me feel happy yet again. While passing the lake I can see Daniel from afar, working with the horses. Even if he's far away, I can see how much he harmonises with his surroundings, and that his ability to tend to the horses in his special way is based on exactly this fact.

Here at Annandale, everything seems like a dream to me, even if I know it's real. Again, I sense the abundant growth of the trees, bushes and plants. It's a feeling as if all the climbing plants, the mystical dark violet, yellow, orange or pristine white blossoms, the huge trees and palm trees swaying in the wind, are not just living around me but also within me. There is no boundary between myself and the vibrant greenery around me. I blend into it.

Annandale is the size of more than 600 acres which is about as large as a small town in Germany. From the house you enjoy a sweeping view of the vast area. It is part of the green heart of Jamaica.

To move through this vastness in between the abundant, unstoppable growth makes me feel very tiny, a human being just a tiny part of the big picture.

While we're driving towards the farmhouse I suddenly think about Oliver, God rest his soul. In this very moment I can feel the love again that I shared with him and it is caused by my perceiving myself in a very pristine way when here. I can feel a room within that I knew when I was a child, some inner world where mysterious plants and trees were growing, fantastic birds were flying around, a gentle breeze was blowing, a world smelling of flower fragrance and humid trunks, a world I withdrew into when I had to flee the too loud outer world. A world where I was perfectly safe and where I always could find myself again. When I was a teen, I wished for someone to find me there to share this world with me. Because that's how I thought love to be: A magical place, unknown to anybody else, but shared with this one person.

It was Oliver who found me there. He had a key to that place. A place that could be unlocked only by someone with a pure heart. He owned the key to my heart, and we lived in this place for many years. Our children grew up there and we all were part of it.

It is back again, here at Annandale, that feeling of love – Oliver and me and our perfect love. I can feel that this love is still intact. I can feel it now and I feel wonderfully at peace.

Monika provided me with a room in the adjoining building in which I can stay and write. I intend to stay for a few days. The room is in a part of the house where the farmworkers live. I like it, it's perfect for a writer. The pitched roof of the building is made of corrugated sheet and there is a fan mounted on a crossbeam. The wooden slats are slightly inclined and allow enough light in for me to write in sun-drenched air, air that is warm enough that I tie my long hair together to cool my neck.

I hear the mooing of the cows, the neighing of the horses and the chattering of the geese from afar and the scraping of the branches pushed against the roof by the wind. I'm sitting on a small white bench made of wicker, my notebook on my lap.

For the moment I'm alone except for the two farm workers Nick and Mr. Nelson. Monika went to the city and Daniel is at the pasture working with the horses.

Right now, Omar is arriving. I can see him through the window. Omar takes care about the house and cooks for the residents and the guests.

He told me quite a few things about his life, for example that he grew up on a farm and his parents didn't have enough money to send him to school. They needed him to work on the farm. When he was eighteen years old, he couldn't even read his own name. It was at that age that he decided to attend school after all to learn how to read and write, and he managed to raise the money for the fees all by himself. Once, he showed me his certificate of his training to become a cook and he really does a wonderful job.

"Hi, Omar," I call out to him. "How are you?"

We know each other from when I stayed here in January. His reply is his bubbling laughter and a "Whenever you are here, I'm fine."

Omar is a deeply religious man. God is his sanctuary whenever his sorrows become too great. He knows hunger and poverty, he has four children and sometimes he cannot afford their school fees and sometimes he cannot afford to buy food. Since his childhood he hasn't been allowed to just live his life but always had to survive. Sometimes, when he's talking about it, he cries. He told me that he often begged God to take him home for life here on earth is too hard.

His life may be hard, but his heart is not.

"I have a pure heart," he says. "There is nothing I need to regret or apologise for."

Sometime later I see him leaning with his back at the wall of the adjoining building, talking to one of the farmworkers. They talk about theft. He's talking very agitatedly and emotionally as if he wants to warn the other man. "I prayed to God: Take my life, if I ever steal from someone, take my life." He's repeating it again and again. "God, take my life if I ever steal from someone."

These are the two things he would never do he claims: Stealing and begging.

I remember the first time I came here with my heavy suitcase.

I asked Omar then, "Would you help me to carry this suitcase up the stairs?"

He looked at me and answered very clearly, "No!"

"Okay," I said, "it was just a question."

"It makes me feel sad that you ask this", he continued.

I remembered that he had been working the whole day and that he'd told me some time ago how tired he was, and I thought that it had been careless of me to ask. "It was just a question," I repeated.

And he repeated as well, "It makes me feel sad that you ask it."

So, I said it again: "Omar, it was just question, it was careless of me to ask." I simply couldn't understand why he was so upset because of it.

Then he blurted, "How dare you ask Omar if he would carry your suitcase for you? Omar would do anything for you! Omar loves you! Omar would do anything for you. Of course, I will help you with the suitcase!"

That's the way he is. Omar and I meet each other in that place of love, there's no doubt about it.

I think the reason why Annandale is such a special place is that you simply become a part of everything. You're blending in. And that's the one thing love demands: To not stay outside just looking in, but to become a part of it. A part of the joy, a part of the pain. Omar's pain is my pain and my joy is his.

I write all day, eat a sandwich I make myself in the kitchen, chat with Omar and look forward to the evening.

It's getting dark, the frogs and cicadas begin with their performance. I put an end to my day full of writing and I feel content. I close my notebook, put on a pair of jeans and sneakers and walk down the way to the horses.

From afar I see a fire burning, Daniel sitting next to it. He looks at me, gets up and starts walking towards me. Then he greets me with a kiss. I'm positively surprised and I very much like this gesture. Then he puts his arms around me. His embrace is gentle and clear, and I feel safe immediately. He takes my hand and leads me to the fire just as if there was no doubt that the two of us were a pair of lovers. He sits down on a knee-high wall, somewhat distant from the fire and puts a caparison on the ground for me to sit on. Around the fire there's a frame with a chicken roasting on one of the crossbars. He hands me a bottle of Ting, a local lemonade.

"Was the chicken still alive when you brought it here?", I ask.

"A dead one would have started to smell bad after a day in this heat," he answers.

Automatically I start looking around in search of the head of the dead chicken but there are only a few feathers.

Daniel assumes what I'm thinking and holds up a plastic bag with two chicken feet inside.

"I will make a soup out of them. Jamaican specialty. The rest was taken by the dogs."

I think I've never before felt this happy just sitting in front of a fire watching a chicken getting roasted ... Daniel holds my hand. It feels perfectly natural for him to kiss and touch me, and I simply enjoy it.

Later, we eat the chicken. Everything is so easy with Daniel, I'm not anxious, not overexcited but I just feel good – plain and simple good. I let go, allowing the things to happen and so does Daniel. He always seems to know what I like or how much of a certain thing I like. And, so do I. I didn't even know I had that instinct, but there it is. His hand is resting between my legs and I'm pondering the issue concerning the condoms again. I don't have one with me.

Daniel pauses as if reading my mind.

"We don't have to go any further today," he says.

I nestle into his arms and look at the fire.

"I've been thinking about you all day long," he says. "I've missed you."

I'm surprised to hear he feels like this, after all I thought it was just me.

"I couldn't forget you," he says. "I didn't know how to contact you, but you heard me anyway, felt my yearning."

Again, I'm surprised by these declarations of love.

From time to time there is a voice inside my mind wondering if he's pursuing a certain target with all of this. But then I just let go again.

We stay there by the fire for a very long time. I see the heads of the horses behind the wall and listen to the creaking of the bamboo and the music of the insects. It's cozy, the fire is slowly dying. Daniels hands are incredibly gentle, touching my neck, my shoulders, my arms, it feels like warm water trickling over my skin.

"I would like to go to Germany with you," he says. "Will you marry me?"

It feels like a heavy rock splashes into the water, circular waves spreading from the spot where it sank.

I nod and say, "Yes."

ONE LOVE - ONE HEART

Chapter 18 – When Your Heart Opens

The next morning, I wake up in my corrugated-iron room at Annandale thinking: This is one of the situations in life when you urgently need to consult a friend. A real good friend. A friend who knows you better than you do yourself: Felicia.

A short while later I'm talking to her on the phone. The call costs about three Euros a minute and I try to keep it short.

"Okay," she says after I explained everything to her. "That's not an issue that can be solved on the phone." I hear her typing. "I'll arrive the day after tomorrow, 7:30 p.m. at Montego Bay. Will you pick me up?"

I think that my life is currently rushing along at an advanced speed and that I could use a break to think about everything. But that's just the thing Felicia will help me with.

"Cool," I say. "Awesome," I add because only now I realise what a wonderful friend Felicia is in fact. Then there is a longer silence and I wonder if I should end the call now, but I know my friend. She's not just saying nothing but she's hatching an idea. Her intuition is priceless, and she knows me very well.

"Listen," she says. "Two things: Don't sign any contracts before I'm with you." Silence. I wait for her to continue. "And watch out for black hens."

I burst out laughing. "Black hens. Got it."

We say goodbye with a series of declarations of love and friendship and imagined hugs and I cannot thank her enough for really boarding a plane to come to me. But it's also a sign that she sees the seriousness of a situation that's probably more obvious for an outsider than for the one stuck in the very middle.

I'm lying on my bed, looking at the corrugated sheet above me and think about Daniel. About the fact that he asked me to marry him last night at the fire. And the fact that I agreed.

I think about the black hens as well and about a dream I had several months ago. Patrick visited me in that dream and handed me two contracts. Then he took me to the garden of his property and showed me his five new black hens. It was one of those impactful dreams you don't forget.

In addition to that, archangel Michael or one of his trainees had made sure that wherever I went black hens would cross my way, most of the time five of them. The same happened to Felicia, who I'd told about my dream. I'm getting the creeps just thinking about it now.

Early in the afternoon Patrick calls.

"Where are you?" he asks.

"At Annandale."

"Can you come to see me?"

"Okay," I say. I could have added 'no problem' since that's my new attitude. Something inside of me has decided to just go with the flow and simply say 'yes' to whatever may come.

"I'll send a driver."

"Great. I'm looking forward to it," I say, and I mean it.

When Patrick meets me at the gate, I realise at once that he looks more serious than usually. The embrace he gives me feels gentle and intimate. It's not the business-man but just the man who wants to be close to me.

"Would you like a drink?" he asks.

"I'd love one."

Patrick creates wonderful drinks of various fruit juices.

I sit on the veranda and look at the ocean. I'm about halfway up the hill and the view of the sea is incredible from here. The area is as wide as at Annandale, but here it's the ocean. I experience a deep calm different to the one at Annandale, it's of a timeless nature.

Patrick comes out with the drinks.

He puts them onto the glass table and sits down next to me on the bench. Yet another man sitting next to me on a bench.

Patrick starts a light conversation. He is very good at this: lightening my mood, making me laugh, making me feel that he knows me well – knows even my (sometimes) bizarre thoughts.

But I know very well that all of this is leading to a certain question. *The question.* The question if I'm going to share my life with him.

I wonder if it hasn't already been answered by the fact that I told Daniel I would marry him yesterday. But I don't know Jamaican habits and customs very well and I don't know enough about Daniel to rule out the possibility of him proposing to a different woman every other night. I remember a certain scene when Patrick and I'd made a trip to a greenish blue lake in the mountains of Jamaica. Some Rastas were sitting under the roof of a small bar at the shore of the lake, smoking ganja (marijuana). They asked us where we were from. When I'd told them I was from Germany, one of them said, "I want to go to Germany with you. Will you marry me?"

And Omar had also asked me several times if I would take him to Germany and marry him.

But I'm straying from the topic again. The conversation with Patrick has stopped.

"You didn't answer my question when we were at the Escargot," I say, changing the course of our talk. "I asked you: Why me?"

Patrick tilts his head. He knows exactly what I'm talking about. He lowers his gaze and I can feel his awareness turning inwards.

"You're the most genuine woman I have ever met. Your love feels true." He's silent for a moment as if he needs to look even further inside to find the right words. "Never before, and I really mean never, has a woman shown me this unconditional love. I know for you it is not about my money or my position. I'm not walking through the world, giving my heart away easily. I'm a reserved person, and despite my strong public presence I'm very reclusive in private. You're aware of this. Everything you wrote me in your letters … It's as if you can read me like an open book. Never before have I felt this understood."

Now I'm really touched and a little amazed. Yes, I could feel his characteristics – that is, I always thought I could. But I could never understand why he'd turned away from me after we'd come so close.

"You must have wondered why I broke up our relationship back then," he says.

I realise that perhaps I'll get an answer to the one question that's kept me occupied for the last two years. I realise that perhaps a door to his heart, which I've knocked at for a long time, is about to be opened. And I realise that perhaps it hasn't been solely his work that kept him from contacting me. I sink back into the cushions and my gaze wanders out towards the sea. Suddenly I don't own just two ears but several hundred.

Patrick speaks up: "Everything we had together was absolutely wonderful. A dream. You made me so very happy. Jamaica. Those were the best days and weeks of my life. ... But every single time we had to say goodbye at the end. ... I don't know if you can understand this but to say goodbye is harder for me than for most other people. Maybe it's because I've been alone for so long. After I'd seen you off at the airport last winter, I felt so devastated, I realised I couldn't do this any longer. But how was I to explain it to you? You surely would've thought I wanted to put pressure on you or wanted to take away your freedom. Because it would've been all or nothing. How could it have been possible to merge our lives – you in Germany, me in Jamaica? I simply had no solution for it. I wanted you to be free."

Suddenly he's no longer the charismatic leader, the versed speaker, but a hurting man who'd decided to keep his pain to himself because he didn't want me to feel the burden of it.

His answer is downright shocking. For months I'd been asking myself why he wouldn't answer. And all this time I'd felt that there was a reason for it, that it wasn't because he didn't love me.

It's a shock of truth. Something deep inside me says: I understand.

Patrick gets up and walks into the living room. I'm glad to get a moment of reprieve. For two years I've lived with this uncertainty, for two years I've encountered it with my pure love and suddenly everything is falling into place. As if the world was tilted to one side and is now in balance once more. I feel a little dizzy.

Patrick comes back. He takes two documents out of an envelope he's carrying in his hands and passes me one of it.

"Please read," he says gently.

I take a short look at it and see it's a contract, possibly a marriage contract.

I think about my friend Felicia and about my dream of the two contracts. I think about archangel Michael. And I feel an inner turmoil, an excitement.

"I'd like to show you something," Patrick says, "Come." His face is lightening up and suddenly I can see the mischievous small boy in him. And he's back – the charismatic man, but this time it's a very playful version of him.

He takes me by the hand and leads me around the house. There I can see a fence and a small wooden house with a door about 20 centimeters high.

"I'd like to keep some animals, to change this place into a real home," he says as lively as I've seldom seen him.

There are certain moments in life when there's nothing left to say. I guess you know already.

I lean into Patrick and sigh.

I count them.

Fife.

Chapter 19 – Finding the Essence

I wake up in my corrugated-iron hut feeling deeply at peace. I'm back at Annandale. I didn't sign the contract. I didn't even read it.

My eyes are still closed but I can smell the intense, moist scent of Jamaica that saturates everything, including myself. I'm drifting through time, drifting through my life in a space that's endless. Already in the morning it's warm enough to make me sweat. When I'm here I seem to own a different body and I like that body. It is warm and soft. Its needs are very simple. A glass of water, the chattering of the geese, the view of the endless green vastness. Writing.

I feel that I'm drifting farther and farther away from the place I'm coming from. I think about my late husband who led a double life in Morocco. Did he follow a passion similar to mine? Am I living a double life now? One in Germany and one in Jamaica? One in the real world and one in a dream?

I think about yesterday's conversation with Patrick. For two years I'd waited for his answer. And yesterday I finally got it: Saying goodbye is hard for him and he therefore avoids a relationship from the beginning. And what about me? I'm just like him because my heart clung to him for two years. And when I finally could let him go, he came back. It's not what we would wish for. We wish for our love and our longing to be fulfilled. But reality is different. We meet ourselves. The yearning I'd felt for Patrick, which kept me imprisoned for two years, has taught me this much about love that I could meet Daniel and know immediately I could go anywhere with him and be happy.

I don't need more time to think about it. I don't need to read a marital contract. I don't even need to choose. I'm just going to trust life and I'll go wherever it may lead. Maybe it'll lead to a new unfulfilled longing, a dramatic love filled with pain or a happy fulfilled life – here or anywhere else, with or without a man.

Theoretically, this could be the end of my story, but archangel Michael and his heavenly band aren't through with me. I just received a text message from Daniel: "Are you coming to the horses?"

How could I say 'no'?

And at the same minute a text message from Patrick: 'Can I talk to you?'

How could I say 'no'?

I think of Grandpa, the spirit who called me to come to Jamaica. And again, I wonder, "Why me?"

Grandpa, I assume, is an ancient African spirit. How am I connected to Africa? I think of the Rastafari movement. A movement of people torn from their home, kidnapped or sold and forced onto ships, abused and used as slaves. People who want to go back to their African roots. People whose messiah is Haile Selassie, the Ethiopian emperor. Where is the connection to me?

Why did I give my heart and my soul to two men whose ancestral lines are reaching far back to Africa?

Yesterday I attended the service of the Seventh-day Adventist Church again. They are doing a pilgrimage currently, a crusade.

The service wasn't held in their church but in a huge tent. That's where I met Mike, about my age, tall, athletic, elegantly dressed. It was easy for us to start a conversation – people with an open heart don't need empty phrases. We were quickly getting close with words, gestures, looks and with pure gentleness. Our congenial souls met, and it was beautiful. One sentence he said is still on my mind: "Whenever I feel that something is given to me by God, I don't question it."

It took about two hours for Romaine, the preacher, to finish his (yelled) sermon. His voice was that loud and forceful that I could feel all my cells vibrate and my inner resistance crumble. Mine and that of the other churchgoers. I'm used to well-worded, officially authorized preachers and sermons. Why is it that I find Romaine that exciting? That mere question nearly makes my mind seize up.

The sermon was about Jesus who was travelling on a boat together with his disciples. He was asleep in the boat's stern until his disciples woke him, they were worried for the boat was about to sink. Jesus woke up and politely asked the storm to calm down. Then he asked his disciples: Why do you behave this cowardly? Don't you have any faith?

I think something similar is happening in my current life. I'm not Jesus, but I'm sleeping in the boat's stern and when the storm arrives, I'll ask it to calm down. I'm not Jesus, but I can see now that everyone of us can do that. This knowledge stems from the past – African, Indian, Asian, Celtic, Greek, Jewish, Christian past – and finally from nature. From love.

I feel myself sliding deeper and deeper into this truth. Those two years in which I longed for Patrick felt like a spirit was living inside of me. It was nice but I was also trapped. My whole life was driven by that longing. That longing being the result of the fact I had put my life into the hands of some higher power. They showed me what really affects my life. Whether we're looking for love or faith or happiness – we all know that we can ask the storm to calm down even if it's in the act of sinking our boat.

We all know that love is powerful enough to capture our hearts, that love comes into our lives like a powerful higher will, that we fight against it and that it makes us very soft and gentle in the end.

The spirit who made Patrick and me meet is gone. My soul released him without me consciously deciding to do so.

Funny, how sometimes something becomes suddenly so very clear. Or maybe it isn't funny at all. All the people who attended the service yesterday are searching for this clarity. The preacher hammered his words into our heads and hearts for two hours to lead us to that very devotion. And we were able to find it and left saturated and nurtured.

Whenever I'm here in this peace, this clarity, I can feel what everything's about. And by feeling it, it becomes reality. The storm is calming down.

And I guess that's what the angels demand of me: To trust them. To lay down and sleep when I'm tired without being afraid of the storm.

One of my friends from Germany asked me in an email today what it is that makes me feel this attracted to Jamaica. I pondered that question for quite some time. I think that I want to sink even deeper into this power that's able to calm down a storm. I want to find much more of this essence. And here is the place to find it, here the curtain is drawn open and everything behind it is visible, here I cannot evade anything. No matter how painful or beautiful it may be – it is true, and it is strong.

In the afternoon I visit Daniel and the horses. He takes me into his arms and again there is this inner feeling as if I've known him forever.

"I've missed you so much," he says. "The whole day I couldn't think of anything else but when you would be here."

I'm sorry that I didn't come earlier. I'm hurting because he is. I'm hurting for him.

"Did you miss me, too?" he asks.

I did – but only a little bit and not all day long. I feel sorry again. He has that many feelings for me – and me? I'm sorry. I didn't think about him because I was occupied with writing. And now I don't know what to say.

"How's she doing?" I ask, looking at the mare who is standing next to him, looking at him attentively.

"She's listening to us," he says. "When I started to work with her three days ago, she had a very negative stance. I thought she would be a difficult case. But now she's soft and gentle. That's because of you."

He takes my hand and pulls me against him.

I can feel the softness of the mare and how she seems to melt under his touch.

At that very moment I realize something that, in all the years I've already been working with horses, has never been this obvious to me. Horses are very sensitive beings and their awareness is incredibly subtle. The only way to gain their trust is to become sensitive as well. As sensitive as they are. I think that's why I feel such a kinship with Daniel. We are alike in our sensitivity and subtlety.

Daniel puts his arm around my waist and says, "A penny for your thoughts."

Then he kisses me.

The kiss is so soft and gentle that the mare is also becoming completely soft. Her look is very gentle and turned inwards. Daniel and I keep kissing, I can feel our bodies touching but it's not solely our physical bodies. It's our energy. Never before have I felt it the way I do with Daniel. And the mare feels it as well.

I can feel it because Daniel can. If he couldn't feel it, I would be all alone. Together with Daniel I can feel so much more than I could if I was alone. A wide space I hadn't know before is opening and even if everything is wholly physical, it feels as if my body and his body are flying into that space where new doors keep opening while, at the same time, we are utterly in the here and now. And the mare – I can feel that as well – she is also utterly in the here and now, and yet she's flying with us.

ONE LOVE - ONE HEART

Chapter 20 – Trouble in Paradise

I wake with a feeling of dreadful foreboding. There are many possible explanations for it. In my world there are Sigmund Freud, psychology, spirituality, libraries full of explanations why I wake up frightened and shivering.

Yesterday with Daniel I experienced a tremendously deep contact when my soul found its answer in another person. A man. I was so astounded by that fact. I hadn't known something like that was even possible, but I felt it. The answer wasn't given in words ... I mean words saying one thing today and another tomorrow. No, it was something in his soul and in mine. And it was my complete soul, not just the nice part of it but also its pain, its fear, everything and anything. We both went to that place where everything exists.

And I wondered if it would always stay like this. If everything beautiful I experience will be followed by something painful. If that's maybe a law of nature. If it's the angels saying: Here comes the next test.

At 9:30 a.m. my phone starts to ring. I think everyone of us has experienced that certain situation, had to deal with 'this one sudden message.'

"Your husband and family died at an accident." – "You have cancer and there is no chance of survival." – "You are no longer needed for this job."

Sometimes you're expecting it already, sometimes you

aren't. But either way your life will be different afterwards.

This morning it's a voice, speaking to me in broken English, a harsh female voice.

"Hello." Silence.

Me: "Hello, who's speaking?"

There is noise on the line. I could see that the prefix number was an international one: 212. I've no idea to which country it belongs.

Next, she says something like "Schiefer", but that's not an English word.

"I'm sorry, I cannot hear you," I say.

She repeats it "Schiefer ...Schiefer". Then she asks, "Did you receive my letter?"

I don't recognise her accent, so I don't know where to place it or her.

"Letter ... what letter?"

"Oliver."

Everything inside of me is contracting at once. I feel sick. I think, I going to be sick. I can guess now that I'm talking to Charifa, the woman from Morocco who has a child with my late husband.

"Yes," I say. I cannot find the strength to say any more.

"I need your help," she says.

I fall utterly silent.

"Your son is ill," she says. I wonder why she calls him 'your son'. She continues, "I've lost my work. I need to take care of my son. He needs me. That's why I cannot work."

"My son? Why do you call him my son? He isn't my son. He's Oliver's and your son."

"He is your son."

"No."

"You are the only one who can help him. Oliver used to help us. We are very poor."

"That's not my problem."

"If you don't help us, he might die."

"I don't know you. I don't even know if you're telling the truth. You could be a fraudster, after all."

Silence. A long-lasting silence.

"You have a cold heart," she says eventually. "This is why your husband wanted another woman. Oliver had a good heart. Full of love. He always helped me. You are wealthy and yet deny your help the ones who need it. You don't help your children. You don't have children any longer. God took them away from you."

All I can hear after that is a tooting. She ended the call.

And I'm back at that very place I was when I stood on top of the high-rise in Frankfurt. At that time, I wanted to jump down to end my life. Now I feel like I'm standing on top of some scaffolding that consist of many layers. I crash through the top one, land on the one below it. I crash through that one as well and land on the one below it ... I keep crashing and falling until I arrive at the very bottom.

I'm lying on my bed in my corrugated-iron hut, crying. The tears run out of my eyes and I'm unable to stop them. Just as I couldn't stop them back then when I'd received that news. For weeks, for months.

I say, "Dear angels, you promised to take care of me. Is

this part of it? Is this a way to impress me? To convince me that life here is worth living?"

The angels don't answer. Probably they didn't even hear me.

My body feels as if I really fell from a great height. It hurts so much I'm unable to move. The worst is her accusation that I don't have a heart. That this is the reason why God took my husband and my children. Maybe she is right? Maybe I live in a world in which everybody has a heart – except for me. Maybe I'm simply missing a crucial organ. To feel, I mean. Or maybe I just haven't understood yet what it is that others mean when talking about a heart or love.

I know only one thing for certain: It hurts so much.

For more than three years I did everything possible to get back on my feet. To find love again. And yet I arrived nowhere. I haven't found a home. Maybe there simply isn't one for me?

I look at my watch. Damn ... Felicia will be arriving today. I need to find a driver. I promised to pick her up at Montego Bay airport at 7:30 p.m.

I reach for my mobile phone and check the new messages.

Patrick asks if we can meet this evening. I answer that I'll have a visitor and will contact him.

Daniel writes that he misses me and asks when I'll be back with him and the horses. I don't know what to answer. I feel so lost. I feel ashamed and I don't want him to see me like this. I don't know if he could understand why I feel so depressed. Maybe he would tell me to help the woman and her child. After all I have more money than they do.

I find a driver who will pick me up and take me to Montego Bay and arrange with him that I'll wait at the gate for him, so he needn't drive up the long driveway. I'll walk down there.

I resurface as if coming out of deep water. I look at my watch, there's time left. I could visit the horses on my way to the gate.

I'm afraid to meet Daniel. I'm afraid he won't like me like this – weak and helpless. I'm unable to find my happy mood again, to ask the storm to move on. I cannot shake it off. And I think the angels don't want me to. They want me to suffer. They want me to feel how it is to be on this world. They want me to find love in the pain as well because this is the only way to find all the love that can be found, because it is the only way for me to feel again what they're doing for me. Then again – maybe all of this is just stupid human speculation.

I see Daniel standing in the middle of the herd, completely immersed in himself. The horses have flocked around him. It looks like a beautiful picture from afar. I've seen this several times: When you are truly and utterly yourself, a harmony arises greater than any harmony a human being could create intentionally, and you become part of something greater. The animals, the trees, the clouds – everything responds to you and the same is true for the other way around. And as I'm watching Daniel,

I remember that this is also what I am. That this is my home. As I'm watching Daniel the deep calm returns.

I don't know if he's already spotted me. Maybe ... he doesn't move. I'm still many steps away from him and yet feel his embrace already. Slowly I'm coming back to feel myself, my breath and my body.

Daniel looks at me and I can feel his gentleness.

He puts his arms around me, and everything is safe in his embrace.

"You are sad," he says.

I weep silently.

I look at the horses and I can feel their deep compassion. And it's not only the horses but everything around me that's full of compassion. My tears won't stop falling. I realise that nothing Daniel could say or do would change a thing. It's his very nature that touches and calms me – not his words or actions. Just like the very nature of the horses and the trees which don't have words as well. All my sadness, all my pain and all my helplessness of which I'm that ashamed – all of it finds a place here. Everything is safe here.

I can breathe again. The memory of every single moment I've felt like this before is back – amidst nature and amidst horses.

For the very first time since the accident I'm able to really think of my children. Up to now this has been impossible. I didn't have the strength. But now, for a short moment, I can allow myself to think of them.

It feels as if life itself gave Daniel to me, to make me

remember that I'm not alone. And it gave Charifa to me, whose call ripped open my heart to let escape all the pain and grieve.

I can feel compassion and pain at the same time. And I feel myself healing. Compassion and pain.

It was my compassion that made me feel so blue. My compassion is the reason I feel guilty. It wants to prevent others from suffering – at any cost. There's nothing I want more than to know that the others are happy. And if they aren't, I think it's my fault. Because I feel so deeply connected with them, I feel like I'm the source of their sorrows. Albeit, I'm only feeling for them.

God did not take my children because I'm heartless. It's heartless to say a thing like that. But Charifa's actions are also caused by pain. Her pain and mine are very similar.

Daniel and I are standing in the middle of the horses. Daniel is just like the horses. He moves with the things around him. He's like the trees, like the wind. He's part of it, feeling it.

Now, I understand better what the story of Jesus and the storm is about. Jesus was this much compassionate he didn't fear a thing – not even the storm.

There is only one thing to fear: To be all alone. But we're alone only if we lose our compassion. I don't just finally realise all of this – I feel it.

And I don't need to explain a single thing to Daniel. He feels it, too.

"I'll always be there for you," he says. He says it in a certain way that makes me believe him.

I look into his eyes and then I look around to the horses.
They are all looking at Daniel and me.
And their expression is full of love.
I look back at Daniel again.
And I say, "I think you're an angel."
Daniel says, "I think you're an angel."

Chapter 21 – Love Will Always Find a Way

Yesterday I wrote that nothing has changed in my life since the day on the high-rise. But you know it: In moments like that you feel with absolute certainty that it's the end of the world – with emphasis on 'absolute certainty'. Later, the sun (and the world) may rise again ... and sooner or later they will – also with absolute certainty. That's what happened to me yesterday. With Daniel and the horses.

I also picked up Felicia at the airport yesterday. And today the day has come for me to tell you about Felicia. Because the one thing that really has changed in my life, is Felicia coming into it.

I don't know if you have experienced something like this: You've reached the bottom. You're hurting so much that you're coiling like a snake in a lion's mouth. The pain is so overwhelming that there is only one thing left you want to do: End it. In situations like these the angels are there reaching out their hands, but we're blind, more blind than ever. They're showing us a way out, but we simply cannot believe them. We're not that naïve to not see through this, are we? We know that nothing can help us anymore.

That is how I felt. When I had reached the bottom, I saw the picture of a woman with my inner eye, a brunette woman with eyes full of love. Back then, I couldn't feel her love, I couldn't feel anything for any kind of feeling would have killed me.

But I could see that picture. It was so impressive that it has stayed in my mind until today. A picture that has a place in the gallery of my inner world. I see that woman, she takes my hand and says, "You will stay with me now. I will take care of you."

Nine months later, nine months after the night on the high-rise, I meet Felicia at an event where I'm invited to speak. We chat a little, talk about horses. Some days later I receive a small parcel from her filled with small gifts. I'm a little surprised by it. Her words in the letter she added are very affectionate and personal. I'm astonished and send my thanks. She keeps sending me emails and small gifts. As I'm a public figure I'm accustomed to people contacting me – often with personal requests. But with Felicia it's different. She wants nothing. She just keeps repeating that she's there for me.

"I only want you to be happy and safe," she says.

I get to know her better.

Never before have I known someone who's put that much effort into my wellbeing. She always seems to know when I'm feeling sad and then she'll drop me a few lines. And she always finds the right words.

And some day it suddenly hits me: She is the brunette woman. Felicia does have brown hair and her whole nature is made of love.

Again, while I'm writing these words, I'm deeply touched. Felicia is heaven sent – I'm sure of it. I don't know anyone else who believes in love like she does. "Love will always find a way," she often says. "Love will make everything alright."

I feel that she really sees me – and my hunger for love. She knows a lot of things about me, but she would never take advantage of that, she'd never use her knowledge against me or manipulate me to gain something for her. I always want to give my love to her because she is giving that much love to me as well. I learn about love together with her. I learn that you cannot experience it when you're alone.

My life is different today because I have Felicia, just like the angels showed me with the picture of her.

I've learned that relations between people, friendship and love can be so much deeper than I used to know. I never knew that this was possible.

I understand now why the angels want me to stay in this world. They want me to experience it. They're looking for a way to show me. So, they've sent all the experiences with Felicia, Patrick and Daniel and maybe even Charifa.

I couldn't have planned or searched for any of them because I didn't even know they were existing. Only after they came into my life, I was surprised. Every single time it's a surprise.

Felicia calls it miracles.

A miracle means live bestowing us with something special. Like sending Felicia or Patrick or Daniel.

Miracles open my heart and when this happens the whole world looks different, colorful.

Maybe you're one of those people who are always strong and always shoulder whatever there is to be carried. I used to be one of them. But after all that happened, I cannot shoulder everything anymore. The problem is just – it's all I've ever known. When Felicia came into my life, I wanted to go on with it – shoulder everything there is, but she said, "No, no. no ... I'll help you carry it and I will take it from you when you cannot bear it any longer, always and forever." Felicia's love is unconditional, it comes from God.

I've always known God in my own way but only now that He sends those people into my life, I get to know Him better. "I've made my peace, I'm not afraid of being alone any longer," I tell archangel Michael.

And he sends Daniel and Felicia and says, "Look, this is what you need – those angels in human form, I sent them especially for you. You're a person who needs other persons around and so I'm sending you the right ones."

Felicia is the reason why I'm in Jamaica. When we met back then, I told her about the wonderful love I'd found with Patrick which had ended in an unhappy way. She looked at me and said, "Love will always find a way."

And a little later she said, "We're going to Jamaica."

Felicia isn't just a woman of words but also one of action. She owns such a brave heart. When she senses that something must happen because of love, she'll travel to the end of the world. Just like now, like she did yesterday.

Since the time Felicia and I travelled to Jamaica for the first time, lots of miracles have happened. Jamaica turned out to be the land of miracles.

Yesterday I picked her up at the airport. She put her arms around me and said, "This journey isn't over."

Gairy is driving us, like so many times before. We're

sitting in the backseat and again I have the feeling to be in the right place. The angels slashed a way through the jungle of fear and love for me. A way solely existing for me, a way nobody else ever set a foot on before and nobody else ever will after me. Sometimes I'm lost, sometimes I forget and sometimes I want to just run away. But now, as Gairy is taking us through nighttime Jamaica on our way from Montego Bay to Ocho Rios, as I watch the people sitting in vividly colored bars at the roadside wearing their colorful clothes, as the ocean stretches into eternity – everything is alright again.

We talk about Charifa's call and how much her words hurt. About her saying I had a cold heart and that'd be the reason why Oliver wanted another woman and God took my husband and my children.

"Maybe she's right and we really have no heart, living in affluence as we do," I say. "We just don't realise it anymore. If we had a heart, we wouldn't exploit other countries and people. If I had a heart, Charifa wouldn't say I refuse helping those in need."

"Mhm," Felicia says.

As if he'd understood our German conversation, Gairy tells us at that moment, "Did you know that it was exactly here that Christopher Columbus set foot onto this island when he came to South America for the very first time?"

I look out of the window and see a piece of a wall in the sea and the remnants of an old hut.

"No, I didn't know this."

"It was here," Gairy repeats.

I try to imagine it: Christopher Columbus, right here between Montego Bay and Ocho Rios.

I think about the fact Christopher Columbus being the epitome of somebody sailing into the unknown and discovering new worlds. A little like Felicia and me.

I tell Felicia about the speech of a Jamaican historian I found on YouTube a few days ago. It was about Christopher Columbus. It claims that Columbus travelled under the authority of the pope, that he was a mass murderer who annihilated the complete native population. I can't remember something like that being mentioned in our history classes. That Columbus, again on behalf of the pope, took all the gold from Jamaica to increase the wealth of the Roman Catholic Church. The Spanish took all the gold they could find. That's a fact. And the local population, the Taino, did not survive that era.

I need to ask Felicia all the questions that are so confusing. "Are our friendships and marriages breaking because we are the descendants of that heartless history? White exploiters? And is it like that until today? Is this the reason Daniel wants to marry me and come to Germany with me? Because he hopes for a better life? If so – is my love for him again just an illusion? Is it just a dream of a white woman?"

Felicia listens to all of this, says nothing and just waits. She's wonderful.

"And one more thing," I add. "John told me currently that, when he and his wife visited Barbados (her home) for the first time, her relatives told her to 'Do be very careful, John is Jamaican – he might kill you!'"

Felicia knows John and therefore that a thing like that is completely absurd. John is one of the most peaceful people on earth. Why would the people in Barbados think such a thing?

"John further told me that the slaves were mainly strong young men and that the strongest of them were taken to Jamaica. And in addition to that – but that I don't know from John, but I read it in the book he gave me – so, it says in this book that the plantation owners in fact bred the slaves like animals. They wanted to get strong workers to gain more profit. That's how they treated and called the slaves: Stock. The stock market is named like this until today because that's what it was in the beginning: A marketplace for animals and slaves.

Yesterday I was in Port Royal, the former seaport, where the slave ships arrived more than 400 years ago, carrying also people who had to flee their home countries – religious refugees, political refugees and all kinds of criminals. The city was said to be the most sinful city all over the world and when 5,000 of its 6,000 inhabitants sank into the sea during a typhoon, together with the whole peninsula, people thought that to be God's punishment. Wherever I go here in Jamaica I'm met with stories and not all of them are nice ones. Okay, I'll stop now. Just one more thing: A taxi driver told me the day before yesterday that an acquaintance of him is living with an assassin, a man earning his money by killing people. And today I read on the news that in Freiburg a mother and her life partner sold their nine-year old son to more than 60 dif-

ferent pedophiles for several thousand Euros. So, tell me –
is Germany any better?"

I stop to talk then. Felicia's flight took about eleven
hours and her internal clock is telling her its four a.m.

She's silent. After a while she says, "I know you're hurt
because that woman from Morocco called you heartless.
It makes you sad."

"Yes."

"I cannot answer all your political questions about Columbus and the slaves. But I want to ask you something."
She puts her hand onto my arm. "Am I heartless?"

My indignant reaction is "No!"

"Was Oliver, was your husband heartless?"

"No."

"Your children?"

"No."

"Do you know many people who are not heartless?"

"Yes."

"If they aren't heartless, you are neither."

I sigh.

"Do you really believe that God took your children and
your husband because you are heartless?"

"No ..."

"We cannot know why certain things happen," Felicia
says. "It's not in our hands. I only know one thing for sure:
That love will always find a way."

That makes me smirk. That's my girl, Felicia just like
she is.

"And about that woman," she continues. "How do

you know that whole story to be true at all? Maybe she's someone who met your husband at the vegetable market. Maybe he just lost his business card. Maybe that woman isn't a woman at all but a bunch of deceivers. One thing is certain: I'm not heartless and neither are you. How could we be here together otherwise? We are here because love always finds a way."

I breathe deeply. All these political questions I'm pondering cannot be answered right know, but nevertheless I feel peace. And I think I should only then take a closer look at them when I'm at peace. Because only if I am, I might find the answers which will bring peace after all.

"I'm so happy you're here," I say and put my arms around Felicia. "I always feel better when you are with me. After all, that's why the angels sent you – to make me happy."

Felicia smiles and then falls asleep. I enjoy the dark night of Jamaica.

ONE LOVE - ONE HEART

Chapter 22 – Wake Up and Live

Why is my stomach revolting? My best friend Felicia is here, I'm not alone and I feel closer to love than ever. I'm back in Te Moana, the sun causes every leave and every flower to shine in their most vibrant colours, the ocean expands in front of me like a light blue crystal and the very air feels like it's breathing itself.

But my stomach hurts as if I'd swallowed a whole lobster.

Waves of sensuality are washing over me. From somewhere behind the fence I hear a radio playing Reggae music. It's this very special mixture of Jamaica that you cannot find anywhere else.

But my stomach feels as if some knifes are cutting vegetables in there.

Once again, my body knows before my mind does, I think. And it tells me that I 'ate' too much and that it needs time to process all of it. Or maybe it's something entirely different.

There's a text message from Patrick. He asks if I'd like to come over to have breakfast with him.

It's nine o'clock. He would send his driver. I'd planned to have breakfast with Felicia.

"You see, once again my life is moving too fast," I tell her.

"Tell him you'll meet him in the afternoon."

"He isn't free in the afternoon," I say.

"If he wants to see you, he will find the time," she replies being quite clear-cut about it.

But I am, too. "He isn't free in the afternoon," I repeat.

"Did he say so? Or, otherwise, how would you know?"

"I just know things like that." That's a truth. Even as a child I knew.

"Ask him, at least."

I ask him. He isn't free in the afternoon. "I need to talk to you," he writes.

I look into Felicia's eyes. She says, "Go then. I'll talk to the hummingbird in the meantime." She means it, she'll have a conversation with the hummingbird, and the outcome will probably be astonishing.

Mark, Patrick's driver, arrives twenty minutes later with the black limousine. Mark has chauffeured many rich and famous people and he always has some news and stories to tell.

Today he informs me that the first shop to legally sell marihuana opened yesterday. It's legal to own three ounces (about 100 grams) of marihuana and now you can even buy it in special shops like that one. Furthermore, it's allowed to grow marihuana for medical reasons, and according to Mark all this together will be the new big business in Jamaica. Of course, this is true only for the wealthy as the initial hurdles are as high as usual. You need money and papers – various kinds of permissions you won't get unless you grease the palms of some officials. (That's his slant, not mine. But very many Jamaicans think the same and if there was an opinion poll, I'd probably be the only person to think otherwise.)

So, you need money not just for plants and greenhouses but also for high fences and surveillance cameras, Mark continues. Another business where money makes more money. This seems to be some basic law of Jamaica. And it started with Columbus arriving here, I add in my mind.

The gate to Patrick's villa opens automatically and Mark drives along the paved road towards the parking lot. I step into the garden of the villa through a gate surrounded by palms. Again, I'm welcomed by silent beauty like at Te Moana albeit everything here's more pure, colorful and orderly. There's a pristine white wall with red hibiscus flowers behind it, a white pavilion with a white table and to top it all you have a wonderful view at the glittering sea.

Patrick meets me at the veranda. His sole appearance speeds up my heartbeat. My peaceful, relaxed self from this morning gets blown away like a strong breath of wind. I stumble over a step I'd missed and barely avoid falling.

Yes, I can see why I wrote love letters to him for two years. It's his very own mixture of an absolute free, self-determined mind on the one and a devastating loneliness on the other side.

He puts his arms around me. "It's good to see you," he says. His voice is very soft, and every single word is absolute true.

At this very moment I recall what our connection is based on. It's his story, his history, that shaped him.

Patrick grew up in the poorest parts of London, he never knew his father, his mother was a hooker. Most of the time he lived with his uncle and aunt. He learned very early to earn some money with small businesses, took the bus to the posh neighborhoods where he mowed the lawns, went grocery shopping for elderly ladies or walked the dogs. Even as a little boy he earned a reputation as a reliable service provider. His work ethic was unrivaled: prompt, modest, clean.

He graduated school with excellent grades, and he was the sole student with dark skin. He made his way all alone, without anybody to confide in. When he finally gave his trust to somebody for the very first time in his life, a woman, he had to learn that he was wrong to do so. It ended in a painful divorce and cost him half his fortune.

Patrick looks at me, his expression clear and open and I'm captured immediately. I wanted to write what our connection is made of ... it's hard to stay with myself when I'm close to him ... I also fought my way out of this swamp of outsiders, I know the feeling.

Looking back, I'm quite certain it was my hunger for love that drove my husband into the arms of another woman. I'm too lonely and too insatiable. And I listen to no one, not even to God sometimes. But when I meet someone like Patrick, together in our loneliness, something inside of me just loosens up. It's not easy for people like Patrick and me to find proximity because the proximity we need is deep.

On the veranda a table is already set. Martha, who cooks for Patrick, serves us breakfast consisting of scrambled eggs, calalou (Jamaican spinach) and fried plantains (very delicious and nutritious). There is already a plate with sliced papaya, mango, pineapple and star apple. One of the reasons I would spend my life in Jamaica is the food that is unique and very healthy. Add some coffee from the 'Blue Mountain Coffee' plantation and you get the feeling of: Couldn't be any better.

"There's something I'd like to talk to you about," Patrick says. His voice sounds unusual emotional now and I'm with him at once. Very often Patrick is somehow out of reach and even if he's attractive even then, it makes me feel sad and helpless. But right now, he's absolute present.

"I've never had much love in my life," he says. "My life consisted of work and survival. I told you what happened when I really trusted a woman. I don't blame her. I couldn't see who she really was and what she desired. I didn't know how to handle a relationship. All I knew were affairs and sex and that's it.

I don't know much about women except for the things I read in books." He smiles a little embarrassedly. "I didn't know that connections as deep as you've experienced them are even possible. I was confused when I read your letters. I just didn't know how to deal with it. I was scared."

He pauses and I can feel his confusion. I'm confused as well. I know Patrick as a superior and self-confident person ... but, then again, I'm not that surprised because when I wrote those love letters, I always felt I was talking to this vulnerable part of him.

And I know how it feels. I'm self-confident and superior in most of my relations as well, but when it's getting deeper, I feel insecure and confused.

Yet again, I notice the bright light around us that lends something pure to our vulnerability. And again, I enjoy how that light brings forth the essence of the colours – the light blue of the curtain, the yellow of the coffee pot, the red of the hibiscus, the turquoise of the sea and the never-ending variety of green of the palm leaves, the avocado tree, the mango tree, the aloe plants.

And I smell the unique moist and slightly musty scent and feel the abundant growth all around, feel it in every single cell.

"What are you thinking about?" Patrick asks.

"It's hard to find the right words," I say. I reach for him with my hand and he opens his one to welcome mine. "I just feel so very ... alive."

He smiles. "We've come this far, haven't we? Quite a long way."

I nod.

I remember how I put my arms around Daniel yesterday. That I promised to take him with me to Germany and to marry him and that I feel the same warmth and closeness standing next to Patrick now. That I condemned Oliver for having two women in his life and that I now have two men in my life and that my feelings for both are real.

"I wrote all those things, told you all about my love and longing, because I didn't want to hold back. I wanted to know you how much you are loved. I wanted you to trust me, to trust that my feelings are real."

"Do you still feel the same?" he asks. "After you never got an answer from me?" He lets his gaze wander to the ocean, leaving me every freedom to answer.

I don't know what to say. A "No" would be too strong.

"By writing everything down I got to understand my feelings better and they changed during that process," I finally answer.

"I can understand this," he says and I'm relieved that he isn't disappointed or hurt. "My feelings are changing as well," he says. "They're awakening and that's wonderful. I want you to know that I don't expect anything from you. I just like being with you ... now, at this very moment. I'm learning so much from you, because of you. Because of your love. I can feel it now and it doesn't scare me that much any longer. It makes me so very happy right now and gives me so much strength. And I want to thank you for coming here. And I'd like to ask you to be patient with me."

The warmth and love I feel for Patrick now are so very beautiful. I let go of all thoughts, prejudice and fear. Patrick's hand in mine and the flow of our feelings are all I sense right now. They are absolute pure, absolute true and absolute present. I've longed for him for such a long time and now it is back – the connection between us. He closes his eyes, I close mine, and the moment stretches to eternity. I feel the light of Jamaica within myself. I feel my soul shining, my heart opening. And all the flowers and their fragrance and the sweet air of this island get into my heart and make it bright, light and free.

ONE LOVE – ONE HEART

Chapter 23 – Can You Love Just On(c)e?

The sun. It's the sun which makes me this happy here in Jamaica. To wake up and find myself in the middle of this flood of bright, warm light. In Jamaica everything becomes easy: The sun and the love.

Felicia is making some scrambled eggs and plantains while the coffee is brewing in the machine.

Later, we sit on the patio and I look out to the silvery ocean. Today it's absolute calm, like a blanket of liquid light. The sky's blue is more than just a color. It's the answer to a deep longing inside of me. When I look up to the sky, I can feel it.

"I met the hummingbird yesterday."

"What did it tell you?"

"I wanted to know what this 'One Love' is all about. I read on Wikipedia that on the 22 April, exactly forty years ago yesterday, the *One Love Peace Concert* took place in Kingston, with Bob Marley and other Reggae celebrities. Back then, Jamaica was on the brink of civil war and Marley managed to get the heads of the two enemy parties onto the stage to shake hands – that was the message of the hummingbird."

At that moment I experience something akin to an expansion of awareness, it's like a shock. I don't know why it happens exactly now. I guess, it's been already underway and Felicia's story about the hummingbird finally opened the door. I feel as if I'm suddenly able to see through everything, like I own x-ray eyes. Yet, it's not the physical things I see but the energy. It's an absolute clarity. I breathe deeply.

I tell Felicia about it. She smiles. She smiles like a friend saying, "Yes, that's the way you are."

I'm very glad she's here with me because those moments, as beautiful as they are, are also scary.

"Bob Marley said ... I just remembered it, he said when there is music there is no fight. ... And this is how I feel about the sun in Jamaica. When there is sun and the blue sky then there is peace. Maybe that's what he meant with One Love."

I tell Felicia about my date with Patrick. "Yesterday I realised that love is always on the move. I'd have liked to hold it, but that's not possible. So, I let it go and by doing so, it became even greater."

"So, then this isn't about the two men or the question who's the right one for you?" Felicia asks.

"No, it isn't." I'm a little surprised to hear me say this, but anyway ... "It's about love itself. One Love. About where it can be found."

"But wouldn't that mean you're always a little unfaithful?" Felicia asks. "If love is roaming free from here to there – doesn't it become arbitrary?"

"I see what you mean. After all, I spent many years in a solid relationship myself, but at the end of the day it was in vain because faith was just an illusion. My question is rather: Am I unfaithful to another person or to love itself?"

"Well, for me love is more beautiful when I'm faithful, when I get to know someone better," she says.

"So, am I not allowed to get to know them better, both of them, Patrick and Daniel? Am I not allowed to see Daniel anymore because Patrick was first? Or am I not allowed to see Patrick anymore because I kissed Daniel? Do I have to tell Patrick that I kissed Daniel? Or is all ok because it's just flirtation? And where is the line – when does it become more than flirting?"

Felicia disappears in the kitchen and returns with a plate with sliced papaya, the pieces with the intense orange coloured fruit flesh arranged in a circle and a white flower at the center.

I realise that the answers to my questions have changed just by Felicia bringing this plate with the sliced papaya, that the answers to every question depend on circumstances like the weather, our appetite and our mood, and also on the people to hear our answers.

I understand that this is Felicia's answer: A plate filled with sliced papaya and a white flower. And that on 22 April forty years ago the One Love Peace Concert with Bob Marley took place and the hummingbird told her about it.

"You cannot reduce reality to a few simple rules," I say. "Sometimes it spits out moments of clarity. That's just like eating a papaya."

And again, I have this strange feeling of my life being theoretically over, the life I once wished for. With a husband and children, a family and a home. Felicia still lives this life. She has all of this – a husband, children and a home. My home has become the sun and the blue sky and the feeling that I can finally see everything clearly, almost like the angels. That's where I am now.

"The hummingbird!" Felicia calls excitedly.

I see it, too. This tiny bird, as tiny as if it'd stem from the world called Liliput. And its wings beat this fast, we can only make out a buzzing but no concrete shape.

It's always like this with Felicia and me. When we're together, it feels like reality sheds its skin to reveal a magical paradise. I wouldn't be surprised if a lion and a lamb came out of some corner and laid down next to each other.

"Let's go to Annandale," I say. "I'd like you to meet Daniel."

Her expression darkens – by just a touch, but I notice it anyway.

"What is it?" I ask.

"I'm not sure if I want to meet Daniel."

I'm surprised. "Why not?"

"I think I don't want to."

The moment is back – the one I'm so well acquainted with meanwhile. I discover a new corner of paradise and my best friend tells me she won't accompany me, and I am to go alone. I go back to looking at the sea. On the outside everything is peaceful and calm, but on the inside? Typhoon ahead! It's a perfectly harmless sentence my friend Felicia said, and she has the right to go wherever she wants. And yet, I feel as if I fall off that high-rise and plummet down to the ground for real. But despite being dead and everything being over, I feel excruciating pain.

I'm hurting because of that crystal-clear truth with which I see the energy of my surroundings. A part of me wants to stay with Felicia and find warmth and love, and another part wants to go ... And just as it has always been – I must go alone, I think. When I was a child, I used to be alone despite being constantly surrounded by many people. And that feeling hasn't changed until today.

I'm very, very sad, the feeling nearly overwhelming – all those streets I walked alone. And I fully realise that it'll always be like this – I'll always choose to go my own way. Always had to, alone or with company. But at the end I'm still alone. I really walk alone on this planet earth.

Oliver and the children taken from me is probably the one huge mark that life left on me – just to make one thing very clear: 'You'll always walk alone.'

And after I did so for so long and so often, life added another mark: 'For the one time of your life you thought you weren't alone: Let me tell you that it wasn't a real family. It was an illusion. That's how your life is. Wake up.'

Where did it go? Love? The One Love? I'm so sad.

"Why don't you want to meet Daniel?" I ask Felicia.

"I'm afraid to lose you," she says, "because I can feel how much you like him."

Now I'm astounded.

"Why would you lose me if I liked Daniel?"

"I don't know, it's just a feeling."

I take this seriously. After all, her feelings are real. And maybe I like Daniel more than I'm aware of and she can feel it.

Nevertheless, I have the need to defend myself and to tell her that I can love her and Daniel both. That I can love more than one person, after all. But I'm suddenly so very tired. I've defended myself so many times and it never had any effect. At least, that's how it feels to me. And I feel myself surrendering. I have no energy left to explain myself or to convince somebody else from something that's not in my hands.

So, I say, "Okay, I'm going alone."

I see Felicia's shocked expression and I feel that my decision is hurting her. But there's nothing I can do about it. It's always like this: I must go. Anywhere – to heaven or to Jamaica or to Annandale.

I call the driver, Mr. Johnson. He agrees to pick me up in 30 minutes.

I listen to Felicia. She talks about her fear to lose beloved people and I realise her fear is just as great as mine. I hear it, I realise it and I understand it. But I don't feel it. My heart has withdrawn.

And I realise one more thing: In moments like these I used to sense not my own withdrawn heart but the feelings of the others. Their fears, longings and needs. And then I tried to make them happy. And it felt like love to me: To sense the feelings of others and make them happy. I followed them, never the other way around. I used to believe that it's impossible to follow me because my ways are lonely ones.

Yes, I could possibly make Felicia happy by not talking about Daniel anymore, and by not meeting him. But I did such a thing too often already. This life that woke me up so rudely from my dream of a happy family, of a perfect love – this very life showed me freedom by doing so.

I'm finally free to find love not in the feelings of others but inside my own withdrawn heart. I want to find out why I'm so afraid of being alone.

I lean back on the bench and look up to the blue sky. I'm touched in the very same way than I was before. I was lost for a short while, but now I'm back. I realise this used to be the other way around – I used to be back only for a short while and then gone again.

The sky, the sun and the ocean are rolling through everything, delicately vibrating – and as I'm part of everything, I can feel these vibrations as well. One Love – maybe this is what Bob Marley felt when he wrote his song: One Love – One Heart.

"You know," I tell Felicia, "I don't love you any less just because there is another person in my life or a new way. I may have new feelings and new colours in my life, but love is depending on the ability to let the sky, the sun and the ocean roll through yourself. And I have that ability now."

Despite the pain that Felicia and I are feeling in our individual ways, a pain that we cannot let go easily, we can simply sit here on the veranda of Te Moana and share this moment with the blue sky above and the silvery sea of Jamaica in front of us. And this is what makes friendship so precious.

"I'll come with you to Annandale," Felicia says, sounding conciliatory.

But I don't have a good feeling about it. I could just say yes, pretending everything was alright. Because that's what I've always done. But today I say, "No, I'll go alone."

"Okay."

I trust that our friendship will not break because of this. And I realise that my idea of how or who Felicia is, is changing. Up to now, it was always her standing by my side and giving me new optimism whenever I needed it. But I'm no longer the little girl in need of protection. And this makes it possible for Felicia to finally be simply a person with her own feelings and fears.

I hear a car in the driveway, the dogs are barking, Mr. Johnson has arrived.

"When will you be back?" Felicia asks.

"I don't know," I reply. There are some clothes in my bag and my sponge bag with my toothbrush. And it's just how it should be: This journey isn't planned through to the end. And maybe this time I'll walk my way together with someone else.

Half an hour later we're nearing Annandale and again I feel like a child coming to paradise: There are tree-giants who protect me and endless meadows I can roam without ever being stopped by a fence. I can hike through valleys and climb up hills to meet cows, horses, dogs and birds. And nobody is disturbing this dream of mine.

I can see the horses standing and grazing near the lake, one of them standing in the water. I'm looking for Daniel, but I can't see him.

After arriving at the house, I say hello to Monika. We

have a little chat and some coffee. She informs me my room is ready and waiting for me. I thank her for providing me with this chance to write in paradise.

"Where is Daniel?" I ask finally.

"He didn't come to work today," she says.

That makes me smile. Well done, dear angels, I think and send my greetings to heaven. *Down here on earth, things need a little time.*

I walk to the horses and sit down to watch them. I notice how they're moving, each horse on its own and yet part of the herd. They have the ability to do something that's so hard for us humans: To be on your own and yet not alone. Together and yet free.

ONE LOVE – ONE HEART

Chapter 24 – Receiving Heavenly Gifts

Once again, I wake up with this deep longing inside of me that assaults me like a hungry animal. I feel so very sad. It's the sadness that keeps coming back, has done so all my life. But now it ultimately stepped out of the shadows. And then, suddenly, I'm so very happy. Grateful and indescribably happy. That's Jamaica.

I'm absorbed by the warmth, the dampness and the noise. Outside, Nick is driving a herd of cows to new pastures. I hear the stamping of the cow's hoofs and Nick's chant. "Heyaah!!" It's rhythmic with gaps in between. "Heyaah!!". "Heyaah!!". It's echoing through the valley and together with the mooing of the cows it becomes music, a radiating song.

Omar is preparing a room for some guests in the adjoining building. The haunting voice of a preacher shrills out of the speaker of a radio like the raving sea crashing its waves to the shore, again and again. "Jesus!!" – "Our Saviour!" – "Oh Lord, oh Lord, have mercy!" It's a piercing, vibrating voice that transforms its surroundings into a holy room.

I realise how desperately people all over the world are searching for nourishment for their souls. And that I'm one of them.

When I pass Omar with the dogs by my side Omar asks, "Is this your new bodyguard?" pointing to Chrystal, the biggest of the dogs.

"Yes," I laugh.

"I'm jealous," he says. "You left me and took a new body-guard."

Just Omar.

I let myself go and allow myself to fall into longing. Here in JA I can do nothing but let myself fall into the arms of longing. It makes me gentler, converts me into a gentle person.

I'm familiar with this longing, know it from the day-dreams I also have when I'm in Germany. A daydream in Germany differs from one in Annandale. In Germany it's surrounded by a safe place to which I can always return, and that's always there when I stop dreaming. In Germany I need to somehow make or even steal time to day-dream. Here, in JA, it's just the other way around. It's quite demanding to return to the daily routines, to planning and doing chores. Too demanding. And so, I keep drifting through my dream.

When I woke up this morning, I found myself embraced, held from behind. The embrace felt so intense that I in fact thought it to be real for a moment.

Later, Felicia arrives at Annandale. I'm happy she's here. Everything is fine. Her friendship and love allow me to stay on my way. Felicia allows me everything. I've never experienced a freedom like this before. Our friend-ship is free. I hadn't been free before, I hadn't known that a friendship like this, in which I could be this free and yet loved at the same time, could even exist. Oh, this free-dom – it makes me so very strong. I want to embrace the whole world because I'm so very happy.

Felicia and I are sitting in the sun on top of the wall. I tell her about the embrace I felt this morning when I woke up. "I wonder, who it was," I say.

"I don't know, you have to know. Who was it?" she answers.

That's what I love about Felicia. She never tells me who I am or what I should feel. She's just curious. Love is the reason – that you want to know who the one next to you really is. That's the curiosity of love. That's like an embrace.

"It wasn't just a single person," I say. "It was God or love or the angels. It was Annandale and nature or ... I don't know, I cannot put a name on it. Sometimes I feel all this sadness that's in the people, it's so huge and heavy but then I feel that power to overwhelm the sadness. And here in Jamaica I feel it especially strong."

There is a grove at Annandale, not too far from the main house, that consists of three trees with trunks large enough to sit in like in an armchair. The trunks are over-grown by huge climbers creating those convexities you can sit in.

Felicia and I like to be there because it feels like sitting in the tree itself. When I was there for the very first time, I was overwhelmed by the pulsing energy. I was sitting in the middle of this energy flow and, wow, I was totally astonished. It's because the trees are this huge here – that's the reason they own that much energy.

When I was a child, I used to wish to be inside a tree like this and being here at Annandale, in Jamaica, it's possible.

I did listen to the talking of trees in times past but to sit here in this one feels like being at a tree-marketplace, and all the trees are talking to each other. It's nice to have a friend like Felicia who's also able to hear the voices of the trees or the voices of the angels. We sit in this tree and sometimes we talk about it, and on other occasions we just sit there forever without talking at all. And when we talk about it afterwards, we laugh because our experiences were so alike.

I think we all will re-learn the ability to listen to the trees sooner or later, and when that time has come it will be very natural for everybody. They will tell us many useful things. We will understand that our intuition is much more intelligent than our brain. And from the moment we realise this, we will want to learn. I know many people who already did it, I learned it myself. You don't even need a special talent – it's enough to simply want it.

But so far people like Felicia and me are still pioneers. We're laughed at or people think us to be a little weird. But this changes nothing about the fact that the trees are talking to us. They've always done so and here in Jamaica they're even louder than in Europe. At least that's I'm perceiving it. Maybe it's because they are so huge. That's why I feel so at home here and that's why the angels made me come here – the angels and Grandpa, the ancient African spirit.

To listen to nature, a tree or a horse, is like listening to a song by Bob Marley. I'm mentioning Bob Marley because he brought into the world what can be found here in Jamaica – the spirit, what the trees are talking about. He wrote the song "One Love – One Heart" which was nominated "Song of the Century" by the BBC. The life of Bob Marley is the best example of how to change 'bitter into sweet', as goes the saying here in Jamaica. His success is proof that people all over the world realise the necessity of turning 'bitter into sweet'. Bob Marley reminds us of this – him being the voice of Jamaica.

And this is how I feel sitting in the tree. My longing and my sadness get changed by the tree. I do hear its words, but before I can hear them, something different happens. The tree's pulsing energy is like a power flow and this power flow reacts to my sadness. It's the pain and the sorrow of the people that are bothering me. It's my longing to change this and the tree is helping me with it.

Next, he talks about all the trees I've greeted during my time in Jamaica. I greet trees just like people or animals without distinction. And the tree knows. This makes me happy. He tells me how honoured he feels because I've visited all his sisters and brothers, so very honoured. Now I feel even more happy and at home because he feels like I do: He feels how others are feeling, even if he cannot see them. That's because he's talking about the trees in the botanical garden in the Shaw Park in Ocho Rios I visited some time ago. There I learned about very many endemic tree and plant species. And this tree is talking about them. It's like visiting a friend and talking about all the other friends we have in common.

When I was a child, I was very aware of the fact that

trees, animals and human beings are interconnected. Later I tended to think that to be just imagination because at school we were taught to view things from the scientific side. Now I know it's just the other way around: It's a conceit to think trees, animals and human being are not interconnected.

All my sadness stems from the fact that people are unable to feel this connection. If only they could feel it, they would know that only good comes from it. I can feel it know, the happiness of the tree because I'm here and because of the love the trees feel for each other – One Love. My sadness has completely vanished now.

I tell Felicia about it.

"I don't have to be sad," I say. "I know that there is all this sadness, but I'm not sad anymore. I used to be when I was a child and I was so very sad when I lost my family. But the angels have shown me that I am more than just sadness, that behind all that sadness I'm like the tree – a sister of all beings. Although I'm getting older, I grow. I grow into the sweetness that shows itself when you overcome the bitterness."

The silence between Felicia and me is simply wonderful. Felicia is a tree, just like me. Or a horse or a cloud. She knows, like me, that everything here on earth is one. One Love. And that everything bitter will turn sweet because of this.

My mind is still occupied with Bob Marley, with his story ... because he had this incredible talent to change bitter into sweet. He grew up in Nine Miles, a little village in the countryside in the middle north of the island and came to Trench Town, the ghetto of Kingston, when he was a teen. His father was a sixty-year-old member of the military who he didn't see very often, his mother an eighteen-year-old Jamaican girl. His school education was only rudimentary and when he wrote his songs, he asked his wife Rita to check if the spelling was correct. He never had a music teacher, somebody to teach him how to play the guitar or how to sing. He didn't have the money to pay the recording of his songs and quite often he didn't have the money to even buy food. Despite all of this, his music was – and is – strong enough to influence people all over the world. He holds rank eleven out of one hundred of the best musicians ever in the "Rolling Stone" magazine. Bob Marley had the gift to turn 'bitter into sweet', not only for himself in his personal life but for the people all over the world. In my opinion, his story is a very good example to show us that the things we value so highly – money, support, training, perfection, surety – are not as important as this one gift: To turn bitter into sweet. Bob Marley worked on his music tirelessly. And that's exactly what happens when one finds this gift inside oneself. You become like the tree, pulsing and sending out vibrations so strong that they change everyone they reach.

Here in this tree I find my way again. I can take all my pain and lay it down here. And there it lies, and the tree takes it and changes it into something that grows, sprouting green leaves and changing carbon dioxide into oxygen.

Trees not only change the exhaust fumes of our cars into fresh air but also the fears of our hearts into courage. For this we need the trees more than for anything else because only if our hearts become as pure as the trees, will we treat our earth with more respect.

Here, at the feet of the tree, I can also shed my great fear of losing my friends and beloved people if I stay on my way.

"There is only one love", the tree tells me. "There is light and shadow – and we, the trees, grow into the light."

At that moment I see Daniel walking along the way to the horses. He looks over and waves at me. It's very gentle, I've only rarely seen this from a man. Yes, it's this gentleness … it affects me. Something inside of me starts to melt away. That hard shell I need to protect myself. I don't need it with Daniel. I wave back. When I'm with Daniel I can be as soft and gentle as I like to be, I don't need to be hard and strong.

Daniel reacts to me just like a tree. One Love.

Felicia says, "I think there is an embrace waiting for you."

Daniel stops and waits for me. While I climb out of the tree, I feel that it's more than just an embrace that awaits me. After everything that happened in the years past, the angels sent me a man who reminds me of my own essence, the person I am behind all the pain – reminds me of my tree-nature. Daniel is as sweet as the tree. I can certainly imagine that there has been pain in his life. But that didn't change his essence. I cry a little while I walk down the hill towards him, with Felicia staying back and setting me free without losing her.

This strange feeling, that I don't just embrace Daniel but something greater, is still there. Although Daniel and I are just normal mortal beings, it feels like we're in a much greater space that's partaking in everything.

Now I can feel it – this pure contact between Daniel and me and the large whole. I can feel that this was my longing – to be part of this large whole, and that my longing is fulfilled now.

This one thing in my life has in fact changed: I don't need to flee from my longing anymore. It's not something agonising like a never-ending hunger any longer. The longing is changing from *bitter into sweet*. And it's gotten strong enough to not only change me but also the people around me. After all, it's possible it came into my life only for this reason. To be changed into something sweet. For this to happen you need none of all the things we believe to be important, like money or property.

Daniel's embrace is the sweetest I've ever known. It's gentle and strong at the same time. And what happened in the tree before, happens again: Our energies are melting into each other.

ONE LOVE - ONE HEART

Chapter 25 – What Happens in Seven Months

I haven't been writing for the last seven months. I've been living. Now I'm back on a plane to Montego Bay, Jamaica. And I'm back to writing. I started to write down this story one year ago. How much can change in one year ... One year ago, I was sitting on a plane to Montego Bay, just like now. But now I'm a different woman. To leave Germany felt like leaving hell one year ago. I remember the feeling very well.

There was only one thing I wanted back then: To escape. Today I feel that leaving Germany is like a prayer. There is gratefulness for everything I've found during this year. As if all the people I've met in Germany, France, Austria, Switzerland, Italy, all the countries I've been to during this year, had come to an agreement. I don't think they'd been conscious of this fact, but they'd made an agreement to love me. They loved me like crazy. No matter how great my hunger for love became – they found a piece of bread, an apple or a piece of heaven to saturate it. I'm so full of love that for the first time in my life I can feel who I really am behind all the pictures. A beloved being.

It's scary. It's scary to be loved without doing anything to 'deserve' it. I'm simply receiving the gift of love.

"Love is mercy," they say. But now that it's finally there ... I've searched for it so desperately and now that I found it ... I'm not great enough for it. I need to grow. Love is there all around me, I'm coated in it, it's inside of me, it's above and below like a sweet floating substance, a sweet bread that I can never eat completely, invisible food saturating me in such a way that I don't need anything else.

I drink from this well and the more I drink the more I fear: The love – it could be gone again suddenly. And what will happen then? Then, a hunger will consume me that'll threaten to kill me. Just as it came into my life – the sweet love reaching me from every direction – just like that it might vanish again and there's nothing I can do about it. It might vanish like Oliver and the children. And what will I do if this happens?

I'm like a tree that has already been half destroyed by a storm. The next tempest will surely break the other half of it. Tell me: Is it wise to succumb to love like that?

I'm sitting on a plane flying across the Atlantic Ocean, the flight attendant is wearing a purple dress. Her face looks like that of a miller out of a fairy tale by the Brothers Grimm, her voice is slightly squeaky and has an American accent. Her head is jerking like the head of a bird. Maybe her great-grandmother was a German miller who held her head very still in the spring sun when the first crocuses blossomed.

Right now, I'm feeling as still as that miller, but the storm of love might come forth from any direction at any time. That I keep always on my mind.

Is this love? People see that the tree isn't whole any longer. They see me. Some see the broken tree and love me. Others see the broken tree and want to break it even more. Many don't see anything at all. The animals see all of it.

Animals always love. Humans could learn to love.

I could learn it. To love despite the fear. With fear or without.

At least now I know it's my fear that keeps me from finding love once it's gone again, not Germany and not the others. Love, it's just me searching for love. Me, with my enormous longing. I know that now. Me, who is loved and who loves like crazy.

I'm glad to be back in Jamaica so soon. In Jamaica everything is greater than me. That's where I find love and everything about it.

"God lives in Jamaica," says Gentleman, a reggae musician from Germany. God and the Devil, too. That's where my home is. Love is as great as it is scary. And where fear is real, love is real as well.

That's what has happened in the last seven months. The fear has become real. It's no longer outside but it's inside of me.

Because of love. There were people who saw the fear in me and loved me anyway. Because of this I could feel the fear – inside of me, not outside. I could never have made it on my own. It was possible only because of love. So long as the fear lived outside of me, so did love. Now, both are residing inside.

Patrick is no longer a part of my life. Sometimes I still think of him. But he isn't in my dreams any longer. I met him one last time in Paris in September. He was attending a congress and I had just finished a seminar. We met for dinner in a restaurant near Montmartre. I was there first, sipping my martini when he arrived. He walked through the door and I felt the warmth immediately, felt his silence and the attraction. He embraced me in greeting and again I thought I should marry him. He put a brown envelope onto the table. The one I was already familiar with. Some illegible letters were written on it with a ball pen.

"How are you?" he asked.

I thought that Daniel never asked me "How are you?", he always asked me "What's up?"

I realised that I could talk to Patrick only in a "human-like" way whereas Daniel and I could communicate like human being and nature. And I believe that was the moment when everything was just over. This realisation was the end of us. The truth between Patrick and me had become so great that one single thought could get to the heart of it. And once a thought like this has surfaced, you cannot push it away anymore.

"I'm fine," I say and decide at the same moment that I won't talk too much human to other people in future. I'll stop to speak the human language and therefore to speak with Patrick. He wouldn't understand the language of the animals. He wouldn't understand even if I explained it to him.

"What's in the envelope?" I ask.

"A contract."

I think about the last time he put a contract on a table and wonder if it's the same one. Strange, I think, but fitting. For him relationships are like contracts. It makes sense, it's the world he lives in – conducting business, doing corporate management.

Patrick sits down and looks at the menu, then orders chicken and broccoli. I feel like I have a knot in my stomach. I'm not hungry anymore but I order a salad because I don't want to tell him that my appetite is gone.

"I've missed you," he says.

I really want to reply something but there simply isn't any room for feelings – in that restaurant, smelling like garlic and red wine, silent voices floating through the room, French voices, there is no room for feelings. There is something in the air heavy like lead, lead that clings to your feelings and makes them so heavy that they just drown. And down there, at the very bottom, they become sludge and mud. I have the feeling that I'm wasting my time.

Patrick talks about what he's been doing in the time past.

I'm fascinated by the table lamp that reminds me of a pleated skirt. Patrick travelled around the world making contracts. I think that I would never be willing to wear a pleated skirt. If Patrick ever asked me to do that, I would suffer a real problem. Because I would do it because I cannot say no. But I would lose myself.

So, I listened to myself having a perfect communication with Patrick.

We had crème brulée for dessert and Patrick settled the invoice.

He invited me to his hotel room, and I couldn't say no. On our way there he searched for a special kind of chewing gum, a green one, in a supermarket that was still open. The shop assistant looked very tired because it was so late and because of his rootlessness. I don't know where exactly he was from, maybe Algeria or Morocco but surely not France. That chewing gum, at ten p.m. in a foreign city in a foreign supermarket with a shop assistant living in a foreign country, made me relent.

I know that feeling. It's the moment of the rootless, the moment all rootless people know and share, the moment in which the rootless finds a little piece of home, finds the familiar chewing gum. The green one. That feels like home.

In that moment I felt very close to Patrick.

We made love and it was so very gentle and sensitive. I loved Patrick and I could feel his very essence because he wasn't hiding it. My thoughts drifted to Daniel. When Patrick touched me, it felt like a human being touching another one. I longed for Daniel's touch that felt like a horse putting its head onto my shoulder. And that made me very sad. I could feel Patrick's very soul but something inside of me had shifted. I was called to walk another way. I didn't know which way it would be, but I could feel myself gliding out of this old world and hear a sound inside of me that called me from far away like the sweet sound of a flute.

I thought that maybe I could take Patrick along with me, that maybe this would dissolve his sadness, that maybe we could walk this way together, the way that'd make our souls happy. Maybe that was what life expected from us, the reason why it brought us together, two root-less people.

While we had breakfast at his hotel the other morning, he again pushed the brown envelope towards me. "You asked, what's in there. It's an offer for you."

I tried to read something in his eyes but there was nothing expectant. His routine-self had thought of this. He was resting in himself, in his identity – doing corporate management.

I like the croissants in France. They are crisper there than anywhere else, darker with more crust and less dough. The hotels offer the small ones with apricot jam inside. I feel safe there, finding a home in a foreign place, feeling free. Free to go at any given moment. I got some coffee at the coffee machine because without coffee the croissants are too dry. I did not comment on the envelope. I would have loved to love Patrick, his whole self. But I imagined that was not what the envelope was about.

The table next to ours was occupied by an elderly couple talking French. She wore a crème coloured pleated skirt, he a white shirt with small black buttons and a showy black seam at the collar. My gaze settled on the golden rings on their fingers. The envelope, the appearance of that couple, Patrick sitting across from me with a Rolex on his right wrist, and me with my being-at-home in a foreign country.

It could have been different with Patrick and me. I could feel his soul. His longing. It made me sad and I realised I'd had the very same feeling the night before. That feeling that made me lose my appetite. But not any longer. I enjoyed my croissant and felt at home. Patrick had decided to leave no room for his longing, that was what was written inside that envelope.

I took it and opened it with a clean knife I got from the sideboard. I pulled out a stapled document of a few pages and quizzically looked at Patrick.

"It's the draft of a contract," he said, "Read it."

"Now?"

He just shrugged, staying very calm, taking the situation very serious.

"You can read the details later, if you like. It says you'll manage my villa in Jamaica. You can live and write there. From time to time I'll invite guests and you'll organise the meals and overnight stays – everything to make their stay convenient. You'll also manage the staff – the gardener, the driver, the cleaning staff. And, of course you'll get a car and a salary."

"Does it also say how often we'll have sex?"

Patrick laughed. I'd really made him laugh.

And it was back – that feeling that caused me to love him so much. Our souls touched. I was very sad – not because of his sadness but because of my own. We'd both given up too early. That's the problem with the rootless: Giving up too early, keep moving, keep following the sweet sound of a flute.

Although I'd just gotten up from bed, I felt very tired again. I wouldn't succeed in reminding him of his soul, it was too difficult.

I looked out through the huge window of the breakfast room. A fountain was splashing and babbling in the patio. I needed to talk to archangel Michael, to ask him what I was supposed to do. I felt helpless and lost. Was that the way they intended for me to walk? Was that my task? To remind Patrick of his soul and find my own salvation by doing so?

Archangel Michael didn't reply. He was there, he listened, but his only answer was a deafening silence. I was familiar with situations like that. He always did that when I asked him questions of which he thought I could best answer myself.

I just thought: There is a system error somewhere ... It's certainly possible I'm that error. I put the document back into the envelope and looked at it from every direction. Then I looked at Patrick.

"I want love," I said. "What you're offering is a golden cage."

So, we said goodbye. And I cried. I couldn't shed all my tears at that moment. I had to make sure not to forget anything. The moment of departure is always critical as I tend to leave important things behind. Things like the cable or the charger of the mobile phone, the only thing a traveller really depends on. I took a cab to the airport.

"No comment," I hear archangel Michael say. I had a feeling that everything was alright for the moment. Even if love just had missed a great opportunity.

Jamaica
ONE LOVE - ONE HEART

Chapter 26 – Breathe and Love

1 January 2019. Jamaica. The morning sun shines through the windows and paints stripes on the tiled floor. A rooster crows behind the house and I'm wrapped up by the voices of different birds – high, low, heavy, light, crushed. The hills surrounding me are covered with huge, densely grown trees. The trees in Jamaica seem to be exploding in slow-motion, a power from within slowly breaking fresh ground and the sun is stressing the shapes of their single leaves.

I'm bathing in that warm, moist air and the music someone in the neighbourhood is playing to greet the new year. "Hallelujah, hallelujah, hallelujah." Every single syllable is stressed until it arrives at even the last cell of my body.

I, the rootless one, have arrived. In Jamaica.

I love to be here because life embraces me like a mother. I can feel her arms, legs, bosom, her gentle and yet strong hands everywhere: In the colours, the moist air, the barking of the dogs, in the gentleness in the eyes of the people who look at me. I feel like I'm in a dream and there's no need to wake up. It is not a smooth and peaceful dream, not narcotic. It's a dream of wonderful beauty and real pain at the same time. A dream of pure life. I'm at home. There are lots of broken trees here, just like me, and lots of very young ones, bursting with energy. I'm not a stranger here.

There is one more thing that happened during the last seven months. Life has a certain way of tearing off all the wrong layers I've attached to myself, tearing off all illusions. It makes me feel relentlessly naked and it's been especially true since I became a traveler. As long as I lived in a house, with a family and regular work, life felt like the world was set in stone. When that life was ripped off me, I found myself on top of the high-rise, together with my desperate comrades on our way to end our lives. I simply couldn't imagine there could be another world, except for this stone-set one. And then the angels came to pick me up and let me proceed and that's when it started ... all that's wrong started to fall off.

I wanted to know. Wanted to meet the woman my husband shared his other life with. I wanted to know just how great that illusion I'd lived had been. I wanted to know if the life we'd lived and the love we'd shared were worth it – to end my life by jumping from a high-rise.

Marrakech, city of souks filled to the brim with yellow and red spices, saffron, curry, peppers, caraway, dried mint, garlic. Tea in metal pots poured into gold-rimmed glasses in long, thin streams. The smell of dirt, burned meat, sweet incenses and decay. Rough male voices, loud and callous, music blaring from small radios or cell phones. A feeling of doom. The old Morocco – doomed like every old world. There are, apart from the dealers and craftsmen, mainly tourists there. The young people get their chai latte at Starbucks and their chicken wings at a fast food restaurant.

She is beautiful with long black hair, fair skin and thick black eyebrows. Her body is lush and plump, and she wears a bright green caftan-like dress and massive golden bracelets. Compared to most of the other local women she has her very own style and radiates a somehow European subtleness.

It was a big mistake to come here. I feel my stomach knotting itself. We're sitting in a small shop owned by her uncle, a shoemaker, whose English is quite good because he often visits relatives in England. She took me here. She hands me a cup of tea.

"Sugar?" she asks.

"No, thank you."

My desperation is back. I feel like I'm standing on top of the high-rise again. Back then I hadn't even known she existed. My knees are getting weak. Nothing has changed. That same desperation is still with me. The angels have achieved nothing, nothing at all. Just an illusion.

She looks at me full of compassion, her dark eyes a nighttime ocean. I know she's going to say something that'll hurt me, even if she doesn't intend to. But I don't have the strength to run away. She'll say it without knowing what it will do to me. She'll think to do the right thing by telling me the truth. But it's not. She looks at me with compassion, but that compassion is going nowhere, it's just a habit. Her real feelings are hidden.

A boy appears at the entrance. The light shines at him from behind so that I cannot see his face – and yet I see his father in him – Oliver, my husband.

It will take some time for me to develop a feeling for this special situation. Right now, I'm just blown away. The boy says something in Arabian to his mother and disappears again. I still don't know what to feel but I do know what to think: The story is true, the boy is real, and he looks like his father. I saw his face when he stepped into the room. Oliver's second life had been real.

Oh, wow. I feel like I'm going to dissolve. It was a huge mistake to come here. I look at my feet, claw my toes into the ground, into the leather soles of the sandals I'm wearing. I need to ground myself again because right now I'm floating around somewhere in the room, maybe I'm hovering under the ceiling.

Now she's talking. I cannot stop her.

I breathe in the smell of leather, glue and some incenses. My eyes stick to the ornaments of the poulaines her uncle produces. Many years ago, when I was in Marrakech together with Oliver, I bought shoes like these at a shoemaker's just like this one. I lose myself in those ornaments on the handmade shoes, study the different shapes and the small differences. I'm almost obsessed by them.

Her uncle puts a bowl with pistachios in front of me. "Eat some, you look pale."

Eat? How shall I eat if there isn't even a body to contain the food? Of course, I don't say those thoughts aloud. I just need to somehow survive this situation without the walls tumbling down on me or something else happening that washes me away.

I look into her intense eyes. There's a fire burning inside

of them that has nothing gentle or lovely. What was it, Oliver was looking for with her?

As if she could read my mind she says, "Maybe you're asking yourself why Oliver was happy with me? More than he was with you."

I just knew it would come like this! This witch is only after psyching me out and I was stupid enough to initiate this meeting myself. So dumb! So dumb! Now I wake up again. To be angry with myself is always a good means to an end. No, I don't blame the angels for sitting here and drowning. That's my own fault.

And to be honest – I finally want to know it. I want to know why this Moroccan bitch thinks that she made Oliver happier than I ever could.

"Germany is cold," she says. I groan inside. Loud, so loud that it must be heard all over the souk. She must be kidding. Cold, cold Germany. I feel like I'm hit by a boomerang. Hasn't it been me running around and telling everybody that Germany is cold? Well, it seems Oliver realised that a bit earlier. Shit! Germany's to blame!

"So, you think I'm cold because I'm like Germany?" I ask. "And you are warm because you are like Morocco?"

"I loved him," she says the words sounding as heavy and sweet as Arabian baklava, that mixture of honey, puff pastry and nuts.

I, too, loved him, stupid bitch, I think, but of course I don't say it out loud. I just keep quiet. But, I'm back again, back and ready to be put through the metaphorical Moroccan meat grinder.

"Oliver says, you're no good mother, no good wife, always writing books, always in another world, no take good care of him."

She isn't aware of my weapon cabinet. She doesn't know about my revolvers, pistols, semi-automatic and automatic weapons that won't stop firing once they start. She doesn't know that I will do anything from now on to destroy her. Simply, because she's walking through this world thinking I'm not good, no good mother, no good wife, unable to handle everyday life. I'm not good at taking care of others. Heartless. Cold. Egoistic. It's my own fault that my husband fell for this pathetic Moroccan bitch.

I stand up and the bowl with the pistachios tumbles from the table. I don't know how this is possible because it was placed on one of these silvery engraved serving plates that have this rim to keep things from sliding off. Well, I guess the emotional bomb, that just exploded inside of me, caused it.

The uncle doesn't even bat an eye and I bend down (very German-like) to pick up the pistachios. But she just pretentiously sweeps away my polite gesture.

"Leave it," she says and points towards the door.

I'm so furious I can hardly put one foot in front of the other and yet, at the same time, I'm glad that I'm not floating anymore. That's the good thing about wanting to know the truth: Before, you're immensely scared of the things you might learn and after you've finally learned them, your world is in ruins. But, at least, there is this feeling of honesty.

"You're a bloody bitch," I tell her while I'm walking out of the room. (That English term sounds so much better than the German 'verdammte Schlampe'.) "Don't ever call me again, I don't want to see or hear anything from you! And don't you dare ask me for money again. Snuff it, for all I care, in your fucking Morocco and with your ice-cold love. We don't yield that fast in Germany. Phhh. We know how to build something new out of ruins."

Wow, I think, sounds a little moronic somehow but at the same time quite witty.

"Salemaleikum!" I add. I don't think this makes any sense, but I don't care.

I push through the canopied side-streets, turn around. She's there, following me like a hound dog. I chase her away.

"You bloody bitch!" I yell again. She sticks to me. Maybe I made her furious, offended her pride, maybe she wants revenge. But I'm stronger. She just stripped me of my roots. What the hell did she think would happen then?

I think I've never been that mad before. I snatch a broom from one of the vendor shops – handmade, mind you – and strike out. That's the good thing about Morocco – nobody cares about it, something like this seems to be normal here.

Now she's yelling at me in Arabian.

"I know, why you are this furious," I tell her. "You thought you could make me bend with your stupid comments and then I would open a bank account for you and your son, out of mere desperation, so you could tell me one fine day 'Oh, you have such big heart, you saved our lives, you're not cold anymore, Oliver wasn't right, you have a good heart and so much love to give'. You think I want to atone for having a could heart. But I won't do anything like that!"

"He is Oliver's son, you've seen him," she yells. "You are heartless, just like I said."

"Tough luck," I say. "And wrong strategy."

"You are responsible," she yells after me.

Again, I strike out with the broom – which isn't that easy any longer because I've arrived at the main artery of the souk and I wouldn't want to accidentally hit one of the elder German couples who came here to enjoy exotic Morocco.

But I'm afraid it won't be easy to get rid of her because all of this in fact seems to be about money. Her survival strategy seems to be based on me financing the life of her son, because he is Oliver's son – and while I'm at it, finance her life as well.

"Here is your lesson of how to live in your own world," I yell. I want her to understand every single word. The fair-skinned and English-speaking among the souk visitors watch us intrigued. Maybe that's the actual reason to come to the souks – to watch real-time scenes like this.

I keep yelling and somehow find myself quite witty. I'm not even that mad anymore, I just want one thing: To throw back as many of the daggers she stabbed me with as possible.

"Better start living in your own world, start with being a good mother! And finally take care of your child."

Hey, I don't want to return to my life with my intestines shredded. I prefer to throw back the daggers.

"You didn't come to his funeral," she screams. "You have no heart."

"And I can tell you why. Oliver was a bloody asshole. He lied to me and betrayed me for years. When I heard the news of his death, I couldn't leave the house for weeks because I was burning from the inside. And now I know why. I knew he was a destroyer. Why should I have a heart for a man who deceived me to no end?"

"He didn't love you because you simply aren't worth loving," says the bitch. That's too much. I hit her head, and she yelps. I didn't mean to do this.

"I don't give a shit if you live or die," I yell. "Fuck off!"

To be honest, I'd like her to follow me for a little longer, so I can yell at her some more. But enough is enough.

A strong arm takes the broom out of my hands. I turn my head and see the face of a muscular, young man, trained, maybe a member of the army. I guess he saw how the broom hit her head.

"Enough," he says. "Stop it."

"Keep her away from me," I yell. He understands at once and steps in her way. He spreads his arms and like two iron gates they stop her from further pursuing me.

I run towards the exit. Outside I'm welcomed by sunlight and the singing of the muezzin coming out of the speakers of the mosque. And again, the moment has come when I urgently need a cab to take me to the airport. I need to leave as fast as possible. I cannot cope with more of this truth today.

Jamaica
ONE LOVE – ONE HEART

Chapter 27 – Angel's Kiss

Yes, I'm living in my own world. I'm a writer after all. But sometimes I'm very lonely there. I need to write but I need to love even more. I need love to be able to write. Since that Moroccan woman blamed me for my husband's adultery, claiming it was my fault as I would stay in my own world for too long, I've been lost. Today my ears are like deaf, I'm almost unable to hear anything. That's because I wrote about it yesterday. I'm trapped in my own world. I need to break out. I must find love, the love.

I need do find love because unless I do, nothing can ever be good again. Thinking of how mad I'd been, so mad that I in fact hurt her. That's not like me. But I have it in me. I simply cannot believe that it's my own fault I have lived a lie. And yet … when I'm hearing that judgement, that accusation that I'm unable to care about others because I'm trapped inside myself … Something deep inside of me tells me that's the truth.

I'm furious, but what's more, I'm utterly helpless. Don't I have the right to love? Must I stay alone forever? Will I be betrayed, rejected and hurt again and again? Because I'm living in my own world?

I'm staying at an Airbnb in a quarter of Ocho Rios where the locals live. The owner, Marc, is a steady-on-the-run kind of guy and so we got along immediately, even if his radius of action is more like ten miles instead of my five thousand. He seems to know everybody who's ever sneezed around here. I'd wanted to stay at Te Moana again, but it was already booked, and it seems to be like this for the next years. It's just too nice to stay empty for long.

Anyway, they play good music in this neighbourhood – rap, reggae, soul – and the dogs and birds are talking constantly. There's a school right next door. A teacher sings gospel every morning which can be heard through the speakers. Mama Jamaica embraces me with her sounds – and with her never-ending supply of sunshine.

Last night I dreamed of a mare I rode without saddle or bridle. She felt very gentle and familiar. She looked out for me, making not a single wrong move. All her movements were focused on my sitting on her back safely. I held myself just with one hand in her mane. I could direct her shoulder to one direction or another with my legs and feet only. Now, as I'm writing this down, I feel the walls of my inner world crumbling and my hearing gets a little better again.

Caring about others, to be there for one another. That's what the mare did for me in my dream. And what did I do for her? Didn't I do everything I could to stay smooth and to flow with her movements to not disturb her? Wasn't I there for her as well as she was for me? Am I really that unable to be there for others?

It starts to rain. Mama Jamaica's garden gets watered. I listen to the sound of the rain, a gentle rush. I can hear again. I've woken from my inner prison. I prepare myself a sandwich with peanut butter and make some coffee out of the Blue Mountain coffee beans Marc left for me. It tastes soft and sweet and full flavoured. My mind is wandering, and I think about Daniel. I had to think about him a lot. A few times I was on the verge of calling him, but something was holding me back every time. But now I need to finally know: Am I really that heartless? Is there really no love for me?

It wasn't only the Moroccan woman who told me. Oliver often accused me of it, as well. And not just him: Already when I was child, they told me 'You dream too much. Wake up and make yourself useful.'

That's the reason I was so furious when I was in Marrakech. Since then I haven't been able to find my inner peace. Am I unworthy of being loved just because I have my own world, my own phantasy? This question is killing me. This fear was the reason I once stood on the roof of a high-rise. I don't want to live my life all alone. I'd rather be dead.

This longing to find love … It's too much for one single human heart. I just don't know how to find my way out. I cannot simply switch off my phantasy. That would be possible only if I switched off my whole self. Sometimes I feel so very far away from all the other people, from the things those other people want and feel, that I just give up. I've stopped searching for love.

I take the cell phone with the Jamaican SIM out of my suitcase and search Daniel's number. I dial, my heart is beating like a drum. To hear his voice again, any second –

or maybe not? What's that?!!! An error-message. I really don't like this. I need to have a serious chat with archangel Michael and his trainees. "What do you want this time? Is this the reason you brought me back from the high-rise and into this life? A life where love simply doesn't exist?"

Of course, Michael doesn't react to such a mundane complaint. But I can probably answer this question myself. Do I really want to go back to the high-rise just because the SIM of my mobile phone isn't working? Do I? Is this my whole magnanimity?

Then I remember that the mobile phone contract expired automatically after six months. That's why ... But how am I supposed to contact Daniel without it?

I stand up, walk to the window and feel all the misery coming back. The dagger. I knew it, didn't I? My whole life is an illusion. I'm bleeding inside like I've done all my life. *Why?* I cry inwardly, and although nobody outside will be able to hear me, the cry is very loud within. *Why?* A van is passing by outside my window. I read the ad *DANIEL'S PLUMBING SERVICE*. That makes me laugh. Daniel's plumbing service? Now, of all times? Is this Michael's doing? Was he listening the whole time after all? Do they love me? The angels?

I feel a little better. And I realise I can call Daniel with my German phone as well. That'll cost almost three Euros per minute, but so what? The angels love me. Or, at least, they check on me. Or they make it seem they do. However, I'm not alone.

I dial Daniel's number. My heart is in my mouth. The dialing tone sounds again and again. Nobody answers. I dial again but to no avail.

This triggers my true nature. No, I'm not highly talented, and no, I'm not the only person on this planet who is truly loving. I'm self-indulgent, impatient, bossy, groundless, self-destroying, self-centered and whenever I want something, I want it NOW. Oh, I forgot insensitive. If this was really about love, I would just sit here, waiting patiently and gently holding my mobile phone in my hands. Now and then I'd try to call Daniel again until he'd finally answer – be that today, tomorrow or in ten years. My love would stand the test of time and I would never give up.

As it is, I cannot even write anymore. I'm totally blocked.

I've no idea how the day went by. I was trapped inside a black hole to which not even the angels could find an entrance.

At night my mobile phone rings. Daniel.

"What's up?" he says.

"Can we meet?"

"Where?"

"Anywhere."

"Where are you?"

Adrenaline is cursing through my body. I'm swimming with a huge, towering wave that threatens to break any second. But it doesn't. I'm remaining in this everlasting state of mind. I think of the mare I dreamed of last night, how it felt to sit on her back, the warmth of her body, her soft fur.

Daniel sent a cab to pick me up, a friend of him. Now I'm with him at his home. It's dark outside and the music of the insects is very loud here on the countryside. A fan is rotating under the ceiling, bringing some fresh air to the moist heat. Daniel is standing at the gas stove, frying some sliced plantains. Now that he's near, I'm very calm and I completely and utterly feel the love.

He places the plate with the plantains and a piece of fried fish on the table, then slices a papaya and removes the seeds. He does all this with a calmness that's typical for people who work with horses. We both eat from the one plate. There is nothing foreign or awkward between us. We haven't met for seven months and we don't really know each other. Yet he's closer to me than several people I've known for years.

"It is good to see you," he says. "Why did you come back?"

I put a slice of papaya into my mouth. The fruit pulp is sweet and soft, and I think it tastes like Jamaica.

"Because I love you," I answer.

He brushes his hand through my hair. His body is muscular, but his touch is as gentle as the mouth of a horse softly breathing into my hair, as gentle as the movement of the mare in my last night's dream. I'm in my own world now, but I'm not alone. Daniel is with me. He puts an arm around me and my body leans into his, the wave finally breaking. There is absolutely no resistance within my body. Our bodies move like two dancers who've known each other for many years. I'm not alone any longer, not trapped in my own world anymore.

Someone came into my life and together with him I feel like I've never felt before. I'm suddenly a very gentle, very yielding being. Like water. I know I'm not like so many other women, always approaching others, always caring, like a nurse or a hospital nurse or a Moroccan hot-blooded woman.

But with Daniel I'm present – for him. Everything I am leans into him and it's so very natural. I can feel that this is my nature because my body and my whole essence seem to grow, and I feel so much happiness just to be here – with him and for him. Just to be.

Daniel takes me by the hand and leads me through a curtain into a room furnished with a bed and a wardrobe. The four bedposts are draped with curtains to keep out mosquitos. The walls are painted in turquoise and a light brown. A light breeze, billowing the curtains, is coming in through the fly screens. I feel like I'm in a jungle, or in a world I lived in when I was a child. On the bed there's just a thin white cover and a likewise thin white sheet.

I don't remember how we got onto the bed but now I'm lying there next to him. We look at each other as if we were the first human beings to ever walk the earth. Like Adam and Eve. Man and woman. We are no names, no stories, no skin color and no language – we just are. Man and woman. Every time we touch, it feels like we touch the whole world. It's endless and everything is alive. Animals and fantastic plants live here, and cloud-ships are slowly floating by.

Daniel and I stroll through this world as if it were our home. Our lovemaking is something well known to both of us as we had other lovers of course. And yet it is more.

I'm losing myself in Daniel's touch. Everything I am and everything I used to be just disappears.

It's nothing special to be naked. It's not about having sex with a man. It's about this pure form of existence I'm entering together with Daniel, with our bodies – his male and my female one. I've never been there together with a man, didn't even know such a plane existed.

I'm at home when I'm with Daniel. Our bodies harmonise in a perfect way, as if we were made for each other. Perfect size, perfect energy. I find myself in Daniel. And yet he is another person – a man, and me still a woman.

We spend the night in this tight embrace and when I wake up in the morning, he is still there.

The angels sent this man, I think. I don't want to go back to the high-rise any longer, and I'm not scared anymore that I might not be able to care for others. They just need to be the right others.

I feel a deep peace and gratefulness.

I feel the presence of archangel Michael very strongly now. Tears are running down my face.

"Why are you crying?" Daniel asks.

"Because I touched God," I say.

He kisses me, a kiss like a gossamer wing of a butterfly. An angel's kiss, I think.

ONE LOVE - ONE HEART

Chapter 28 – A Day with the Angels

God lives in the animals. That I know for sure. It's my work, my life. With animals there is always love. With human beings … hmm.

I find love with Daniel. I find it within myself. – Not always.

Since I was with Daniel, I've been very calm.

I didn't write yesterday.

Instead, I spent a day with the angels.

Daniel made us breakfast and then had to leave. The cab took me back to the Airbnb, I took a shower and put on my light pink dress which is dotted with dark pink roses and has a slim waist, and high heels. And a pearl necklace.

In Joy's church, where I'm heading to meet the angels, quite a lot of women – no matter what age – wear stilettos and dresses like a second skin. And hats. My heels are not as thin and I feel a bit strange dressed up for church, but I want to be beautiful – for the angels and the people in the church.

There's a little girl next to me in the pew, maybe around eight years old. The way she looks at me makes me feel like I'm a foreigner. I'm the only white person in the church and I guess she isn't used to see white people. Joy, sitting to my left, says, "That's the girl with the pink dress you liked so much last time you saw her." I take a closer look at the dress she's wearing today. It's white with thin pink stripes and small flowers. I gently point to the pink color on her dress and then to the pink color on mine. She looks at me a little startled. Then I point to the small flowers on her dress and to the ones on mine. She smiles and I smile back at her. Now I'm no longer so alien to her and neither is she to me.

She wants to know my name. "Viola," I tell her.

Her name is Ariana.

I'm glad I chose the pink dress.

I feel someone touching my shoulder from behind, pushing back the straps of my bra under my dress. I don't see who it is and simply wait until she's done. Then I turn around. A woman about my age smiles at me. It's very natural for her to do such a thing. She doesn't think me to be foreign at all.

"Thank you."

I like being among these people. This feels exactly like being among angels, I think.

I haven't met Joy since the last time I was in Jamaica in April, but we embrace each other when we say hello and it feels as if we'd said goodbye only yesterday. There is no feeling of foreignness between us. She's brimming with energy as usual, nearly eighty years old but filled with twice as much energy than me.

I'm back in the angel's house and it feels so heavenly here. The people are convening in small groups to pray, holding hands, and any person of the group respective just starts to pray – no fix phrases but simply words coming from their heart. Some people are very shy and would never look me in the eyes. But that's not important because I can feel their closeness and they feel mine.

This is how it feels to be among angels. To speak without saying a single word but to talk with your heart.

There is also a choir, coming to the stage now. It's gained a lot of members since the last time I was here. At least thirty singers. The colours of their clothes resemble the lush colours of Jamaica. I don't take any pictures, nobody does. You can write about the angels but taking pictures doesn't feel right.

So, the colours: They are monochrome, I don't know if they arranged it, but there isn't a single piece of clothing with stripes or flowers or an Adidas logo. Only pure colours – dark green, corn yellow, violet, light blue like clouds, earthy brown, orange, lilac, blood red, dark blue. For a long time, I look at these colours and marvel at how they're harmonising. There are colors and combinations of colours in Jamaica I've seen nowhere else. No, that's not true. I've seen them in my childhood when I used to look at post cards from foreign countries and marvelled at the colours of dark pink and turquoise.

I close my eyes and listen intently to the singing. I've never heard a choir like this. The ones I've heard sounded as if they'd practiced a lot to find an accordance. This choir doesn't sound like a lot of practicing. There are voices of young women and young men, old women and old men and everything in between. Sometimes somebody slips a bit, sometimes a single voice gets quite loud and rough.

When the men sing, it sounds coarse. Sometimes someone will take the microphone and sing as loud as possible.

And yet there is a constant accordance, a harmony carrying everything, a tapestry of sound despite nobody carrying this tapestry, it just is. As if the angels would sing along with them. The intensity and strength of it makes me cry. These people aren't singing with their voices but with their hearts. They aren't singing by themselves but altogether, together with their hearts. Their hearts aren't withdrawn, you can hear it in their voices. There is no wrong and no right in the voices of those who sing with their hearts.

A young woman takes the platform and welcomes the community of about two hundred people. She uses a microphone and talks to the people as if she was talking to her best friends, sitting on a meadow and chatting. Her voice and her attitude have nothing official and she's not afraid of talking in front of that many people.

After the service she stands at the exit to see off the people. I tell her that I really liked her talking and how self-confident she is. She looks at me and doesn't understand what I'm talking about. She isn't aware of her talent.

She also greeted the 'visitors' during her welcome, asking them to show themselves and then somebody sitting next to them to introduce him or her. 'Visitors' meaning the guests who are not part of the church community. Like me. Some visitors are introduced, they all come from other cities in Jamaica. A woman sitting in the next pew introduces me.

"This is Viola from Germany," she says. The speaker laughs and says, "Oh, she's a regular." That really blows my mind. I feel so welcome here. After all, I'm sticking out because of my fair skin and it wouldn't be too farfetched if they saw me as an intruder, just like the people with dark skin are looked at in Germany.

Joy, who brought me here initially, is laughing hard. So, I'm not totally unknown to the angels anymore.

We sing all together and I don't mind it at all despite the fact I actually don't like singing. No, that's not true, I do like it, but I'm convinced that I'm the worst singer on the planet. Here, I'm *so very me* that I don't care, I can just sing, like when I'm with Daniel or with very good friends.

I not alone trapped in my own world any more. I am in this own world, but there are lots of other people with me, people who are no strangers to me.

My world is no longer a world known solely by me. All the people around me know it as well, and they like being there as much as I do. I think that's the reason they're here, in this house of angels.

Once again, I think about the young woman, the speaker. Her talent is rare. I know this because I've trained actors, because I've lead workshops about charisma, because I know how hard it is to train someone to become a good speaker or actor and how rare natural charisma is. She is not aware of her talent – and neither is anyone in her near vicinity. Otherwise, somebody would have told her, and she would know.

The sermon starts, I remember the preacher from last

year. Last time he told us about his newborn, fighting for life because it was born too early and had to stay in an incubator. The whole community prayed for the child back then. Today he tells us his wife recently gave birth to another child, she'd become pregnant again shortly after. The first baby is fine as well, Joy tells me later.

He talks about two young men from the community who drowned a short time ago. About the children they left behind, about their families he'd visited. It was a tragic accident. Those young men overestimated their ability to stay afloat in the open sea. I think about the fact that most Jamaicans cannot swim despite living on an island. Nobody teaches them how to do it, not at school and not at home.

He also talks about a text from the book of Hebrews, number twelve, that is about running with patience. "Let us run with patience in the struggle we are destined to fight." The sermon is about Usain Bolt, the multiple sprint world champion from Jamaica, about his rigorous training, about the fact he didn't stop even when he was bone tired and even had to throw up because of sheer depletion. Why? Why did he carry on? He was 15 years old when he became famous.

What an incredible spirit must live inside a 15-year-old to motivate himself like that? He won his first gold medal when he was 22 years old, running with untied laces.

I don't really listen to the exact words he's speaking, but rather to the mere sound of his voice that gets more passionate and louder and more urgent the longer he speaks. He states that evil will pursue mainly the innocent, that faith always demands sacrifice, that those who look for the easiest way will perish. His voice and his words feel like a waterfall, the water thundering onto my head, my face in my hands to protect it. The water clashes onto my back and I feel its power.

The world around me, the world I once lived in, disappears. I'm in a different world now, I'm at home. I'm in the world the preacher is talking about. It's in his voice, in his heart, inside of him and filling all space. It's in the heart of all people here and it's so strong that all of us are looking for shelter, like with a great mother who protects everyone. It doesn't matter if we call her God or something else. We are her children.

Ariana, the girl next to me, lays her head onto my lap. I cradle her by carefully moving my leg up and down. We all are cradled by the great mother.

I hear the preacher talking about being powerless, about being hopeless, about wanting to give up and about carrying on – running on – with patience, just like Usain Bolt did. About the hopelessness vanishing if we do so. I can feel it, so can Ariana and everybody else, too. I'm not in an alien world where I must be alone any longer. I'm at home, I'm no longer alone. I know now that I don't have to stay alone. There are so many here with me. Maybe this could be a home to all the people. If they left behind their alienness, they all could be here in the bosom of the great mother. The people here in Ocho Rios are no different from people all over the world: young, old, man, woman, educated, uneducated, fat, thin, healthy, sick, faithful, unfaithful, poor, rich. And searching for a home.

I believe that whenever somebody runs like Usain Bolt, or sings like the choir in this church or talks like the young woman – it's the angels doing. It makes you win a gold medal with untied laces. Makes you sing without missing a single note. Makes you talk to every person like to a friend.

After the service I search for John who picks us up. I get into the car, we embrace and laugh heartfully, simply because we are this happy to meet again. After that a lively discussion breaks out – just as it always does between John and me. A friend of him passes by, says hello, and John asks her about her son. John tells me that she had to struggle hard, brought up two children by herself, but she managed to make something of herself, nevertheless, went to school and trained to become a nurse.

That leads us to our next topics – how everything has gotten easier for women, to the question why God is said to be male and to the fact that it's solely men who preach at the services. I also ponder the fact that three thousand years of philosophy I once studied at a German university didn't contain one single text of a woman. And how different this world could be if the talents of women would be looked upon as important as the ones of men.

I don't agree with the bible text of today about corporal punishment. That a father beats his son because he loves him. Daniel told me only yesterday that the uncle he grew up with often beat him when he was a child. That he had to work all day and yet was beaten, that he didn't possess one single toy, that he was only rarely allowed to attend school. That's Jamaica, too. ‚Evil pursues the innocent'. I've never heard something like this in a German church. I've seen it often, but nobody talks about it.

Here evil is real. Poverty, exploitation, prostitution, crime. The German travel agencies advise people to not travel to Jamaica.

If women had had a part in writing the Bible, if there had been female prophets and not just a son of God but also a daughter – maybe we could read in the Bible that there is no need for pain and beatings to find love. No punishments. No yelling. No sickness. That the only thing necessary is an embrace.

"God lives in Jamaica," the Italian reggae musician Alborosie said in an interview I watched lately, "And, so does the devil." That sentence has stuck in my mind. Alborosie has lived here for many years.

And somewhere in all of this, there is love.

After the service I'm invited at John's and Joy's, at the "Little Farm in Eltham", as John calls it since he knows that I can always be found on some farm.

We enjoy an afternoon full of sweet chatter.

"Love and peace," John says when we part.

He always does.

ONE LOVE - ONE HEART

Chapter 29 – Soon Come

Today is black. No word from Daniel for two days. He doesn't respond to my WhatsApp messages and when I call him there isn't even a voicemail to talk to. Felicia, my friend I'm usually exchanging daily messages with, didn't write yesterday either. And today she wrote she thinks it's not necessary to write daily and we should take a break from time to time.

Felicia – don't you know that I cannot live without your daily messages? I'm suffering from a severe writer's block. What shall I write? That I found love only to watch it wave goodbye directly after? Talk about extremely short dis-integration time … I didn't get a wink of sleep last night. No, not true – I did sleep for a short while, only to dream one of the worst nightmares I ever had: Every single person who has ever been important to me left me. And me? I told them to "fuck off … I don't give a shit about you!" After that they told me that I will be completely alone from now on, my greatest fear.

I'm standing at the window of my Airbnb room. Marc just gave me some calalou (local spinach), plantains and two mangos and I prepared some breakfast for me. Now I hold the plate in one hand, a fork in the other and wait for the moment when I'll taste something, anything. No, in fact, I'm waiting for the angels to send me another sign, like the car with the slogan *DANIEL'S PLUMBING*.

I'm pissed off!

Angels are the most unreliable partners one must endure in a relationship. They're like some nasty lover, winding you up just to disappear right after and not to be seen for some time again. A most certain way to become addicted. From time to time they will show themselves in their divine grace, but whenever you really need them, they're just nowhere to be found. Even if you'd search the whole globe for them, you wouldn't find them. They're hiding behind their own invisibility.

And about Daniel – he is visible at least, made of flesh and blood. I could call a cab and go to his village. But I won't. After all it's possible to find him in the arms of some Jamaican beauty who tells me I don't know how to take care of a man. Yes, life is good at making up things like that. Especially reruns of nasty and absolutely crushing scenes.

I'm just no use to this world. It needs cooks and nurses and cleaning ladies or women with a lush body, walking around on high heels and willing to have sex at any given moment. But my kind of love is not needed here. I told you, heaven was a better place for me than earth. The high-rise was the perfect place for me. I'm no use to this world – or the world to me. Yes, I know, I'm repeating myself.

John sends me a WhatsApp with a picture of the two young men from the church community who drowned in the sea. He writes that one of them swam out to save his brother-in-law. That makes me cry. On Saturday during the service I thought it to be something tragic, but I didn't realise that it had happened for love ... he swam out to save his brother-in-law because he loved him.

I cry for the other people who love so deeply that they're willing to give their lives. Yes, that was the angel's doing. They do things like that to remind us human beings that there is love on this earth. They pick the innocent, the ones whose hearts are too big, the ones who have too much love to give. The ones who drown because they want to save someone else.

A little later a cab stops in front of my door. It's Daniel's friend, the one who took me to him once already. I stuff a fork with plantains into my mouth and finally I taste something. Normally, I would drop the plate, hurriedly put on jeans and sneakers, storm out of the building and jump into the car to get to Daniel. But I don't.

I'm not running around like a headless chicken. That's a saying Marc used this morning. I'd asked him once again one of my super-daft questions of curiosity. "Do say, Marc, what do you think is the difference between Europeans and Jamaicans? I mean, you meet so many European guests, I thought you'd know."

He answered without blinking an eye and he wasn't even trying to be funny when he said, "The Europeans run around like headless chickens."

In other words, chickens that have already been slaughtered, yet still think they're alive. (He didn't say that, but it's just the situation such chickens find themselves in, don't they?)

I stay at the window and eat my breakfast, because

now it tastes good. The driver has seen me, and I wave to him. He isn't in a hurry either, we have all the time in the world. 'Soon come,' is the Jamaican expression for it. Chicken with head. Although Usain Bolt is the keeper of the sprint world record, I never see anybody running around 'headless' here just because he or she is in a hurry.

I could sit down to write now and maybe would produce one of my best chapters of this book, but, after I empty the plate, I calmly put on my jeans and sneakers and walk out to go see Daniel. I step into the cab, a chicken with my head still attached.

Once inside the cab I need to clarify some things with the angels. It's quite a long ride, so there is ample time.

"Bloody amateurs! Michael, you loser, again you sent a rooky to take care of me. And he's thoroughly letting me down. And what I really, really don't like: First you wind me up and then you drop me like a hot potato. If you go on like this, I'll quit. I'll come home. Just to have some personal words about this. You have a lousy outfit up there and you have no idea how life on earth feels like. It may be looking funny from up there, but it isn't if you're stuck with a human body."

"Are you ok?" the driver asks and turns around to look at me while the car is slamming into a fat road hole.

"Yeah, yeah," I say and look out of the window where the valley is giving way to an extensive landscape. I'm gazing directly into this green – not just green as a color, but a green that's ascending like a cloud from the tropical woods. It makes me relax. The Toyota, a car every expert would deem as not drivable any longer, is floating and crashing above and through the road holes. Sometimes I think that cars and human beings are driven by spirit alone here. No, I don't merely think they do, I see proof of it every day.

I wonder if Michael's trainee forwarded my complaint. The problem is, if you complain to them, they sometimes think of something even worse – just because they think it to be healthy. Healthy! Beneficial!

The driver stops in front of Daniel's house, sounds the horn, and after a while (I guess he also finished his breakfast first) Daniel steps out of the house carrying a machete and one of those black plastic bags that flood the island.

The driver takes us to Annandale.

"She has a new horse," Daniel says. "A difficult one."

He doesn't explain why he didn't respond to my messages and calls. And I don't ask. I already put that in with my complaint to the angels who, that much I've learned, don't like it if you repeat yourself. I'm terrified that they could think of something even worse. And today I can't take any more heartlessness. My nerves are frayed as it is.

The new horse is standing in a roundpen, separated from the other ones. It's a chestnut (reddish fur and mane).

"They attacked him," Daniel says. "That's why we separated him." He's talking about the other horses.

"Where is he from?"

"He's one of the horses that go out to the sea with the tourists. Too young. Too many tourists. He attacked them. A man was hurt. They want us to fix him."

"What's there to fix?" I ask. "He's just too smart. He knows that he doesn't have to tolerate everything." You just need to look into the eyes of this horse to see that he has more survival intelligence than any human being.

"Then he'll go to the butcher. He's useless."

"How old is he?"

"Six, they say."

"What's his name?"

"Oxygen."

I laugh. What a fitting name.

Daniel takes a halter and walks into the round pen.

Oxygen starts to move without Daniel doing anything. Oxygen moves with an energy as if he'd convert oxygen more efficiently than any other being. I like him immediately. He's got more energy than his body can deal with, I think.

Daniel doesn't intervene, just lets him run. Oxygen is afraid of human beings, that much is obvious. He doesn't trust Daniel, although Daniel has the one thing horses need to feel save: An absolute grounding. But Oxygen's distrust is so deep, he cannot feel anything subtle right now.

Daniel isn't in a hurry. I try to imagine how Oxygen carried headless chickens on his back and how that must have felt. After a long time, he gets calmer and moves towards Daniel, sniffs a little. Daniel still has the halter in his hands, but he doesn't use it. He puts it aside and touches the horse's back instead. Oxygen jerks, but Daniel's hand is very calm, not too pushy but neither overly cautious. Then he puts his other hand on Oxygen's back as well. Steady, simply there.

Oxygen can feel this. He snorts and calms down. He stretches into Daniel's hands and those answer to the movements of the horse's body. It's not just the hands, it's his whole body, his whole being. The horse feels it. And it doesn't take long for him to recognise that this human being is different from the ones he already met.

Daniel stays with him for a long time. I can see how the horse in fact seeks his touch, wants it. It seeks with his body for Daniel's hands and Daniel gives back exactly what's needed. He doesn't leave the horse, not for a single second. Finally, Oxygen drops his head, his eyes getting sleepy. Daniel draws back gently and slowly, Oxygen lifts his head, looks at him and goes back into his calm.

I'm touched by what I've witnessed and feel pretty dizzy. So much love. To be there for the other without smothering him or her, to feel the longing and give your complete essence with a touch.

Daniel seems to be tired as well. He sits down on a fallen tree trunk, takes two coconuts out of the black plastic bag and cuts them open with the machete. He hands me one and I put it to my mouth and drink.

I'm agitated, would like to talk to Daniel, a thousand sentences are swirling inside my head but not a single one comes over my lips.

"I know you were worried because I didn't answer your calls," Daniel says.

"So, what kept you?"

"I don't want you to get involved in this," he replies with utter calm.

"In what?"

He laughs. "You have no idea."

"What do you mean?"

He looks at me and his expression is saying something like 'you're really quite naïve'.

That irks me. I don't like it if somebody thinks I'm naïve. Makes me rather rebellious. But I don't say a thing about it because after all he didn't say anything, just looked at me and maybe I'm just imagining it.

"I love you," I say instead, with all my heart.

He laughs like a happy child. He cracks open the coconuts so we can eat the fruit flesh that feels like jelly. He shapes a spoon out of a piece of the split off nutshell so we can scrape everything out.

"I told you that I'm blind in one eye already, and the other one is about to get blind as well. The doctors told me I need a surgery that costs 100,000 dollars. And after the surgery, chances of being blind, nevertheless, are fifty percent. Without this surgery I will be blind in three to five years. Then I won't be able to see your beauty. I won't be able to work with horses. I won't be able to work at all and I will be very poor. Do you want to pay for my pension and pay the costs for the doctors when that time has come?"

It feels like a kick to the gut. "Fucking angels" I scream within my head. First, I don't say anything. I'm silent. Then I say, "I love you. I feel at home with you. Everything will be alright."

He turns away from me just like Oxygen did when Daniel stepped into the round pen. As if he was running away from me even if he stays very calm on the outside. He's very far away, beyond reach. Nothing and no one in this world can bring him back right now. I'm also far away and something strange is happening to me. I cannot believe what I just said. I said "everything will be alright." Hell is breaking lose inside my head. How can I make such false promises? Give false hope? Did I only say this to avoid the pain of reality?

I'm simply unable to accept that I cannot fix everything. Cannot solve every problem. He probably feels just how presumptuous my promises are. The European headless chicken. What do I know about his world, his life, after all?

And it's getting even worse: I found the courage to voice my feelings. That's what everybody's doing here all the time, isn't it? No matter if it's appropriate or not. And what's the end of it? I'm about to be at the receiving end of a sermon about how naïve I am, about being realistic. Just like in my last night's dream when all my friends warned me.

My stomach feels like one huge knot. My hand holding the coconut spoon is unmoving. My sense of smell is gone as is my vision for colours, I can't taste anything and the only noise I can still hear is the very thin twittering of the birds in the trees.

Oxygen looks over to me.

His gaze is resting on me as if he hadn't looked away for billions of years. I'm amazed by his alert expression. And touched. He wants nothing from me and yet is just there for me. My stomach is still hurting like crazy, but my heart is getting lighter.

My heart is crying. And now tears are running down my face as well. I cannot hold them back. My body is shaking. I cannot stop it. I want to hide them, I'm ashamed. I …

I feel Daniel's arms around me, and I let myself fall into them like into a bed made of feathers. There's an uproar inside of me, I feel like all the mud of my life has been stirred by a huge catapult. All the shitty details. The fear that I'm not useful or right. That they'll take me to the butcher, like Oxygen, if I cannot finally be fixed.

"I love you more than you know," Daniel says with his clear, gentle voice. And he means it. Everything he says. Again, I feel the home I'm sharing with him. The boy and the girl – we know nothing of the big wide world. And yet we know everything. We don't know more than a horse could know. And yet we know everything a horse does.

I can feel the angels, they're back.

"It felt strange," Felicia writes in the evening via WhatsApp. "Somehow you were gone for the last two days. I thought I'd better leave you alone. But that was a stupid idea. Just wanted to tell you: I'm always there for you."

Damn it and damn it again! Life on earth is totally crazy. Love is totally crazy. It takes everything from me, crashes me with its machete until I'm unable to hold a spoon any longer and then it blesses me. Until I can feel its truth. Until I can say, "I've found it – and it's utterly real."

Jamaica
ONE LOVE - ONE HEART

Chapter 30 - The Horseman

I don't know who I am anymore. I took the plunge with love, but it doesn't feel like a bubble bath. It feels raw. Helpless. I haven't felt this helpless for a long time. I feel alone, but it's different now. I feel love and it's real. It's deep inside of me.

And I can feel myself. That's what love does to me: I'm perceiving myself in a different way. Helpless, defenseless. I'm not even sure anymore if I want to see Daniel again. His world is so very different from mine.

I hear the honking of a horn from the street below. Electric current shoots through my body. I walk to the window. It's a Route Taxi and a woman from the neighbourhood gets into it.

Suddenly I feel sad. Something inside of me broke open yesterday, but it's not just lavender feelings. It's also something dark that was buried deep inside of me.

I've just ended my breakfast when Daniel's friend sounds the horn of his cab. I get into it.

Daniel takes me with him to Oxygen.

"I want you to work with him," he says. Somehow, I'm honoured but above all I don't know how to feel about this. I have no idea why he wants me to do it.

"Okay."

Oxygen is in the round pen. He looks at me. And again, I see his alert, billion years-old expression. I feel helpless and weak and there's nothing I can do about it. A small voice deep inside of me tells me not to go in there. My heart is beating madly and my whole body is tense. And yet I feel that everything inside of me is searching for relief, for silence and peace. Maybe Oxygen can help me find them. I take a deep breath, smell the moist earth, hear the rustling of the huge bamboo in the wind. Maybe I will find peace and quiet with this horse.

Oxygen approaches me curiously. He doesn't seem to be afraid of me. He sniffs a little. I keep very still. I hear my heartbeat, smell his fur, sweet and warm and earthy. A shiver runs through his body. I can feel it in mine. I feel a timeless space opening for us and know that I'll meet Oxygen there. His spirit.

"Watch out," I hear Daniel yell. And only a fracture of a second later I find myself lying on the ground, a piercing pain in my cheek. Oxygen is standing next to me. Daniel comes into the round pen, takes my arms and sets me back to my feet. Then he leads me out of the round pen.

I'm dizzy. "What happened?"

"He attacked you."

"Why?"

"Because you are a woman." Wow. I take that personally.

"What has me being a woman to do with it?"

Daniel doesn't reply.

I sit down on a trunk to find back to myself. I'm shivering. I cautiously check my cheek and there is a little blood on my fingers.

"He bit me," I say. "It happened so fast I didn't even notice. I only remember you calling." Daniel must have seen it coming. I didn't.

The back of my head is hurting. Not from today's fall but from another one. I didn't fall onto the back of my head that time, but onto my side. I fell from a horse half a year ago. My body remembers that now and I feel miserable.

"You shouldn't have gone in there," Daniel says. Great, I think. It was his idea, not mine. He could put his arms around me and ask me how I feel instead of reproaching me.

"It was your idea," I tell him. I can see that this sentence has a certain impact on him. He says nothing. He's angry because I blamed him. But it was just my tit-for-tat response because he reproached me instead of comforting me. If I'm not careful now, something might explode between us.

I put my head in my hands and try to calm down. The horse is grazing calmly in the round pen. I feel something deep inside of me breaking, not a part of the body but my soul. Something is trying to reach the surface. I do my best to hold it back. Now is not the moment to bring to light something that's buried deep inside my body's memories. I don't have the strength to deal with it right now.

Daniel sits on the same trunk about two meters away from me. Motionless.

Neither does he go into the round pen to fix the horse, nor does he do anything to fix me. Apart from our short fight nothing happens. He isn't lost in his thoughts either, he's just there. It's a strange feeling I'm not familiar with.

In my culture somebody would approach me, ask me if I'm injured, if I need something, try to comfort me. In my culture, I think, Daniel would be deemed heartless, but I don't think he is. His behaviour seems strange to me, yes, but also friendly, pleasant, giving me the chance to just sit here and calm down.

I watch the other horses grazing around the lake. How peacefully they're moving, each one on its own and yet together under one big dome. A flock of white birds is sitting on a tree beyond the lake, white spots in the middle of a pulsating green. Suddenly they fly up and over the lake, each one on its own and yet together. Not like with military forces with a fixed pattern, but taking their natural space. I wonder if it's similar in the army. Everybody taking his or her natural space. The difference is just: When I watch the birds – they are not interchangeable. If one bird changed place with another one, the complete picture would change. Each bird so very unique and yet at home in the flock.

"What are you thinking?" Daniel asks.

"Not much," I answer. How could I explain, after all? It's too complicated.

"You think it's too much for me to understand," he says.

Huh, I think, he can read my mind. But I don't tell him that this is exactly what I thought ...

"I watched the horses and thought about the harmony of the herd," I say.

"I won't take you with me to the horses again," he says suddenly. "It's too dangerous."

I'm shocked. Why does he say a thing like this? That's a low blow. It hurts. Why? I feel humiliated, marked as incapable, as a weak woman. Horses are my profession, damn it! I want to defend myself, but the words are stuck in my mouth.

I think about Oliver telling me, "I won't go on vacation with you anymore. You don't do anything but write, anyway." I don't know why I remember it just now. Maybe because it felt similarly final. If I'm not allowed to go to the horses together with Daniel ... I feel like I'm thrown out of life itself. I'm boiling with rage. And apart from that – it was a lie! I never wrote when we were on vacation. An unfounded accusation, just like Daniel's. Nothing happened. The horse just shoved me away, yes, things like that happen with horses. How dare he be so arrogant. And apart from that I've learned it the hard way that Oliver wanted to go on vacation by himself just because he wanted to be with his second family. A whole landslide of thoughts and feelings is crashing down on me.

I want to leave, just go away. I don't want to find love any longer. I just want to be alone. I was just surmising things where Daniel is concerned. Bullshit. Pure imagination.

But I don't find the strength to stand up. My mind is running wild, my body is hurting all over. I can neither say nor do anything. I feel helpless.

"Come," Daniel says and takes my hand. It feels good, his hand. The only thing that's feeling good right now.

We walk up a hill across a wide meadow. At first, I try

to adapt to the rhythm of his strides, but soon I give it up because I'm too weak. I realise he's leading me with his hand. It's so subtle that I notice it only now. He leads my whole body, every single one of my steps, solely with his hand. I let go.

We trudge through high ferns towards a forest. I constantly need to mind my steps to avoid the nettles that are growing everywhere. Luckily, I'm dressed in my sturdy jeans and sneakers.

Daniels bends down low and I mimic him. Inside the forest, in the undergrowth, it's darker and cooler. I find myself in the middle of a jungle, among climbers with huge leaves, aerial roots winding and stretching into every direction like snakes. It looks like there are no solitary trees in here as everything is part of something else, plants and trees embracing each other, entangling each other. Everything is brimming with life, growing and proliferating.

I feel at home at once, like in the middle of some intense dream. Surrounded by a greenery that is impenetrable, that is luring me in deeper and deeper.

My pain is forgotten, I'm wide awake. My hand is still entangled with Daniels. He leads me gently, step by step, over dead branches on the soft ground, even deeper into the jungle. He seems to know his way.

Then he stops. He lets go of my hand and brushes away dead leaves on the ground to reveal a skull. When I take a closer look, I see it's the skull of a horse. I lower myself next to Daniel.

"I started to work with horses twenty years ago. Before that I tended to cows. There was a horse, his name was Solo. He wasn't huge, like Oxygen, and he was more intelligent than all the others, wouldn't let himself be trained. No saddle, he got rid of every single one. I got thrown of uncountable times. Until I woke up one day. I'd always thought I needed to teach him." Daniel looks at me now and I've never seen such an animated expression on his face, even if he's still motionless. All his movements seem very restrained but when I take a closer look to his facial expressions, I can see the changes there and can guess what he feels.

"Solo came into my life to teach me."

I listen to Daniel and feel our silent connection again. I'm very calm now. "He always stayed a good-for-nothing," Daniel continues. "Except, that he was there for me. Whenever I arrived, he saw me from afar. He watched my every movement. Like Oxygen, you saw it." Daniel seems lost in memory now, focusing inwardly.

"I always felt that he watched out for me. Like a huge eye watching over me. I do until today." He laughs.

I laugh as well and look at the skull.

And I feel something inside of me changing. My heart is beating rapidly, but this time with joy. I think back to my encounter with Oxygen. When I'd approached him, I'd been very stressed which he'd felt and pushed me as if to wake me up. Talking about Solo with Daniel now, I can feel Oxygen's spirit. I think back to the moment when that timeless space had opened – right before he shoved me away. As if he was pushing me further into that space. And now I'm there. I'm in that space and – oddly – that's where I find love.

I take a deep breath. And I'm amazed. Oxygen, Daniel, Solo's story. It's as if they can see me in my very raw nature. The sun is shining through the leaves, lighting up the jungle with a hazy shine and enhancing the outlines of the single leaves. That thing I've been afraid of since this morning, that somehow eerie feeling slumbering inside of me: It came to light and they saw it. It's an uncanny feeling: It's love.

ONE LOVE - ONE HEART

Chapter 31 – Freezing Point

Two days later. I've waited for the cab to pick me up. Waited all day for something that might never happen. I think back to my old life when everything was predictable. I'd write a chapter of my current novel during the day, Oliver would come home from work, just normal family life. Every day. Now there is nothing constant in my life anymore.

Yesterday I couldn't write. I'm totally pegged to Daniel. I feel dependent, needy and a myriad of other things I never wanted to be. Where has the love gone? I thought I'd found it but it's seemingly a one way feeling. Daniel doesn't share it. If he did, he would contact me. But I cannot simply forget everything and move on. Instead I'm suffering from one more writer's block.

What will I do with my current novel? It's about 250 pages now and nearing the end. But what end? Unhappy ending: Love not found.

It was a bad idea to stick so close to my real life this time. Life is just too depressing. Novels are meant to take the reader into a fictional world where there is real love – and where, above all, life makes sense. Where the events happen in a logical succession and aren't just a pointless list of happenings. Car accident, losing complete family, find out husband led a double life. Wonderful Jamaica, the offer of a golden cage, meeting the perfect man who then disappears again. It's impossible to create an exciting story out of these ingredients.

I promise, dear reader, next time it's gonna be well built fiction again.

Marc, the owner of the Airbnb flat I live in, drops in and hands me some beverage. Marc is so sweet, he pops in every day to give me something: Coffee, a papaya, plantains, today it's a bottle with a label of Jamaican rum on it: John Wray & Nephews. When I open it, the content is foaming like sparkling wine. "Homemade," he says, "Give it a try," and looks at me like a child having just gotten a new toy.

I do. It tastes like a mixture of vinegar and mud.

"How does it taste?"

I tell him.

He laughs. He finds it very amusing to look at me while I'm making a face.

"What's in there?" I ask.

He explains that the juice is made of tree roots. I'm impressed. I can feel the juice running down my throat, burning as if it was some high-proof rum.

"Does it contain alcohol?"

"No alcohol."

He tells me not to take more than three mouthfuls of it, because "it's a medicine."

This tree root essence is a class of its own. I feel like I'm flushed out. As if roots would grow inside of me – I can just picture it. I've never drunk something with an effect like this.

"How is it produced?" I ask. "Are the roots pressed out?"

"Boiled out," he answers.

"Do they cut off the roots? If so, how can the trees live on afterwards?"

Marc feels criticised by my question. I can tell for I know that expression by now. Of course, he would never admit it. He just doesn't answer. That's beneath him. I just implied he and his fellow countrymen would kill trees to make juice of the roots. So, I answer the question myself.

"They only cut off what the tree can handle so it will live on."

He grumbles something. It's the Jamaican version of "yes." You rarely hear the word "yes" here. Instead there is a variance of mumbled or grumbled noises, sometimes it's a small melody like the song of a sweet little bird or a very gentle "Mhm."

I feel the medicine working inside of me.

Marc informs me there have been some cases of dengue fever in Jamaica and that I'd better stay out of the jungle. And always use some insect repellent because it's transmitted by mosquitos.

Again, I think about the unhappy ending of my novel and my life. Did the angels deem it right for Daniel to break up with me so I wouldn't go into the jungle anymore and cannot be infected with dengue fever? No, they're not that inept.

Marc gives me a hug when he leaves. It's a very nice feeling. He is tall and athletic, and his embrace is gentle.

Marc has left and my loneliness is killing me. Everything

used to be fine, I think. If only I hadn't gotten involved with love. Then it wouldn't have the power to torment me so much. The tree root juice makes me feel like Obelix who just took five spoons of the Magic Potion. I feel like I'm able to do something unheard of and even get away with it.

I call Daniel. I'm brave enough now.

"What's up?" he says.

"I miss you," I answer.

Silence.

"Don't you want to see me anymore?" My heart is beating like drum now because if his answer is "No" I'm sure gonna die.

Silence. I start to wither away. The Jamaican "No" is no gentle murmur like the "yes" but it hits you like a mace. Thankfully I have tree roots inside of me now, they will help me absorb the shock.

"Why would I want to see you?"

I'd thought my question to be legitimate, after all we'd slept together. But no, not for Daniel.

"Why don't you want to see me?" I ask. I need to know it. Six months ago, he asked me to marry him and take him to Germany.

"I told you I'm in a difficult situation," he says.

"I could help you," I answer and could beat myself with a frying pan at the same moment. Just the most possible stupid thing to say.

"How?" Daniel asks.

Better to say nothing more. I've navigated myself into a dead-end road. There's nothing left to say.

"How do you intend to help me if you are even worse off than I am?"

"What do you mean?"

Silence.

Worse off than him? Now I'm speechless. That answer catches me off guard.

I wonder if he's making fun of me, but his tone of voice sounds very serious. As if he's about to put an encroaching horse into its place.

"Why am I even worse off than you?" I ask very naïvely.

"That horse could have killed you – and next time it maybe will."

I'm rapidly losing my courage. Normally I would defend myself now, would tell him that it's happened before, that it's normal to get pushed by a horse, that I'm not that easy to kill. But his "You are worse off than I am" – knocks me off my feet. It galls me immensely. I'm furious about how I'm treated. How he makes me look like a complete loser. How exorbitant that is! How arrogant! Who does he think he is? To talk to me like this! Has he gone crazy? Or was I completely wrong and he's just a huge asshole?

"Later," he says. His usual way of saying goodbye.

And now he's ending the call! I don't even get the chance to defend myself! I'll be damned.

Fuck love! I think. Fucking angels! Fucking novel! Fuck my life!

Never before have I been insulted like this.

No, that's not true. Oliver often insulted me, especially during the last years. Those words could have been his. He often stated I was a bit out of touch with reality. It's always the same. I'm lacking ... hm, what exactly is it, I'm lacking? A sense of reality. Ah, yes, and I'm unable to maintain a relationship. And unable to care about others because I'm so very self-absorbed. And Daniel came to the same conclusion in record time. I'm in fact badly off. Horses are pushing me around because I don't have any standing, no sense of reality and I'm unable to maintain a relationship.

I think today is the worst day of my life. There is no escape for me, I cannot find the exit to a normal life. Nobody on this planet earth loves me just like I am. They are all searching for someone ... normal. And I'm not. I'm simply badly off. No living person on earth wants to have anything to do with me, not even in Jamaica.

It's getting dark. The insects are starting their daily performance.

I can't think of anything better to do than to check my emails. It's two a.m. in Germany. I don't know the address of the sender whose subject line says: "Who are you today?"

I hesitate. Chances are high it's just junk. But the wording sounds so strange. It reminds me of the question that had to be answered by every new member of the FB group "When everything ends." – "Who are you when everything ends?"

"Hi Viola, it's Michi," I read. "Maybe you remember me. The rooftop of that high-rise? Alex stumbled upon your online novel. It's about us, among other things."

I stop short. What's this? A hallucination? A side effect of the tree root drink?

"WhatsApp?" I ask per email and send my phone number. What's there to lose after all? Could be some weirdo who read my novel. Could live anywhere in the world, still awake at two o'clock in the morning. My greatest fear is that I'm about to talk to my own hallucination. But what do I have to lose? Everybody knows that I don't have a sense of reality and that I'm badly off. So, what difference could it make?

I know this voice! It really is Michi from the rooftop.

"You're alive!" Yeah, not very witty.

"We all are," he answers.

"Wow," I say. "Alex, Severin, Hannah?"

"Yes. Because of you."

"Because of me?" I'm baffled. I hear Gloria Gaynor's song "I will survive" playing in the neighbourhood. "At first, I was afraid, I was petrified. Kept thinking I could never live without you by my side." How fitting. Has somebody made that up or is it just a perfect hallucination? Again, I can't shake the feeling that all of this seems a little unreal.

"Viola?" I hear Michi's emphatic voice. I've always liked him, he's so caring. Yes, he's a person born to take care of others.

"Yes, I'm here," I say. When the sun sets in Jamaica the clouds turn violet. I think this will never seize to impress me.

"I thought the line went dead."

"No, I hear you," I say. "What do you mean – you are alive because of me? I'm so sorry. You'd planned to end it, after all."

"You don't have to be sorry."

"What happened?"

I make myself comfortable on the sofa. I'm so happy to hear a familiar voice. Even if 'familiar' is a bit much to say, after all I heard it just once, on the roof top. But I know his story – from the FB group. And with voices it's just like that: Once I hear a voice, I'll recognise it anywhere. Even if a long time has passed. To be precise, it's not the voice I recognise but the person behind it. Yes, it's the person I re-recognise.

"Well, you suddenly kind of 'spaced out' there on the rooftop. Then you started to talk – about angels. You seemed to be in your own world, and – sorry – but it was so exciting that we all wanted to listen. The angels, archangel Michael and at the end even the devil. It was quite impressive."

"I was talking aloud?"

"Yes, it sounded so real. Like a wonderful world and we all were kind of absorbed by it. It felt like we were part of something holy, yes, that's how it felt. It was so strong that nothing else was important anymore."

Now I'm totally dumbfounded. I remember my meeting with the angels very well. But that I'd been talking aloud? I hadn't known.

"You signed a contract with them," Michi continues.

"And then?"

"We took you home. You were completely out. I mean, you could have harmed yourself, you know."

I burst into laughter. "Sorry Michi, for laughing like

this but we were there to end our lives – and you were worried I could harm myself?"

Now we both are laughing loudly. Cackling. Thinking of the time we spent together.

"You could have been run over by a car, that would have been without style somehow and maybe you would have lived on. We had to take care of you. And, apart from that, we were curious about the rest of the story."

"Ok, so what happened next?"

"We took you home. Your address was on a business card we found together with your keys in your bag."

"And then?"

"It got really ugly in the end. Satan showed up and it felt a little like in the movie "The exorcist.""

"Please tell me I didn't throw up!"

"No. ... We thought about taking you to a psychiatric ward but decided against it. We were a little worried that they might keep us all there."

Again, we start to cackle, laugh like it's only possible amongst suicides who have nothing left to lose. I use the opportunity to laugh away my pain about Daniel and my failed quest for love. Well, not completely, of course.

"And then?"

"And then you woke up, looked at us and told us: It's all just a big lie" ... No idea what you meant with that, but you sounded very sure about it."

"A big lie?"

"That's what you said."

Strange I think, I cannot remember this.

"It's good to hear your voice," Michi says.

"I feel the same," I reply. "Why did we lose track of each other?"

"You didn't want the contact anymore. Wanted to start a new life. I could understand this. What had us once brought together held no value for you any longer."

I lean back on the sofa in my Airbnb room. It has gone completely dark while we were talking, and I look at the lights on the hills surrounding me and listen to the barking of the dogs and the crowing of a roster. That one is crowing non-stop day and night. And I think about the one sentence: 'It's all just a big lie.'

"Michi, can I ask you something?"

"Sure."

"Do you think I'm somehow missing a sense of reality? You know, like, when we first met?"

"Well, you do have plenty of imagination, but I don't know if I'd call that a lack of sense of reality. Why do you ask?"

"Because that's something people state quite frequently."

"Maybe those people are simply suffering from a lack of imagination."

That's Michi. He always sees the best in everyone.

"I like you, Michi. I'm happy you contacted me. And you chose the perfect moment to do it."

"I'm happy to hear this," he says. "I like you too, Viola. You are just a little different than most people. You need more love than they do. All of us do, you know, us meeting there on the rooftop. That's what tied us together."

His voice sounds so warm and honest – and suddenly it's back – love. I can feel it.

Chapter 32 – No Love without Truth

Michi has stirred up my past – which I don't want to look at. Neither do I want to write anymore. I just want to hide and close my mind to everything, but it doesn't work. And that other thing? It doesn't work as well: To open. Because ...

It's a wonderful morning in Jamaica. Through my open window I can hear the pupils talking to each other while they're walking along the street. I stand there watching them. The girls are wearing blue dresses at calf-length and white T-Shirts, their hair is braided in fanciful patterns. The boys are in light brown military-like short sleeved shirts and trousers. I'm crying. I'm thinking of my children. I mustn't do this. I must not open this particular door. I realise that my soul needs incredible strength to keep this door closed, but it's all I can do. At least I'm writing again. I must not give up.

Yesterday and the day before I spent at Sugar Pot Beach. I went swimming. Just like one year ago when I began to write, in Te Moana, my cottage by the sea.

When I'm in the water, I feel alright. At Sugar Pot Beach the waves are rolling in and breaking at a slight bank. I place myself in the middle of it. Over and over my body braces itself against those waves only to yield in the end.

I forget about time, my skin and my lips are salty, and I have seawater in my nose, my ears and my eyes. The water, the endless water, that ocean that embraces me gives me a deep feeling of being at home, being safe. I breathe in the smell of seaweeds and sea salt. I feel the sun burning on my head, heating up my hair. I'm gazing into the distance, into the clear blue sky. My vision becomes soft and my eyes soak up the endless space.

Sugar Pot Beach is a secluded place, not the typical place to go for mainstream and cruise ship tourists. More a place for the dreamers, for people who left their old lives behind, for those who prefer to stay on the sidelines. Josh, the Belgium guy who made his dream real when he bought that piece of the beach some years ago, is sitting on the patio, having some beer and soda together with some friends. He keeps an eye on me but it's very discreet. No control, just gentle awareness.

Here, in the water, bracing against every new wave, in this huge ocean that swallows every pain, every tear, every resistance, I give in.

That world made of concrete, Germany, I can feel it inside of me. And I feel hardness. It scares me and yet I feel closer to myself. I don't push my feelings to the outside any longer. I find and embrace them within. I'm aware of myself more intensely.

My quest for love: I've found love in human beings, in animals, in nature – and today, for the very first time, I feel something like love inside myself. Just me, no other person or animal next to me. The sea does this to me. I listen to my inner voice and I find something there. Like the bottom of the sea with mysterious plants growing there.

They're floating back and forth with their oh so thin skin, like dresses of a ballerina, their gossamer calyxes in pink, violet, pale-yellow, playful details like small balls, geometric ornaments, curly rims, whole colonies of gently floating orange coloured corals. They're talking silently. And I'm listening. It's soothing.

I wade out of the water, dry myself and lay down in the shadow provided by a tree. I let my mind wander, my thoughts seeking their way like the water, coming in waves.

I get stuck at my communication with Michi the day before. That one sentence about everything being 'a big lie' keeps coming back.

I cannot remember saying it, but I have no reason to doubt Michi. I remember the angels calling me a difficult case when I first met them. I remember something devilish happening and them stating he had ensnared me. What did they mean with this? Why am I a difficult case? Why did Daniel say I'm even worse off than he is?

Yes, it's true, I avoid dealing with the pain. I just want to forget. I'm proud of myself for managing to start a new life. Yes, that's what I did, and I think that's quite an accomplishment.

I think Daniel sensed it, the pain that's buried deep inside of me and how I'm covering it up. I cannot even resent him because of it.

And where is the love? Can there be true love if there is so much pain? And can the heart ever open up if a part of the soul remains locked?

And why does some part of me think that everything is a big lie?

I simply don't get any further, my mind gets stuck at that situation every time.

I order some fish at the bar. A young woman with this typical Jamaican accent, stretching the vocals, asks me what kind of side dishes I'd like to have and what I'd like to drink? It takes a little while for the meal to be served as everything gets prepared freshly. At the rear wall of the bar is a portrait of Bob Marley, the very symbol of Jamaica for peace and One Love – One Heart. And right behind the beach the jungle begins with its abundant growth, the trees and plants entangled around each other, smothering each other and searching for a way to freedom. Green in every shade imaginable, shimmering and vibrating and luring you into its depth.

Everything here makes me relent; the water, the blue sky, the jungle, the people. The concrete inside of me doesn't stand a chance, it's broken up and overgrown by the jungle. I'm getting smooth and flexible like the climbers that find nooks everywhere, holes and niches to grow into and out of, that never seize to grow, constantly sprouting new shoots. That grow huge leaves overnight in a color so vividly green and shapes that soften my eyes. I feel like I'm that never-ending growth myself.

I feel like Daniel again, too.

I feel the harshness with which he rejected me. His harshness that clashed with my own. I feel that he didn't intend to hurt me, he was just responding to something inside of me, something I wasn't even aware of. Just like Oxygen, the horse, did.

I think I will see Daniel again.

After I've found a little more of that truth that hides behind the lies.

The next day. I'm back at the beach, Sugar Pot. Back in the water. The waves are even higher than yesterday. I stay for a long time. Stay in the arms of the ocean, my body wanting to relent like it does when in Daniel's arms. I can feel his embrace again, as gentle and endless as the sea; nothing in it trying to hold me back, nothing wanting to let me go. It just is – like the sea. In his embrace I can feel myself, my very self. I recognise this now while I'm feeling the embrace of the sea. Is this love? Will I find it here, that One Love? That love all living creatures have in common? That love I find in the ocean, in the sky. That love that creates something beautiful of everything, that causes everything to shine, that bestows the sky with this distinct blue and infuses the green of every leave with its light. That love that makes the people believe. Like in the church in Eltham changing life into wonder.

Again, I rest on the beach and let my mind wander. Back to the scene in the souks of Marrakech, to the shop of the uncle, the shoemaker. There was something in his voice, a kind of tiredness, a cautiousness in his behaviour as if he was despising the very act of speaking, as if every word coming over his lips meant an effort to him. The voice of the Moroccan doctor, who called me to inform me about the death of my family, sounded exactly alike. Tired and as if it was immensely hard to speak at all. The same voice. Maybe a typical voice of a Moroccan man? My knowledge of the Moroccan people is too sparse to be able to judge this. And yet ... there are voices you recognise immediately, and it's not only the voice itself as it is but a means to express our whole nature. I feel that nature in the voices. Suddenly my stomach feels knotted again. And the feeling stays for the rest of the day, the nagging ache won't go away. No fish today.

And again, something sticks to my mind: Charifa's letter. She sent it about one year ago. Three years after the accident. Why would she wait three years to tell me I had a family in Morocco? Why would she call me three months later to tell me her son was ill, and she needed money? Why wait this long? Because the son fell ill three years after the accident? Then she'd send me a friendly letter, then wait for three months to ask me for money? There's a lie hidden somewhere in all of this. I just can't tell where exactly. The knot in my stomach won't go away.

In the evening I stroll through the market in Ocho Rios. My gaze is drawn to the guys wearing dreadlocks down to their hips or put into hats that look like beehives. And to the other men wearing sunglasses and massive golden necklaces.

There is always reggae music. Chronixx, Busy Signal or one of Bob Marley's sons; it's a fantastic generation of reggae musicians, successors of Bob Marley. Songs with strong messages like the one by Ziggy Marley:

Heaven can't take it no more
They're killing for money, they're killing for power
They're killing for religion, they're killing for color
Some say they're killing for peace, but the wars won't cease
When everyone is wrong, no matter what kind of bomb, yeah
Heaven can't take it no more

(Songwriter: David Nesta Marley
Songtext of Heaven Can't Take It © Ishti
Music Publishing)

I stick out with my fair skin. Men are calling after me. "Hello beautiful." – "You are a rare beauty." – "I love your body, do you want a boyfriend?" Some try to draw me into a conversation. If I don't want to talk to them, I tell them, "My boyfriend is waiting for me over there and it's better if he doesn't see us together." That always does the job.

In the eyes of these men women are territory that needs to be defended. Nobody wants to rile up a man who has taken a woman under his protection and considers her his. I buy papayas and sliced pineapple and two avocados for breakfast. This market in Ocho Rios feels different than the souks of Morocco. Lighter, brighter, left to take a place in its own time. Even if there is surely an order of powers beyond the surface as well.

Although Jamaica is a country of sunny spirits when looked at from the outside – from within it is directed by crime and corruption.

"You cannot trust anyone here," Marc, in whose apartment I'm living, says. "Everybody is up to something all the time. Before you know it, you've been robbed."

What makes Jamaica so special for me is the fact that the people are shining, nevertheless. Despite the poverty, the daily struggle to survive. They are a hard people and yet soft. Their smiles are radiating like the sun. Their friendliness is never artificial. And their harshness is as unrelenting. Just like Daniel embracing me and at the same time telling me to my face I'm worse off than he is.

The people at the market, the market traders, the vendors, always answer to me like I'm behaving towards them. If I'm friendly, something friendly will be returned. If I'm brusque, something brusque will come back. Nothing artificial. Only honesty.

The people are in their essence, whether they're absorbed by their work or talking to each other. They do one thing at a time. It gives them beauty and dignity.

I feel at home among them. I think they are free, even if they perhaps don't think the same.

I'm glad I can simply be myself here, be just who I am. I can tolerate Daniel rejecting me like he did. It's not evil,

it's not a strategy nor is it a lie. Is it love then? No love
without truth?

Chapter 33 – I'm a Mother

Another day has begun. Again, I'm standing at my window looking at the school and the teens. Who would I be if I didn't avoid the pain any longer? If I dared to look in its face? My children would be the same age now as the kids down there, coming together in small groups, making fun of each other, telling secrets, making friends, looking after girls, loving and hating school.

I'd be a mother. Even if Oliver left me to live with his Moroccan family, I'd still have my children. I'd share their lives. I'd be at home on this planet earth. I'd find the love that is most important for me, the love for my children. Now I really start to dream.

I climb onto the roof of the house. I have a good view of Ocho Rios from there. And I can see the ocean! That makes me happy at once. The ocean, that huge storage tank of dreams. Everything is allowed in the ocean. I can simply plunge into it, into this clear blue and my dreams will levitate like drops spreading over the ocean and shining in the sunlight.

Wow, what a feeling. In my mind I go for a walk on the beach together with my children. Saskia and Leo. They would be eleven and thirteen years old now. How they've grown, how graceful they've become. What fine people they are. I see their hands, their feet, their delicate bodies showing more and more signs of becoming a man and a woman. I even hear the sound of the sea. It feels so very real, as if my children were really here with me. I hear Saskia's voice. 'Mama'. I see her smile. I feel her putting her arms around my neck. I hear the twittering of the birds mixing with the sound of the sea.

Right below my window a few kids are getting into a Route Taxi that'll take them home. I imagine Saskia and Leo, here with me in Jamaica, attending school. Or would they attend school in Germany? They wouldn't have a visa for Jamaica, that'd be an issue. Or would I find a way to make it possible for us to live here? Would they like it here? And would the school be of the same quality than a German school? It's wonderful to ponder all these details, just like a mother always does. I allow myself to do it. No pain, just a wonderful dream.

I hear Marc calling my name. Very silently at first. He's far away as I'm sitting on the roof and he's probably on the ground floor. He calls my name again and again, I climb down.

"Someone's here for you," he says.

"For me?" Who would visit me here in Jamaica in this Airbnb? I look around seeing nobody.

Then he comes around the corner.

"Daniel!"

I feel him all over my body. I start to shiver. Daniel? And I stop to think. I simply stand here and ... stand here.

Daniel and Marc exchange a few words in Patois, talking too fast for me to hear anything but a cloud of words. They high five and Marc disappears.

Daniel looks at me like he would look at a horse. With this attentiveness so typical of him, that just is but demands nothing. Now, here together with him, I can utterly feel myself. I'm completely calm and so is he. I smile, he smiles. All the thoughts I kept pondering, about him and his behaviour, about him and me. They're gone. Floated away like soap bubbles.

I lead him up the stairs with the intention to invite him to my apartment, but then I change my mind and take him up to the roof.

We sit down on the knee-high wall surrounding the water tank on the roof. I'm so excited I cannot think straight, much less talk. I look at the house next to us where metal rods are protruding from the roof. Armoring irons for the next level the owners are planning to build some time. My mind settles on this Jamaican oddity. On the people starting to build a house, only the lowest level, and already putting in the armoring for the next level. Whenever they've saved enough money to go on, they'll build the next level and again put in the armoring for the time they'll be able to expand again. One layer after another. One step after another. It's not necessary to do everything at once, I think, it's not even necessary to plan to the end.

Then I look at Daniel's hands that are very slender; I've never looked at them this thoroughly. I think of him touching me and again start to shiver.

I'm so relenting right now that I've no strength left in me. My whole being is trying to regain my poise. That's how I feel with Daniel, the impact he has on me. I lose myself completely, try to hold on but I can't, and then I let go ... to find myself.

Daniel is very quiet, just sits there and breathes calmly. Time seems to be of no importance to him. The birds, I'm listening to the birds, their twittering very close now, like they were sitting right next to my ears. Their voices sound like fine flutes, playing one caper after another as there are so many things they need to tell. A huge network of messages, enclosing the whole residential neighbourhood and probably much more. How they're pushing out the air, as if their beak was a trumpet. Firing salvos into the air. Speeding up and slowing down their fluting. One of them holding an even whistling basic rhythm.

My gaze wanders back to the sea, this light blue infinity.

I'm sure Daniel won't be the one to start talking, I think. But he also won't avoid it. He doesn't spend his time pondering something like this at all.

More and more pupils are surging out of the school onto the street. Their voices are getting louder and drown out the singing of the birds.

"You came back," I say.

"I've missed you," he answers.

"Really?"

"Would I say so otherwise?"

What stupid questions you ask, Viola. But during a conversation in Germany that would be normal. I'd say "Really?" to express my joy about the fact that he missed me, and he would say "Yes, of course," to emphasise what he said. With Daniel it doesn't work like this. With him it's about facts, spoken in a direct way and clear manner – like with a horse. It's not even because he's bossy but it's just his way of talking. I need to stop this carousel of my thoughts, I'm just too excited.

"You look better," Daniel says in his calm and warm way.

"Thank you." I wonder if he's talking about me being not that badly off any longer. And if so, why. Why does he think differently about me now?

I raise my eyes to look at him. This peace and quiet in his expression, as if the sun has been shining on him all his life and he's never seen anything else but green. As if his eyes have never seen a world in which human-made things are greater than nature. What would he gain if he accompanied me to Germany? What could he find there that he doesn't have here already? Would it even be a violation of his beauty and dignity?

Why do I look better? What is it he sees or senses that I'm not aware of?

He takes my hand, gently caressing it with his fingers. That warmth, that gentleness. I'm totally calm now. Everything's alright.

Nothing needs to be said.

I sense Daniel is completely present. His touch is neither intrusive nor indifferent. He isn't holding me down, but just holding me. His hand is touching mine – that's it. And it's everything.

I exhale deeply.

"My children," I say. "I saw them."

I know it doesn't make any sense to him, but I tell him anyway because it's affected me so deeply, because it's so new for me that I'm able to think about them at all. Because it is so very important to me – and, additionally to this, Daniel showed up, that's a lot of happiness to deal with at once.

Daniel doesn't even know the story of my children. I never told him about them and how they died in an accident. And it's basically not important if he knows about them or not.

"Do you have children?" I ask.

"Four that I know of," he answers and smirks like men do who are aware of their power and powerlessness at the same time.

"Do they live with you?"

"No."

"Do you see them?"

"Yes."

"How old are they?"

He shortly thinks about that question. "Three, five, Serena is eleven now, I think, and John is seventeen."

"Different mothers?

"Yes, three."

This is more of the normal case here than the exception, I think.

"Why do you ask?" Daniel wants to know.

Again, I look down at the street and watch three pupils get into a Route Taxi.

Then I see a cab driving around the corner. It stops in front of Marc's house. The car door opens and two teens with fair skin step out of it. They carry backpacks like the Jamaican pupils, wear jeans and sneakers and t-shirts. They look around, obviously searching for something. The driver points to the house on which roof I'm sitting, they look at the house, but of course they cannot see me up here.

I cannot clearly make out their faces from my heightened position, but the girl's hair looks just like Saskia's – dark blond with thick curls. And the boy – his hair color is a very light blonde, the same as Michael from Loenneberga's – in that movie with Pippi Longstocking. It's highly unusual for boys to have hair this color, but my Leo does.

Something inside of me is breaking apart. How is it possible to see my children getting out of a taxi down there on the street? That they seem so very real? I'm not imagining this. This is not a story I'm making up with my imagination. Am I going crazy? Are the boundaries between reality and imagination getting too thin? I knew something extreme would happen if I allowed myself to think about my late children. I permitted myself nearly everything during the last four years – except this. And now?

I watch as the other kids look at these two fair skinned ones. They seem to see them as well. They seem to be real, not my imagination.

"Seems your children have just arrived," Daniel notices very rationally.

I feel like my brain is going to explode.

I stand up, climb down the ladder, run down the stairs to ground level, towards the door, open it.

My heart is beating like a drum.

"Mama," I hear Saskia's voice. Then she throws her arms around me. I reach for Leo and pull him to me as well.

Oh my God, oh my God, oh my God ... What is this? What is this?

The love ...

Chapter 34 – The Love of Fish

We're here, Saskia, Leo and me. And Daniel. We're sitting on the rooftop. Every noise we hear is very distinct, the talking of the pupils, the screeching of the birds, a motorcycle roaring past. And we hear the beating of our hearts. We are as close at this very moment as is humanly possible. There are no questions, no wishes, only love.

I have no words for what is happening right now. Only feelings. My children. They're here. With me. This is not a dream. I'm here in Jamaica. Jamaica, my paradise. Where the impossible is possible. Where the angels are so close. Goats are grazing on the meadow across the street, a shepherd watching over them. A big black bird is circling above the living quarter. My gaze is following its flight and for a moment I can see a curtain lift, allowing me to glance at its second nature: Its feathers are pure white – and he is one of archangel Michael's trainees. The one who picked me up on the rooftop of the high-rise.

"Good job," I tell him, watching him as he does an extra circle.

Right now, I'm not a difficult case. Right now, I'm simply so very happy.

Marc learned what happened and you know, he's a real kind-hearted spirit. And he's one of these people whose schedule books allow for unplanned happenings because they're not filled to the brim.

As a result, he carries in a box containing fresh fish, taken from the sea only minutes ago – a doctor fish and three others – the names of which I keep forgetting. And a black plastic bag filled with red peppers, fresh coriander, coconut oil, mangos and papaya. In my fridge we find a pumpkin, carrots, tomatoes, onions and garlic. Marc is about to start cooking, but Daniel nudges him away.

"Let me do this," he says. "I'll call you when it's done (mi a tej ya, when mi a readde)." At least this is what I get, yes, I'm getting more accustomed to the local dialect.

The kids and I are hanging around in the kitchen with Daniel. Daniel prepares the food just like he works with horses. Totally absorbed in what he's doing.

"Where did you come from today?"

"Marrakech."

"Wow! How did you get into the plane without an adult?"

"We weren't alone," Leo says.

For a moment I feel a searing hot flame inside my body. The mere thought that Oliver could be here as well.

"Who ...?"

"A colleague of papa."

Suddenly Saskia is very excited. "Leo found you ... on the internet. Your novel, you wrote about us."

Again, my brain feels like it's going to explode any second. How does all this fit together?

"I thought you were dead. That doctor called me and told me papa and you had died in an accident."

"That was no doctor, mama," Saskia tells me. "That was the uncle."

"Charifa's uncle?"

Saskia nods. I think about how I thought I recognised his voice, that tiredness in it. Again, there is a blast inside my brain. I shake my head. How does all this fit together? I dig deeper: "The uncle wanted me to believe that you were dead?"

Saskia nods again. Then I see tears in her eyes. Her gaze is getting hazy. She tightly clings to me and I hold her protectively in my arms.

"Nothing can separate us now, nothing can keep me away from you," I say. "I will always be there for you. Always. From now on."

Leo rummages around in his backpack and pulls out a piece of paper.

I'm baffled.

It's my handwriting. But the words are not mine, I never wrote them. Somebody faked my handwriting.

The note says:

"Dear Saskia, dear Leo.
You both need to stay with your papa now.
I cannot be your mama any longer. I have another family and I'm the mama of other children now. Papa will take care of you as will your new mama, Charifa. She loves you very much. Please don't search for me. Take care."

I read those lines and feel like I just left my body. It's a feeling I know well – from my childhood. It was always present when I was a child. And now it's back. I know it because I remember the feeling of how my neck is tightening. As if my neck wanted to tether me while I left my body and went looking for a place where I could find peace.

I'm paralysed.

"Hey," I hear Daniel's voice. It cuts through the fog. "Come here," he tells me strictly; it's the voice he uses when he talks to absentminded horses. "Peel the yams and cut it into slices."

Daniel has a feeling for whenever I'm drifting apart. He gets me back. I stand up and peel the yams, big bulbs, like potatoes but with a thicker skin and a harder interior. You need a big knife and strength to do it and it brings me back to the here and now.

While I'm cutting the yams my thoughts drift along: That's not possible. Oliver made up this whole shit. He wanted to live with that woman and their son in Morocco and he wanted to take Saskia and Leo with him. He just disposed me off. I thought I had lost absolutely everything, but it was just one huge rip-off!

I feel sick. I feel I'm drifting away even further.

"Hey," Daniel says. "What are you doing?"

I've cut the yams into very small pieces.

"Slices, I said."

"Sorry," I mumble. I feel like I'm going to break apart any moment.

"Go to your children," Daniel says. "Aren't you happy that they are here?"

I see this expression in his eyes that tells me, "You are worse off than me." But maybe he doesn't mean it like that.

I can feel it now. What the angels said. I can feel why I'm a difficult case. And why Daniel tells me I'm badly off. If something happens, like now, I cannot find stability inside myself. Looking back at my life in moments like these I can see how exhausting it is to return to this world again and again just to cut the yams into slices. While something inside of me is constantly trying to get away from this world.

The flavour of fried garlic is drifting past. I'm sitting on the sofa, holding both of my children in my arms. The moment stretches into infinity.

Why had it been so very easy to deceive me? Why didn't I feel there was something wrong? I wanted to end my life because the pain was so unbearable. And all this grief was caused by something unreal! The only thing I would've had to do was to travel to Morocco and search for Oliver. After all I knew the name of the company he'd worked for. Then I would have found my children.

"How do you like the fish?" Daniel asks me later.

Marc has returned and we're having dinner together.

"Honestly, I've never eaten fish like this." The flesh is pristine white and sappy, a little jelly-like, it kind of dissolves on my tongue. And there is something else as well. This fish isn't just food or something to taste. It's pure energy. I can feel its energy inside my body.

"It's like medicine," I finally say.

Daniel nods satisfied. I notice that, apart from salt and fresh coriander leaves, he didn't use any spices. Everything I eat has its own pure taste. The carrot. Have I ever eaten a carrot that tasted this pure? But maybe all carrots taste different in Jamaica, because they grow under her sun. The carrot, too, is energy and I feel it affecting my body.

A gate of perception has opened inside of me and I sense all things as one living organism.

"Now you understand," Daniel says.

I nod.

I'm back. Fully and completely back, surrounded by people I love and who love me back. Together with Saskia and Leo, with my children. With the truth. Such a wonderful feeling. Even the fish gives me his love in the way it nourishes my body with its medicine. I can feel it, this gift of the fish. The gift of the carrot, of the tomato.

I can feel the angels. They're here as well. Together with us at the table. They are very happy. I've never felt before how they exactly are, I mean, their character. They are light but not like a light bulb, more like a happy light, a light that laughs and likes to make fun and likes to be happy for you. Wow, what a wonderful moment!

I take Saskia and Leo to bed. Later I will lay down beside them, the bed is big enough. I will never again leave them. They are finally here and I'm here as well, I'm their mama.

I'm sitting on the sofa with Daniel. I'm so happy it's him, I wouldn't want to share this moment with anybody else.

We are sitting very close, our legs are entwined, my

head is lying on his chest and he has put one arm around me. We always find the one position that brings us as close together as possible. This is how we are. You couldn't fit a breath of air between us.

"I have a question," Daniel says. I'd told him about the letter and about Oliver staging the whole situation.

"Shoot."

"You must have other family, parents, sisters or brothers. And he has a family as well. Did every single one of them believe he was dead?"

"I called his family after I'd recovered from the first shock. They didn't want to talk to me. They never liked me. They thought I wasn't good enough for him because I'm not as sophisticated as he was and didn't have a 'real' job. I've no idea what they know or don't know. I couldn't reach them."

"And what about your family? Weren't they asking questions or offering help to find your children?"

"I don't have a family." I take a deep breath. The secret is out. The one thing I've kept to myself for so long. I haven't told anyone. Not even you, dear readers …

"You have no family?"

"I'm an orphan."

"But you told me about your family once, how kind they are."

"That's what I tell everyone, so nobody is bothering me because of it."

"Then you're lying – just like your husband?" Daniel looks at me appalled and sits up. "I cannot be with you if you are lying."

Now I'm afraid. He doesn't understand. How can I explain it to him? I feel I'm drawing back again.

"Hey," he says. "You haven't answered my question."

"Do you never lie?" I reply.

He gives some thought to this question.

"There is no need for everyone to know everything," I say.

He nods. I see him nod and I'm back again.

We stay there for a long time. It feels like honey. I can still feel the fish inside my body, the good energy it is sending out and I think about Marc, who gave so many fresh and tasty Jamaican things to me. And about Saskia and Leo who are lying in the bed in the room next door, sleeping. And about the fact that life is so good.

"Now I know how love feels," I tell Daniel. "I've always been looking for love, especially when I was a child. Sometimes I could witness it when I watched other children and their mothers. I always wished that I would find something like that one day. Then I thought I'd found it with Oliver. I was so proud, having a family had always been my greatest wish. With Oliver and the children, everything was fine. It was everything I'd ever wanted."

I stop briefly and then go on, "When the accident happened, when they were gone, I was suddenly an orphan again. I was alone again. This hunger for love I've had all my life – I couldn't deal with it one more time. And I thought I wasn't meant to have a happy family. That's why I didn't want to stay any longer."

Daniel simply listens. He doesn't interrupt, doesn't say

anything, just listens. It's strange with him. I never feel judged even if I tell him something, I'm sure I would be judged for by anybody else. No matter what I tell him, he simply listens. Listens in a manner I'm not accustomed to. He isn't just hearing my words. He listens to my heart-beat.

I'm quite surprised myself by the next thing I say. The fact that I can say it at all – has something to do with Daniel and the way he listens. And it feels true, so very true.

"It's not important anymore if I have a family or not. My happiness is no longer depending on a family. I feel love – it's within myself. Not somewhere out there. It's more than a family or a single person. It's not just one moment. It's something permanent. I feel that I can take it with me wherever I go. It doesn't matter where I am. It stays when everything else is leaving. It's permanent."

I think that's what the angels wanted to show me.

Looking back, there were so many moments when they tried to draw my attention to something distinct, when I could feel love. And now it's piled up in front of me and cannot simply disappear anymore. Even if I lived an illusion where Oliver was concerned. I don't even care about that any longer.

Jamaica
ONE LOVE – ONE HEART

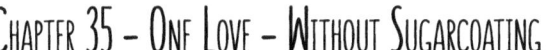

Chapter 35 – One Love – Without Sugarcoating

The next day I call Felicia to tell her what has happened. I tell her about Saskia and Leo and that I'm sure about love now, that I can see love even in a dead fish. Almost everywhere. The comment about the dead fish makes her laugh. She knows love very well. Felicia is like the angels, since the day we first met she's kept explaining to me how love works. And finally, I get it. I realise that there has been one person in my life who has always loved me: Felicia. And as I can feel her love so much stronger now, I'm also able to feel the love of other people which has been there all along.

I'm sure Oliver loved me too – he just felt like doing something else after a while, and when he wanted to get rid of me, he forgot about the fact that the feeling of not being loved is my weak point.

Doesn't matter any longer. My weakness is about to become a strength.

"And what about Oliver?" Felicia asks. "Is he still there? And the kids – did they run away?"

I laugh. "No, you know, life has a subtle sense of humour. Oliver did die in a car accident. But much later, when he and the children already lived in Morocco. It was shortly after that had happened that Charifa sent me her letter. Her money source had suddenly disappeared, and she thought she could tap into me."

"And the kids?"

"They lived in a village in a rural area, learned to speak Arabian and attended school there. They didn't have mobile phones or internet access. Oliver made sure of this. But that changed after he'd died. Leo started searching for me then."

"Crazy," Felicia says. "As if I'd known it all along ..."

"What do you mean – you knew it?"

"That whole story was just too ... it didn't feel right."

"And yet you didn't say a thing?"

"I did."

"You did?"

"Yes – but you didn't want to listen. As soon as I spoke a thought pointing into that direction, you clammed up. Oliver was like a saint to you."

I hear voices coming from the bedroom, Saskia and Leo just woke up.

"For me, he had to be."

"I told you several times to go there and investigate a little, but – no chance."

"I didn't have the strength. I preferred the lie. I'd appointed Oliver to be my saviour and it needed to stay that way. I just couldn't go back to that loneliness. But after all, Oliver was just human like we all are." Phew, I exhale heavily.

"When will you come to Germany?" Felicia asks.

"I don't know yet."

"Well, then I have to come to Jamaica, I guess."

"That would be wonderful!"

Saskia and Leo come in through the door.
"How about breakfast?"

This is the end of my story. I finally found it – love. It's finally come to me and now I can see it everywhere. But I want to tell you a little more about Jamaica before I finally leave you because this island saved my life – along with the angels. It's hard to explain what makes Jamaica so very special. I've tried to do exactly this in the last few hundred pages. And yet I cannot shake the feeling that it's so much more.

I live with Daniel in his village and I write. The kids like it here, they already know rural life from their time in Morocco. They play with Daniel's children when they come for a visit. I'd like to tell you about the festival Daniel took me to yesterday. Something happened there that I couldn't imagine happening outside Jamaica.

The "Rebel Salute" festival took place for the first time twenty-five years ago. Since then it's been celebrated for the duration of two days every January. It's a stage for reggae, the music Jamaica is known for all over the world. At the "Rebel Salute" festival you can experience reggae in its most elementary form, without sugarcoating. Reggae growing right out of the earth, rising from the souls of the musicians. Here I sensed what reggae really means: It's raw, coarse, utterly passionate. The singers perform as if there was no audience, no tomorrow, no yesterday. They seem to dissolve within their moves, their voices.

Driven by the relentless rhythm of the reggae you find

no vanity here, only power. There is no specification except for the riddm (rhythm). Only that beat, building the base of everything with a myriad of different variations. Reggae is merciless individuality. Maybe this is the reason for its spreading all over the world. Every artist writes his or her own texts and songs and performs them with a distinct voice. It's not about how good or bad a singer or a band is, it's about passion, about shouting out truth. The reggae you hear at the "Rebel Salute" festival is not some cheerful background music to listen to while sipping a cocktail on the beach. It's an eruption of feelings and raw truth coming from the bottom of their souls.

And I realise with absolute finality that Jamaica is not the country of the happy, stoned hippies or the always cheerful islanders, of the white beaches and turquoise ocean, where everyone is dreaming the day away. Nobody here can afford to float through a world made of dreams. I'm talking about the locals, of course. There is no comfort zone, no safe place for fun-loving music. Reggae means survival on a small blessed piece of land. A land full of sun, fruit, beauty, exploitation, poverty and wealth. And if I feel like I'm in a dream here, it's not the kind of unrealistic or naïve dream. It's a dream about life itself – vibrating life, hard and soft, dark and light, divine and destructive.

So, what I wanted to tell you about: The performance of Queen Ifrica on the "Rebel Salute" festival. She is announced with the title "Queen", "Empress" even. This title is bestowed upon women who have a certain power and exude feminine charisma and an inner beauty, women who thoroughly are women, who own self-love and are not afraid to show themselves in all their beauty and greatness.

And she really is an Empress, this Queen Ifrica. If you've seen her once, you will never forget her again. She's an impressive woman with a deep, coarse voice.

Andrew Holness, the Jamaican Prime Minister, is among the audience sitting in front of the stage. She addresses him.

Tells him that the next song is for him. That she isn't just some mere entertainer, but a voice of the people. Even if it hadn't been her choice, the people chose her to become their speaker because she loves her country and the people who live in it. That the song she's going to sing isn't meant to be disrespectful.

"But I want you to listen to my words: 98 percent of the people who live here are black people. But they gain only little benefit of the things coming to Jamaica." (She's talking about economic profit.) "Our island could be a role model for the whole world. If only our government would recognise the needs of little girls and boys, the needs of the very poor, if only it would give those people a home and something to feel deep inside, something that would make them strong ..."

Queen Ifrica sits down at the edge of the stage, directly in front of the Prime Minister, the microphone in her hand. The cameras capture her so that the people farther back can also watch her on two huge monitors.

"Jamaica is on the brink of great changes," she says. "Please let the people be a part of them. Thank you for feeling me and for seeing me," she continues, still speaking to Andrew Holness, the Prime Minister – who stands up, takes a step towards her and embraces her.

I'm deeply impressed by this behaviour. That a Prime Minister would embrace an artist voicing critical issues. The mere fact that three important members of parliament (apart from the Prime Minister the Minister of Culture and the Minister of Defense came, too) would come to a festival, and that the country's most powerful politician would embrace a rebel singer – that's unheard of.[1]

Mutabaruka, who hosts the festival, is a legend, a Rastafarian poet, a man who has never worn shoes in all his life. He asks the Minister of Culture to come to the stage and tells her that all over the world reggae musicians perform in big music halls – except for Jamaica, where there isn't even a roofed place for this world-famous music. She promises to change this.

Whenever I think about Jamaica my heart is about to burst. There is so much beauty here and so much pain at the same time. So much truth. And therefore, I must stay. Jamaica and I – we are alike. Beauty and pain. Fear and love. Death and survival. Severe need and exuberant abundance.

Oneness and contradiction. The slaves, who were

---

[1] By the way, there is a movie of that performance on YouTube – Queen Ifrica at the Rebel Salute Festival in 2019

brought to Jamaica by the Spanish and the English, were people who'd been separated from their families, their ethnicity. It was made sure that the members of a tribe were separated so that they couldn't find or create a common culture or build a resistance. Apart from those slaves, people from all over the world found their way to Jamaica: from India, China or England, from Europe. There is one city where almost only German immigrants live. And yet this variance of different people has one thing in common: Reggae.

Reggae is political music, profoundly spiritual music with roots in Africa and it stems from the Rasta-movement. Things that have always been integral parts of the Rastafarian's life are slowly finding their way to the western world nowadays: They live a vegan or vegetarian life and are closely linked with nature in a deep nature-related spirituality. Their unique identification is the dreadlocks, their symbol is the lion, their flag is yellow, red and green. They heal with herbs and smoke ganja (marihuana). Their music is reggae. They are the soul of the country. They are the reason for Jamaica being a place beyond comparison. Their message is peace: "Out of many – we are one. One Love – One Heart."

So, what's next in my life? Now that I've found love. I have a dream, a vision.

I want to create a place, here in Jamaica, where human beings and animals can live together. I'd like to invite people to come and experience something called paradise. To work together and just be together – people, animals, nature.

To cook together: The goods of nature, freshly picked from a tree or bush, roots the ground bestows us with. Fishes that were swimming in the ocean just minutes ago and now gift their souls to nourish the people.

To eat together at a big table, live together with animals without urging or even forcing them into doing something, feel how loving these animals are. To remember who we are: One Love – One Heart.

To make it possible for all of us to find it again: Love.

So that love won't stay a vision but become real to touch, taste and live it.

Because love is the one thing that remains, the one thing that reveals what or who we really are when all the fog has lifted.

Thank you, dear reader, for accompanying me this far. This story is coming to an end now. And it means a lot to me. I woke from a nightmare. By writing it. I can write again. I can love again. And I have a home again.

It has been a very long way – and yet I've finally arrived.

And I wish the same for you, no matter on which road you might find yourself right now. It's possible for you to arrive as well – at yourself and in love. That much I know.

The angels are there for you, too.

They're inventive, as you can see from my story. They'll stick to their guns and if it must be Jamaica? Be it.

This novel was published as a blog and I'm grateful for the ideas of my readers, their comments and their inspiration that reached me via the website and so many emails. Thank you, dear readers, you were a huge motivation.

This morning I talked to Felicia on the phone – about project "Paradise Garden", that place where it will be possible for people to experience paradise, and the dreams we shared were vivid. She'll come to Jamaica soon. And then we will verify in detail what can be accomplished.

While I was writing today, I received an email from a beloved (and quite wealthy) friend. A year ago, we'd talked about a visionary nature-human project in Jamaica. He asked me in his email how far I'd gotten along – looks like he knows me quite well ... Wrote he has quite a bit of money that's waiting to be invested.

By the way – his name is Michael.

ONE LOVE - ONE HEART

My Wish

This novel contains biographical parts, yet overall it is fiction.

The names, places and events in this novel have been changed to some extent in order to protect the privacy of the people concerned. But the feelings are genuine.

I'd like to thank all those who have accompanied me on this way, who have inspired and – above all – loved me unconditionally.

Love lets us survive when we are at breaking point – no matter where it's coming from.

I was searching for paradise as life on earth had seemingly become too unbearable for me. I thought I would find it in heaven, but I was wrong. I found it down on earth, in Jamaica.

I've always been attracted by the beauty of God's creation and in Jamaica I find an abundance of it. And at the same time, I find many horrors human beings are capable of.

This is my nourishment as a writer: Light and shadow, beauty and glimpses into the abyss, the strength to overcome every fear and keep moving on.

If you are as desperate as I was, you need people with a huge heart to help you come back to this world. I've met such people. They are existing and they are there for you when you need them most.

This is the greatest gift of all: Love. Being there for each other – you, taking care of the others, and they, taking care of you.

May this book give you beauty, faith and love.

Ocho Rios, Jamaica, February 2019
Ulrike Dietmann

About the Author

Ulrike Dietmann, born in Bad Mergentheim, Germany, is author of numerous novels and specialist books. She is head of the publishing house 'spiritbooks', the writing school 'Pegasus' and the 'Spirit Horse' company (Spirit Horse – Persönlichkeitsentwicklung mit Pferden – personal development with horses). She travels a lot and trains people in many countries. In summer she hosts the 'Horse & Spirit Festival.'

www.ulrikedietmann.de

ISBN 978-3-9815421-4-1
10,99 EUR

Ulrike Dietmann
On the Wings of Horses

What if we purposefully tap the horse's ability to make us better humans? Ulrike Dietmann offers a heartwarming, empowering program for doing just that. In this book, she uses the model of the hero's journey, developed by the late author and mythologist Joseph Campbell, helping us consciously, and thereby much more efficiently, access what horses have been silently teaching riders, heroes, pioneers, leaders, and artists for millennia. Her graceful, intelligent writing is also clear and easy to understand as she makes some normally complex personal development principles surprisingly accessible.

Ulrike is a great translator of horse wisdom.

ISBN 978-3-944587-00-4
11,90 EUR

Ulrike Dietmann
The Medicine Horse

After her daughter has died in a riding accident, Valerie's world becomes completely unhinged. Suddenly a horse called Gitanes turns up and declares he is a medicine horse and has come to heal her soul. The horse owner, Tom, a half-breed Indian, invites Valerie to join him on a journey to Arizona in the USA. There amongst the descendants of native Americans Valerie undergoes spiritual initiation into unknown worlds. Gradually she becomes aware of the special gifts horses have …